pussy's bow

Neal Drinnan was born in 1964 in Melbourne, and was dubiously educated at various (now defunct) high schools and Camberwell Boy's Grammar. He has worked in publishing for many years, and also writes for a number of magazines. He is the author of *Glove Puppet*.

What reviewers said of *Glove Puppet*:

'An impressive work. Imaginatively drawn and psychologically vivid.'
Australian Review of Books

'One of the most exciting literary debuts in years.'
Outrage

'A thoroughly absorbing read.'
Courier Mail

Also by the same author

Glove Puppet
Quill

pussy's bow

NEAL DRINNAN

PENGUIN BOOKS

For Tim, Khym and Anthony,
May you always be safe in your worlds.

Penguin Books Australia Ltd
487 Maroondah Highway, PO Box 257
Ringwood, Victoria 3134, Australia
Penguin Books Ltd
Harmondsworth, Middlesex, England
Penguin Putnam Inc.
375 Hudson Street, New York, New York 10014, USA
Penguin Books Canada Limited
10 Alcorn Avenue, Toronto, Ontario, Canada M4V 3B2
Penguin Books (NZ) Ltd
Cnr Rosedale and Airborne Roads, Albany, Auckland, New Zealand
Penguin Books (South Africa) (Pty) Ltd
5 Watkins Street, Denver Ext 4, 2094, South Africa
Penguin Books India (P) Ltd
11, Community Centre, Panchsheel Park, New Delhi 110 017, India

First published by Penguin Books Australia Ltd 1999

10 9 8 7 6 5 4 3 2

Designed by Anitra Blackford, Penguin Design Studio
Cover photography by Garry Moore; digital imaging by Paul Fenton
Author photograph by Tim Mansour
Typeset by Midland Typesetters, Maryborough, Victoria
Printed in Australia by Australian Print Group, Maryborough, Victoria

National Library of Australia
Cataloguing-in-Publication data:

Drinnan, Neal.

Pussy's bow.

ISBN 0 14 028247 5.

I. Title.

A823.3

www.penguin.com.au

Acknowledgements

Huge thanks to Laurie Critchley for all her time and enthusiasm with this book, and to Helen Pace for her work in the later stages. Thanks also to the many others who helped to fill it with fun, facts and festive filth: Roger Fordham, Kim Rosser, Ross Lester, Les Carroll, Phil Hammond, Keith Shreeve, Anthony Rich, Tim Mansour. And thanks always to everyone who keeps me bed, fed and entertained whenever I'm in that groovy city of Melbourne: Mark Bedford, Matthew Wheelan, Lorraine Banks, Sean Corrin, Michael Broderick, Michael Daniel, Jonathan Seares, David Nair, Genevieve Milton, Simon Abbott, Kirk Drinnan and Kate Spratt.

Also special thanks to everyone at Hares and Hyenas Bookshop and Bookshop Darlinghurst for their ongoing support, in particular to John Donnon, Chris Sims, Graeme Aitken and Susie McConaghy.

Prologue

'Missy, Missy ... Come inside.' Claudette stood in the kitchen doorway, clutching her kimono against the descending chill of a winter evening. As was her habit, she glanced up, acknowledging the presence of the turret that loomed over her house and garden. Perhaps it was the light, but its mood tonight was dark. With a shudder she remembered the sticky end it had offered one sorry resident many years ago.

'Missy,' she called again, spooked now beneath its gaze. What her current neighbours got up to in there she could only half-guess. Male homosexuals were such abstruse creatures.

'Rather like you, Missy,' she said as a ghostly bundle of pale fur glided between her legs. 'And just like you, puss, they're charming, handsome, seemingly respectable, yet capable of such depraved nocturnal curriculums.'

Missy stopped at her bowl and devoured some fishy muck – oblivious to Claude's ruminations. 'They might be fun to play with, and pretty to look at, but they don't really cater to all of a girl's needs, do they?' Claudette sighed. 'And this girl ain't getting any younger.'

Missy had no interest in vain speculation or human anthropology. Nor did she possess any of her mistress's inherent caution. With fish on her whiskers and agendas of her own, she spared a momentary upwards glance for the offending monolith and ventured back into the garden.

'Well stay outside if that's how you feel!' Claudette bolted the door and returned to the cosy comforts of her private world.

one

'Ask about the neighbours before you buy the house.'

Yiddish proverb

Poets' Corner

'Elwood: too charming not to flatter, too modest not to blush,' proclaimed a gaily lit billboard for a shoddily renovated sixties apartment block.

'Too fucking modest not to blush! Have you ever heard such a load of contrived estate agent codswallop in your whole life? How, pray, does a suburb blush? You'd have to nuke it,' observed Dixon from the passenger seat of Doc's 1972 Citroën DS. The car's uniquely curved, European styling suited Dixon Brearly who liked to surround himself with beautiful things. Doc, hands on the wheel, just shrugged, his attention elsewhere as they glided along the wet Melbourne streets.

Dixon, too, had once been a thing of beauty. These days he was feeling rather chipped. Thirty-four was neither young nor old, he reassured himself. Not an optimistic age perhaps but neither did it warrant the opening of a vein. He stretched himself out like a long winter tea-time. His tall, slender frame settled into the sheepskin seat-covers while his toes kept themselves warm as toast against the heating vents.

He studied his shadowy reflection in the car's side mirror. His hair, a floppy, dirty blond, was definitely receding. In need of highlights, or something, he decided. But his eyes – ah, his eyes. Devastatingly blue, an icy European azure that time had not withered nor years condemned. 'Soul-searingly sensual,' a lover had once remarked, and the image had been powerful enough that he'd forgiven the alliteration. Dix narrowed them now for a blurred, timeless perspective. They were still a little puffy from last night, and the night before – not to mention a lifetime of other nights. His English skin and Roman nose were threatening their first blooms and splotches. Time was poised, torn between its choice of neck or jowl. The outcome was uncertain, but the plans were being laid. Dixon dragged his gaze away from the mirror to the view beyond.

They were driving through some of the most bankable, blue-chip real estate in the city. Victorian, Federation, Nouveau, Deco and Spanish style architectures all shared Elwood's wide leafy streets with contemporary, innovative townhouses and greedy rental piggy banks which had snuck in during less auspicious architectural periods. 'Pinch Yourself', another realtor's billboard proclaimed. 'Don't dream it. Live it.' It was exactly the sort of suburb that attracted homosexuals, their friends and, of course, their enemies.

One of Melbourne's Anglophilic forefathers had named a section of Elwood's streets after dead English writers: Keats, Tennyson, Dickens, Milton, Wordsworth . . . A patriarchal bastard, he'd made no references to any of the scant women courageous enough to take pen to paper in centuries gone by. But what femininity was lacking from the street names could be found on the buildings. The homes either had romantic, opera-inspired names like Norma, Ysolde, Iolanthe, or else boasted sturdy, simple ones like Janet, Betty and Anne – perhaps named for the builder's wife or the stonemason's daughter.

'At least they've got European appliances,' said Dix as they drove past yet another motley development.

'So did Auschwitz, but you'd hardly pay a quarter of a million to live there.' Doc, deeply immersed, didn't take his eyes from the road. 'I'm so glad I bought Juliette when I did. You can't lose money on property around here.'

'Unless some trash-bag ex-boyfriend takes you to the cleaners for half of it after living with you for all of five minutes.'

Doc laughed nervously, his shoulders noticeably broader than they had been six months earlier. Dixon regarded his companion surreptitiously. Doc was a different type of thirty-four, better maintained but somehow older. His stocky, sculpted shape, his straight-acting movements and his immaculately clipped hair elicited difficult and conflicting reactions in Dixon.

Dix had originally been one of Doc's pick-ups. He'd been staying in a small hotel in St Kilda and within a week of meeting Doc, had moved into his bayside home. Dix quite liked Doc, but in his heart of hearts he knew he'd been whoring for survival at the time – using more than just his English charm to negotiate his way in this odd choice of a city. Dixon, a once hopeful English scholar, had foundered in his academic career and, for reasons best known to him alone, had ended up as far from England as he could get. He'd flown down from Sydney to chase up a job in the Melbourne University history department. The job had fallen through, but Doc had known someone at the *Toorak Courier* who'd offered him a job writing about rich people's homes and gardens. He'd needed the money and blithely ignored the commandment in his passport: thou shalt not seek work while in Australia. Since then a year had flashed by. Dixon had overshot his visa and his tax file number was fraudulent, but no one had caught up with him just yet.

'You know,' Doc continued, 'our Juliette is considered by some to be one of the finest examples of Deco architecture in the area. A few boring critics maintain the turret and the English leadlight windows are impurities – unfortunate displays of wealth and folly by the rich Jewish architect who built her – but I think they really suit the house.'

'Yes, you've said.' Dixon pulled a joint out of his pocket and lit it. 'Joy,' he groaned, sucking greedily. 'A piping hot spliff in a cosy car on a winter evening. What could be finer?'

'You smoke too much,' said Doc, 'and I've told you, don't smoke in the car, it stinks for days.'

They glided into their crescent-shaped driveway, lurching to a stop at Juliette's large entrance which offered a sheltering annexe to one side of the car. The double stained-glass doors glittered from the lights within. Coloured pieces of leadlight inlay shimmered like brightly coloured lozenges, offering blurred, fragmented glimpses into the hallway. A kaleidoscopic peek into a psychedelic world.

Claudette's cat, Missy, meandered across the entranceway as if she owned the place. Doc wondered sometimes if she wasn't a reporter, sent in to cover any events that Claude might otherwise miss.

'Sssssscat. Go and piss in your own garden,' he hissed at the feline figure which had perched on the low garden fence dividing their two properties. Doc looked up at the house and felt a familiar glow of pride. Juliette's name was set into her masonry with a classic twenties typeface. The letters formed a noble curve around the top of the large white vestibule of the house. She had been built in 1924 by a man who lost everything in the Depression. Legend had it that he took his own life after the stock market collapsed by noosing himself in the strange turret of his own design. This same turret stuck up like a rude finger from the otherwise sedately designed single-storey house.

Doc loved all the stories about Juliette, and would regale people for hours at a dinner party if they let him. He felt proud to own this piece of history and loved to watch Deco enthusiasts photographing the house on Saturday or Sunday mornings. Juliette often appeared in magazines, and had a permanent spot on the Deco website.

Dixon took one last toke of his joint and flicked the butt onto the wet lawn.

'I wish you wouldn't do that,' grumbled Doc. 'What happened to your vow to give up smoking?'

'And your vow to give up minor tranquillisers? The addiction's become more fierce, I can't seem to control it. Help me, Doctor, sedate me!' Dixon took his landlord and occasional lover by the throat, pretending to choke him.

Doc pushed Dix away as he reached for the house key. 'I only like asphyxiation when ejaculation is imminent.'

'Dream on white boy . . .' sang Dix, carrying the shopping bags through the door.

Sittings and Stirrings

'Honey, we're home!' Doc and Dix burst through the front door. Bustling into the kitchen, they found the slender figure of their housemate bent over some legal documents.

'What are you doing?' asked Doc.

'Oh, just forging my grandmother's signature.' Dũng straightened, his cherished privacy and calm shattered.

'She's dead, isn't she?'

'Yes, but *they* don't have to know that.'

'I'd better keep my prescription pad under lock and key then.'

Dixon laughed. 'Giving you a prescription pad's like giving a junkie an AMEX.'

Doc flushed slightly. 'Well I'm off to the gym as soon as I've cleaned up and changed.'

Dix quirked an eyebrow at Dũng. 'Don't forget to wash your hands,' he called as Doc vanished into his room.

As soon as Doc had gone, Dix shed his gear to pose for Dũng, their artist-in-residence. Dũng slept and worked in Juliette's third bedroom and had done so for some months. His room was at the very back of the house and was blessed with a whole wall of latticed French windows looking onto the small, immaculately kept garden. It was large, long and made for a perfect studio. Dũng never minded sleeping with paint or turpentine fumes – he'd been weaned on Agent Orange.

His last exhibition, *Giết sụ khoan dung (Slaying Tolerance)*, had gained him national notoriety, a major art prize and $75,000 in painting sales. The National Gallery in Canberra now housed one of his largest works – a purchase more bigoted forces in the country saw as 'a public purse apology to recently vilified ethnic groups'.

Doc had been one of the buyers at this exhibition and while both Dix and Dũng agreed their landlord was essentially a philistine, they both loved his house and preferred to have their party drugs injected by a qualified medical professional. The painting he bought, *Viêc làm đem lai tư do*, (*Work Makes Free*), looked truly remarkable over Juliette's huge Deco fireplace.

Dũng's paintings were a strange combination of styles, partly recalling traditional Orientalism and partly inspired by Russian communist propaganda from the thirties. *Work Makes Free* depicted Melbourne's wealthiest Vietnamese restaurant owner in one of his chic and modern Victoria Street establishments. He was holding up his obese, rosy-cheeked son while, in the background, stylishly dressed Vietnamese couples sipped wine and nibbled *gỏi cuốn*. Behind them, paintings on the walls depicted Vietnamese war atrocities: people being suffocated with plastic bags, babies on the ends of swords, the usual sort of thing. Some of Dũng's paintings had made him less than popular amongst the Vietnamese community. His family, well, they were a-whole-nother story.

Dixon's painting seemed to require an inordinate number of sittings. As he lay there, Dix looked over at Dũng's next major work. A particularly Gothic piece, *Murmurs of Genocide* seemed to combine every horror of prejudice known to man from the Spanish Inquisition through to Pauline Hanson, and included a distressed-looking Hassidic Jew about to throw himself from Juliette's turret. Dix didn't dare mention to Dũng that it was highly unlikely Juliette's original owner was Hassidic.

'What do you think?' Dũng noticed the perplexed scowl on his model's face.

'It's too hysterical a response to contemporary Australian racism to have any intrinsic artistic merit. Where's your usual subtlety, Dũng?' Dix's voice was laden with sarcasm.

'You stick to your gardens, literary references and Toorak matrons – I'll deal with the painting of life as I see it, alright?'

Pauline Hanson was what Dix couldn't stand. 'The mere depiction of that woman parochialises and lowers the tone of the work. She doesn't deserve a place amongst the likes of Pol Pot, Stalin or Hitler – you flatter the woman more than she deserves by counting her amongst them.'

'Even Hitler had to start somewhere and the German people were probably more shrewd than the Queensland rednecks,' replied Dũng, unswayed by Dix's counsel.

'She's so God-awful. Who's going to mount her on the wall?'

'Who's going to mount her anywhere?' said Dũng with an evil grin.

Dixon looked across the room to that cruel mistress, the mirror. Age had altered the set of his face. 'They say your nose keeps growing until you die – that's a depressing thought.'

'They say your nails and hair keep growing even after you die,' answered Dũng.

'Yes, well, "they" have a lot to answer for.'

Dix laughed at his own vanity and narcissism. He wondered if homosexuals were merely creatures of the spring. 'Perishable amusements – the castrati of a thankless contemporary world,' his friend Soren had once claimed. Dix comforted himself with the thought that most homos aged better than their straight male contemporaries and amused themselves far longer. Still, he was pleased his immortalisation was taking place now, before the rot could set in any further. He shuddered at the memory of fifty-year-old queens with sun-seared lizard skins lolling about in G-strings on Melbourne's summer beaches.

Dũng paused from his painting, remembering different things in association with aging. He thought about Reg, the hideous old letch he'd lived with for a year when he was eighteen. He remembered how Reg had showered him with jewellery, aftershave and Lloyd Webber shows, only to abuse him whenever Dũng wouldn't do as *she* was told. 'Oh, so she's not happy being Miss Saigon, now she wants to be the fuckin' queen of the Orient. All pearls and diamonds, but no put-out.'

When Dũng had tried to go home to the commission house where his mother lived in Preston, things were no better. She'd driven him into the arms of that slimy creep with her histrionics. He shuddered, remembering how she would chase after him, grabbing at the jewellery he wore, shouting abuse in a concoction of English and Vietnamese.

Dũng sighed and came back to the present, his hands smearing splashes of deep red and fleshy pink on the canvas. He never allowed his reveries to engage him for long. What did the past matter?

Dix watched as Dũng focused intently on his work. His hair, a short, wavy bob, refused to stay behind his ear, and he had a cute way of flicking it back so as not to get paint in it. Dũng's body, too, was in great shape. It didn't have that dogged look that Doc's had. Muscles rippling sinuously beneath the tattoo of a Celtic cross – an absurd design for one so obviously Asian.

Still, its owner was quite exquisite, he conceded. Nearly thirty, successful and wearing all the correct hallmarks of the ruling gay tribe, Dũng was quick, angry and political. All the same, Dix understood that Dũng's artistic earnestness masked a healthy appetite for the ways of the flesh and a real hunger for love.

Dũng's eyes were eager to recognise his housemate's desirous glances. With his success and the gradual Anglo acceptance of Asian beauty, he'd grown increasingly accustomed to such looks. He felt his body respond and silently cursed his involuntary self-betrayal.

Dix noticed the slight bulge in the front of Dũng's white trousers. Bless him, he thought, and allowed his own cock to increase in size just the teensiest bit.

Dũng smiled, acknowledging the compliment, but realised nothing would come of it today.

For his part, Dix knew his own naked asset was the real reason Dũng was so keen to paint him. Why, he thought, did every gay boy go weak at the knees when they saw the size of his schlong? The legendary appendage had saved Dix from having to make too much of an effort in other ways, socially or sexually. Doc thought he should get a mould made. 'We could market it as a dildo, like Jeff Stryker, only yours could be called "Dixon Brearly – Really". Whadaya say, Dix, shall we take a mould?'

Dixon didn't want to think about sex while so flagrantly exposed, and so he turned his mind to work – and his recent visit to Asquith House. Dix was quite a hit as Toorak's local lifestyle journo. He felt that working for a free weekly rag, which had the sole aim of shifting real estate, was beneath him, although the ladies thought him divine with his degree from Cambridge (never finished) and his husky well-bred English voice. They were only too happy to while away the hours of their dotage with this charming man.

Lady Penelope Asquith had proved no exception. The eighty-eight-year-old biddy was the daughter of some department store magnate, and owned a seven-acre estate right in the middle of Toorak, neatly tucked away down near the Yarra River. It was hard to believe so much unrealised development potential still existed in such a prime location. Dix had only to close his eyes to see the white villa apartments rising up on the riverbanks. The bidding on each one would start at 750K.

Lady Penny could no longer look after the place but refused to sell it off. She had a chap in to see to the two acres surrounding the house, but the rest had been left to turn into something more brambled and sinister.

'The children love to play down there. They must get torn to shreds on the blackberries and I dare say they think I'm a witch,' she'd said as she hobbled with him to the outer reaches of the formal garden. 'You go ahead, dear. I'll make some tea for when you return, I can't walk back up that hill any more and I can't bear to see how wild it's all become down there. You can imagine how the garden was when I was younger. Do look out for the convict-built well, it's nearly 150 years old.'

A well, thought Dixon, unimpressed by the age but intrigued by the prospect. 'Do you mind if I take some cuttings from down there?'

'Not at all, my dear. Take the secateurs with you.'

He wandered through the winterscape of the garden, noticing again how much more foliage Melbourne gardens managed to sustain compared with their English counterparts. Dix's history honours thesis, 'Ewe Can See for Miles: The Gardens of Capability Brown and the Evolution of English Country Life', had qualified him quite nicely for this Australian job. He felt that gardens were the perfect adjunct to the less wholesome side of his nature, but it was their aesthetics and not their maintenance that interested him.

Wet bracken moistened his trousers as he sidled through the profusion of neglected plant life. There were collapsed pavilions, decaying belvederes, scum-lined ponds, even a swimming pool that looked as though it hadn't been filled since the sixties. From there the path took a sharp descent towards the mist-covered Yarra River. Dix felt he was in some sort of Miss Haversham–Norma Desmond theme park. As he rounded a bend in the path, he noticed a driveway that came in from a dead-end street – one servicing all the other expensive houses with river frontages, he guessed.

The old garages and servant quarters were in a terrible state of disrepair and to their side was the well Lady Asquith had mentioned, a sandstone structure, surrounded by very old, hand-made brick work. It was partly covered with corrugated iron, a corner of which now creaked in the wind. Dix stuck his head in and yelled 'Hello!' His voice echoed back, and he was struck by the musty, cold vapours that emanated from within. He fished in his pocket for a coin and pulled out a dollar. Too much, he thought, and tried again. Finding a twenty-cent piece, he tossed it in, wishing for a wild weekend. He thought first of the Doc, but then changed his mind, as images of Dũng reared up in his head.

Dix pushed through the remnants of a rosebed and took some cuttings of Rambling Rector and Rosa Mundi for Claudette, who was trying to establish some roses down the back of her garden. He looked across the river to Richmond. A whole lot of road works were going on, new tunnels, more freeways.

On his return, Lady Penny served him tea and ginger cake with gnarled fingers that boasted exquisite jewellery. One piece in particular, a huge diamond and emerald ring, looked worth a mint. They sat in a drawing room, which housed a magnificent Steinway baby grand. Dixon longed to have a play, but listened instead to the lonely old woman.

'That well was properly sealed last time I saw it, to stop the children getting in. One little horror put my daughter's cat down there years ago. It's had iron on it ever since.'

'Can you drink the water?' asked Dix, trying to avoid a third cup of tea. His bladder felt ready to burst.

'Lord no, not since the thirties. The water table has changed and it is quite poisonous now, there's seepage from the river and there's all sorts of nasty gasses coming up through it. But that well was where all the water for this house once came from years ago.'

Dixon nodded and yearned to get away, back to the real business of dope-smoking, trashy socialising, cocktails, sex and fashionable urban oblivion.

Now he pondered the seeming downward mobility of his life, a pale reflection of the slowly ebbing fortunes of his Toorak hostess. A farcical sham, he could imagine his father saying of his present existence from the comfort of his leather lounge chair. But there were blissful moments of Bohemian sanctity, like now, when he was posing nude for Dũng, ripped to the rafters, his cock draped across his belly.

Deep down, Dix knew he was wasting all his advantages, but he'd never asked for them. He'd abandoned all that family-based hetero-babble for something else. And his life in Melbourne was rather dapper, wicked, cool and very stylish – even by harsh British standards. He let a puff of smoke escape towards Dũng's ceiling. 'That's all we are,' he muttered as it dispersed into a haze of question marks.

Family Planning

As he drove to the gym, Doc's fears resurfaced. Ricky, the junkie from hell, had been in again today. How he hated being used by trash like that. It had been a couple of years since the incident and Doc was still paying.

Ricky Drouin had come into Doc's practice the Tuesday after a dance party, a day Doc would usually have taken off himself. He'd seen Ricky a couple of times for minor things, a cough, a sore throat. This time Ricky had maintained there was something wrong with his bum. Ricky, a gorgeous twenty-year-old, had had all the other boys in the waiting room secretly glancing up from their *Who Weekly*s.

'We'd better take a look then,' Doc had said and ushered him towards the examination table.

He was feeling quite light-headed himself from two days of excessive drug consumption. Still, he was quite capable of donning a rubber glove, taking a swab and checking for inflammations and swellings. Ricky perched on the table and bent over like a porn-star. Doc, moistening what seemed like an already sticky anus with some surgical lube, inserted his finger. As he did, Ricky looked over his shoulder. 'Aren't you even going to kiss me while you do that?'

Doc laughed, he'd heard that one before. 'People reckon I should keep amyl here for this procedure,' he added with a smirk.

'I don't think there's really anything wrong with *it*,' said Ricky, looking over his shoulder as Doc prodded and fingered the anal walls for anything amiss. 'I think it's just that I've been getting well and truly rogered, pretty much constantly since the party, if you know what I mean.' There was something guttural in the way he said this that made the drugs kick back in and Doc's cock harden inside his tight, pale moleskin trousers.

'Well, perhaps, you need to give it a rest,' he advised, beginning to slowly withdraw his fingers.

'Aahh, not just yet,' moaned Ricky, shunting himself back onto Doc's digits, a Chesire-cat grin spreading across his face. 'You know what it's like, eccies and Rohys all weekend long?'

Doc didn't commit to an answer.

The boy's hand shot out and began rubbing Doc's now visible bulge, his arse working rhythmically on the outstretched fingers. Doc was about to stop him, but he was momentarily weakened, enjoying the boy's fingers touching him through increasingly restrictive pants.

Suddenly Ricky was up – off his haunches and off the table like a shot. He began to look agitated. 'Um, I'm sorry, I don't like what's happening here and I feel you've seriously abused our professional relationship.' Within seconds his pants were on and he was out the door.

Doc was left standing in the open doorway of his office with a glistening glove, an erection outlined in his trousers and, worst of all, a five-cent spot of pre-cum visible against his near-white trousers.

He dabbed at it quickly and uselessly, before snapping off the glove and pursuing his patient. Ricky was at the desk complaining to Rhani, the receptionist.

'I'm afraid I'm going to have to lodge a formal complaint. I feel a bit freaked out at the moment, I need to get myself together after something like this.'

As Doc appeared, he could feel Rhani's eyes burning into the bulging stain on the front of his pants. Ricky had been talking loudly and the people in the waiting room had found something much trashier than tabloids to tune into.

Doc could feel his face crimson with embarrassment, a wordless confession.

'Ricky, would you please come back into my room.'

'Oh, yeah, right. What are you going to try and do this time?' Ricky looked towards the three waiting patients, as if for support. 'I don't think so. You'll be hearing from me. Anyone else want to get felt up by the doc?' he shouted, pointing at the glaring wet spot. His eyes filled with tears and he left the surgery.

Since then, Doc had struck a deal with Ricky. The initial payment had been five grand, which Doc had thought a small price to pay and an even smaller price to ask. He knew how much something like this could have cost him. He'd been writing scripts for minor tranquillisers for two years now and Ricky, a fully fledged speed freak at twenty-two, had a much easier time of his drugs thanks to Doc's intervening medication.

Of course Doc had never been able to look Rhani in the eye again. She'd left soon after and he'd been relieved. Was it his paranoia or had she really made him feel guilty? He knew, like all Catholics, that he was eternally sinful, a weak recidivist doomed to the ways of the flesh and all the suffering that that entailed. His compulsions were constant and almost robotic. His fear and remorse, secret, Gothic and terrifying.

Doc pulled into the gym determined to exorcise the demons that plagued him. Putting Ricky firmly from his mind, he thought of his latest decadent distraction, and a guilty, joyous smile played across his lips.

Ever in search of new luxuries, Doc had placed an ad in the *Melbourne Star Observer*. He wanted a houseboy, but he would have to convince the others that they wanted one too. Friday night was the best time to broach the subject since they generally ate together then, so he bought them all noodles on the way back from the gym.

Juliette's dining room had a domed ceiling, presided over by an exquisite and utterly unique light fixture. Sixty opaque, hand-blown glass lilies – each containing its own bulb – loomed over the dining table. Dixon, Doc and Dũng sat bathed in its light, eating their take-away noodles from American-style boxes. Dixon was reminding them of *The Lost Boys* and how the noodles turned to worms.

'Yuk,' said Dũng, 'I'm glad we're not tripping.'

Doc just smiled into his food. They'd planned a few quiet drinks at the Duke after dinner but Doc had already added something to the wine.

Dixon stretched his leg out and ran it along Doc's thigh. Doc felt his sphincter contract – in memory, fear, or anticipation, he wasn't sure. He coughed and took the plunge. 'Guys, I think we need someone to look after this house. To cook, clean . . .'

'Butle and plough,' slurped Dix.

'No, I was thinking of someone like a student. You know, someone who needs a place in the city and who can't afford rent. We've got that extra bedroom, he could go in there.'

'Oh, so it's going to be a he, is it?' protested Dũng. 'As if we don't have enough resident testosterone already.'

'Claudette lives next door and she's my oldest and best friend. It's just too complicated for a girl, that's all,' insisted Doc.

Dũng peered up disapprovingly from his food, chopsticks aloft. 'I see, so by adding a "young boy from the country" it's going to be less complicated. HELLO? Doc, your fantasy life is insatiable.'

'I'm not the only one in this house with a porn stash. Look, I'm serious, we all work really hard . . .'

'Speak for yourself,' choked Dixon.

'We're forever eating take-away. House-keeping would be a great way for someone to live in a really nice place. We could pay him something each, or he could get a part-time job, or something.'

'I'm not paying him,' said Dix at the first mention of further subsidy. 'Besides, we all know who'll be the first to get his money's worth.'

Dũng and Dix smirked at each other before simultaneously thrusting their hips in a grossly indecent way.

'It's arrogant and exploitative,' protested Dũng mildly.

Dix returned to his noodles. 'Well, as long as he doesn't spend forever in the bathroom – *we* don't have an ensuite like the Lord of the Manor.'

'Does that mean we can get someone?'

Dũng shrugged. 'Go on then, you'll do as you want anyhow.' He felt the first flutters of something in his stomach. That was the thrill and the terror of living with Doc, you never knew what he'd concocted.

There was a knock at the door, a tell-tale Claudette rat-ta-tat-tat, which Dixon went to answer. In she swept, hair newly styled and lips aflame.

'It's frigging freezing and my bloody car won't start,' she pouted. 'Do you think I look like Ally McBeal?'

'More like Elle McFeast in that dress,' laughed Doc.

'I'm talking about my hair, you arsehole!' She bashed him on the head.

'If you're fresh out of booze, Claude, you can just come in and ask for a drinkie, you don't have to make up stories about the car,' said Dixon handing her a glass.

'You want to get rid of that heap. I told you old European cars are nothing but trouble, and mechanics always rip women off. It's good money after bad,' advised Doc in stern, fatherly tones.

'You're one to talk. What about your Citroën? You're a doctor – aren't you supposed to have something reliable so you can deliver babies and enemas and things?'

'Don't do babies, Claude, you know that.'

'I don't hear him denying the enemas though,' added Dũng.

'This is nice wine, Doc. What is it?' Claude took a hefty slurp.

'Something French that Dix bought.'

'You feeling homesick for the continent, hon?'

'No, it was just cheap. Mind you, I could do with a week on Ibiza right now – depressing bloody Melbourne winters.'

'As opposed to the warm, bright, happy English ones you mean?' she teased.

Dixon laughed. 'There's no pleasing the English. I hope you didn't come in here expecting us to start your car.'

'As if. I was only going to drive to the bottle shop anyway. This will do very nicely, thank you.' Claude settled herself at the table and smiled into the chalice of red.

Fox Hunting

On Wednesday morning, somewhere between Wangaratta and Benalla, Shane Hutton became Murray Fox.

He spread himself out in a nearly empty carriage, gazing with fresh wonder from the window of his Melbourne-bound train. On the eerie-looking, man-made Lake Mokoan, thousands of dead gum trees offered moorings to rotting sheep, drowned cows and other unidentifiable domestic debris. Faded billboards showed families busy at play amidst this bizarre aquatic recreation site. 'More hours of sunshine per year than the Gold Coast' one boasted. But there was no sign of their famous sunshine today. The dead trees looked silver against the gun-metal grey of the sky. To the left of the train were distant mountains – on a clear day he'd be able to see their snowy peaks. He had done this trip plenty of times before, but this time it was for good.

The journey always gave Murray a peculiar wide-open Australian kind of feeling, one which was sad as well as exhilarating. He looked towards a distant shabby motel by the lake, a vestige of the water-skiing sixties. It was the last place his father had been seen with that sixteen-year-old. 'Filthy piece of vermin,' his mother had called her.

Shane remembered how she'd appeared as if a ghost six months or so before his dad had left them. Sharon, or Karen, or something, her name was. She'd hung around, at the garage where his dad worked, at the milk bar, on the corner, or even in the lane that ran along the back of their house. Once she'd got a taste for his dad she wouldn't go away. She'd never said anything, though she'd known who Shane was all right. She'd just stand there smoking a cigarette, her mousy hair streaked with blonde, her lips shiny with lip gloss. She always wore a button-up, napkin-sized denim skirt that was quick to get on and off.

'They'd all been through her, everyone of the blokes at that garage. Yer father was the only one fool enough to run off with her,' his mum had told him.

He'd caught his dad with her once, in the shed out the back. She was sitting up on the bench, her skirt, a tiny picnic blanket, spread open like her legs, whimpering as he went at her. His dad had his back to Shane but she'd seen him. She'd started exaggerating her whimpers as if to boast a victory, poking her tongue out, while his dad, muscles thumping mechanically, strained, sweated and flushed. She was so small, she looked like a toy. She'd kept watching him until he turned away. His father never saw him. A good thing, too, it would have meant quite a hiding.

What a bastard he was, thought Murray, leaving us all like that without a word, driving off in that panel van full of engine parts. Not that he'd ever shown much interest in Shane or Treecia. She was only two when he left anyway.

They'd moved house to Albury soon after his dad's disappearance. Murray's mum couldn't bear the humiliation of being left for the town bike.

Murray was old enough now to have worn that sweet-sticky girl fragrance, eagerly tendered by several waitresses at his work. He knew there was something about him that made them keen. He'd also sampled the testostoro-musk fragrances offered silently by anonymous men down by the riverina at night, a beat that went off after dark. He'd tasted the same white power surges from them that the girls had seemed so eager to take from him.

'Watch those girls, Shane,' his mum had warned. 'They're only after a wedding ring. You don't want to get married just because you have to. The last thing you need is a couple of screaming brats before you're twenty-five. You're smarter than that, love.' He thought about his mother's words – advice that seemed to have fallen on deaf ears with most of his friends around town. He'd escaped though. He'd packed in his job as a kitchen-hand at Vienna World and spent the last week saying goodbye. His mum would worry about him in the wilds of the city. She just had twelve-year-old Treecia to look after now. Murray worried that Tree wouldn't look after the vegetable patch he'd been growing for the last five years. She was already more interested in older boys and Spice Girls. They'd been through tough times the three of them, but a nineteen-year-old dude could go crazy stuck in a place like that.

The train creaked and lurched, the sound of its wheels tempting him to sleep. His eyes nearly closed, he wondered how he'd go in the big smoke. You can get away with murder in the city, he thought.

Five hours later, Murray caught a tram to Commercial Road and booked into a hotel. He decided he could live it up for three nights, then it was the youth hostel if nothing permanent showed up. He had sold his bomb of a Cortina for almost nothing and saved $3000, but he knew that wouldn't last long in Melbourne. He looked through a copy of the *Melbourne Star Observer* while grabbing a serious caffeine fix. He looked at the haircuts and clothes, the snapshots of cheeky party boys out clubbing, and figured he'd have to reinvent himself a little more. Then he glanced at the classifieds. He skipped the personals and flipped to rentals.

Unusual Opportunity. Unconventional, professional guys in magnificent Deco house seek live-in housekeeper with cooking skills and open mind. Free accommodation and expenses covered. Ideally suit uni student or traveller: pref non-smoker.

He pulled out a pen and circled the ad. He'd worked in a restaurant, he'd kept the house and garden tidy – why couldn't he do the job? Back at his hotel, he rang up and arranged to go by the following night. He pulled out a joint – 'Rutherglen Rip' as his friends called it – flopped onto the bed and chilled.

Later, he took himself out for a stroll, looked at the flickering lights and walked past the bars and cafés, all firing up for the night. Candy Bar, Diva, JC's. He looked at the boys rugged up in fake furs and leather coats, their hair immaculate, their clingy shirts suggesting sculpted bodies, their noses in the air. He watched with curiosity as pale girls with lots of lipstick vaguely satellited some of them. Everyone seemed to be chewing gum, talking loud and fast. They'd have their heads kicked in Albury.

Murray looked down at his trainers, his trusty Levis and the ugly parachute-silk jacket his mum had bought him 'because it rains all the time in Melbourne'. He overtook a group of conspicuous and up-themselves queens who snickered as he went past. He felt his heart sink. Was this the sort of tribe he wanted to join? He moseyed on to the Exchange. People in there didn't seem quite so full of attitude.

A big, handsome guy of about thirty emerged from the smoky haze and started chatting him up. Shell-suit aside, Murray was pretty gorgeous. He was no good at making first moves, but once someone started talking to him, well, he opened right up.

'Yeah, mate, I'd love another beer.' He eyed the guy through the gloom.

Turned out the bloke was staying in a hotel too, only his was in the city. They went back there and Murray noticed he was wearing a wedding ring. Damn, he thought, he could have it off with a wedding ring back in Albury. The other guys in the park used to laugh about them. 'You think they'll be all fuckin' butch and wanna top you, but they're always the ones who want to be fucked – up the proverbial wedding ring.'

But this guy wasn't like that at all. He was a salesman from

Perth, and more aggressive than Murray bargained for.

'You like getting fucked?'

'Oh no, I've never really got into it.'

'You should.'

Murray kept sucking his cock – it would keep his mind off the other thing, he thought. The engorged dick was too big and not the sort of thing he wanted to be shafted by for the first time.

The guy was squeezing Intensive Care lotion all over his hand and rubbing it into the valley between Murray's buttock cheeks. His middle finger took a savage lunge into Murray's shy rear passage. It contracted violently, but as the lotion ran round to his balls and the guy started taking long greasy strokes of his hardening cock, Murray found the finger less of an imposition. Unngghh, he exhaled from somewhere inside, closing his muscles on the invading finger pushing as if to expel it like shit. But the finger had plans; it pushed and worked its way further in. Another finger joined it and he felt the hot terror of too much intrusion.

Suddenly he stopped, the burning fingers shot themselves free. For a minute Murray thought it was over. Then big arms turned him over; the salesman clearly had invasions of a larger scale in mind.

'No!' cried Murray as the man plunged into the tiny, glistening fret of flesh. It was pure white pain. 'It fucking hurts.'

'You love it, all that cock up your greasy arse,' the salesman grunted.

The white pain fragmented into hundreds of colours. Murray meditated on it for a time. The searing, raw tearing of flesh suggested the possibility of internal damage. He felt cut inside. The guy was pumping harder like he was getting close. Murray moaned painfully, rhythmically. Whether they were sounds of pain or pleasure made no difference to his assailant. He was fixed on his goal. Spurts of white into crimson chambers.

As the guy topped the crest of his thrusting, Murray twisted free. The glistening cock burst from Murray's seared viscera and waved about, showering the bed with a beaded rain of pearly sperm. Murry's arsehole spasmed and burned. Tears escaped his eyes, absconding shamefully down his cheeks.

'Shit, you made me pull out too soon,' gasped the salesman.

'Too fucking right. I didn't even want you in there.'

'I thought you were into it.'

'Yeah, right. What part of NO don't you understand? Haven't you heard of condoms? Fucking AIDS?'

'Don't sweat, I hardly ever do guys and I'm nobody's bottom, if you know what I mean.'

Murray was putting on his clothes, eager to get out.

'I'm in town for a couple of days, you want to get together tomorrow?'

'I don't think so.' Murray grabbed his coat, nearly speechless at the gall of the guy.

He found a bench hidden by the towering shadows of Collins Street's monoliths. He curled up and began to cry, the sound obscured by the crash of a nearby fountain. He felt sore, torn, shamed and stupid. He wondered if he was bleeding. He felt sick. He heaved up some beer and cried some more. What would his mum think of that effort?

Suddenly he missed her, and cried about that as well. He wandered past shops towards the tram stop, each store window a shimmering winter palace. Every one a shrine to the splendours of city life. His eyes dried quickly in the sharp cold of the night as he waited for the last tram.

Back in his room, he sat on the cold white porcelain toilet, and cried some more. 'Shut up, you girlie sook,' he said to himself. He remembered how his father had used those very words when, at five, he'd refused to go beyond his depth in the Hume Weir.

'I can't swim, Dad, I can't swim.'

He'd begun to cry then because he didn't know what he'd do when the water was over his head. His dad saw the tears.

'Oh, you're not fuckin' crying are you, ya useless little sissy?'

Murray cried harder.

'For Chrissakes, shut up, you girlie sook,' his dad had exploded and then he'd swum off further, leaving Shane sobbing. He hadn't said another word to him all day.

Remembering this now, Murray shed a few more tears into the handful of toilet paper he'd grabbed. He wiped himself clean and flushed. He never looked behind or turned the light on. In darkness, blood is always grey and sobs muffled. He had an appointment in the morning about a house and job. He needed to be together for that.

Auditioning for D3

A large picture hung over the fireplace in Claudette's house. It was of a woman in a black rubber suit and pornographically high stiletto boots. She held a whip and her waist was corsetted to an impossibly small girth. A long tongue curled up to taste her black lipstick, her make-up Malcom McLaren inspired. The photo was of Claudette sixteen years ago, during the height of glam/punk. Her old friends all knew who it was, but newer ones didn't recognise her at all. She wasn't that thin any more. 'I never was,' she'd drawl at their surprise. 'I nearly died getting into that outfit.'

These days Claude went more for a glamorous-arty-tarty look, accentuating her beauty rather than ridiculing it as she had in her Gothic incarnation. She'd deserted her tepid love affair with textbook feminism a decade ago when she realised that there was a type of woman already sipping champagne in the boardroom while the sisters were still bringing a plate. It had dawned on her then that her skills were much more suited to that corporate climb than the cooperative collective.

Claudette was thirty-four, still got into a size twelve and was quite outspoken about the reigning female body-type which she called 'starving-for-attention'.

'Go into any of those shops in Chapel Street, ask them what sizes they have, they'll tell you both: six and eight,' she'd mock.

At five foot six, Claude was voluptuous, the type of woman one noticed when she got herself up. Her hair, usually dark, had lately had all sorts of blonde, copper and red streaks through it. Prevailing fashions had her spending far more time drying and voofing it up than she would like. Her face, finely featured – chiselled, one might say – was somewhat reminiscent of a European folk doll, she presumed her Jewish grandfather had something to do with it, though she'd never met him. A little make-up went a long way on Claude and when she put on her lipstick she was always thrilled at the transformation. She'd mix all the freebie perfume and aftershave samples she got from doing department store catalogues together with tiny amounts of neroli or patchouli oil. She did it so well that people walking behind her were often tempted to follow. Dix liked her style and so did Dũng. Doc tended not to notice women unless he was forced to.

Claudette invoiced at $75 an hour. A photographic stylist and freelance advertising consultant, she made sure food and merchandise looked good for magazines like *Vogue*, *International Gourmet* and *Good Weekend.* She sprayed glasses of room temperature Chardonnay with a fine mist of water so they looked crisp and chilled for the camera. Her busy fingers and long nails could bring a limp piece of lettuce momentarily back to life, or make a Christmas hamper with only five meagre items look abundant.

Her skill permeated the rest of her life. Her back garden was alive with the stuff and colours of the magazines she worked for – Provence meets English country. Her kitchen was remarkably reminiscent of Tuscany, and her boudoir mysteriously Oriental. Her house was much smaller than Juliette, a small Federation-style cottage in red brick with an extended garden.

She'd lived in it for twelve years. Originally it had been a share house but the time came when she could afford to buy it. Eight years ago it had cost her $160,000. Now it would be worth two times that at least. It was she who'd noticed when Juliette came on the market four years later.

Claudette had never thought of herself as tough but perhaps she was. She'd made it on her own, unlike Doc who'd inherited the money that had bought him Juliette. Doc was from a well-to-do Catholic clan in Armadale and had inherited a mint from his grandfather. He still had truckloads left, she suspected. Her mortgage had given her vertigo; she hadn't believed the bank would even lend her as much as it did.

Now she sat at her computer putting the finishing touches on a major catalogue quote and wondering whether to up the price. The phone was ringing but she let the machine take it. She listened to her own voice, husky, like a smoker though she hadn't smoked in ages. 'Hi, this is Claudette. (Her best friend Bella's dog barked in the background, convincing any potential intruder that she had one.) You've also reached the offices of Hot Biz. I'm busy or out so leave a message or call me on my mobile . . .'

'Claudette, it's Doc, are you there? Claude? Hello! I'm not going to ring the fucking mobile when I can see your car in the drive.'

She picked up the phone. 'Hi, Doc, what's up? Why aren't you at the surgery?'

'No pox, no appointments, what about you?'

'*Vogue* have put off their wintergreen salad and brittle toffee pudding until tomorrow.'

'So it looks like we'd better do lunch on Acland, what do you say?'

Claudette could see him in her mind's eye, all ready to go. He'd have just been to the gym and was probably ready to eat a horse. It annoyed her sometimes the way he assumed that just because her car was there she'd be free to do whatever he wanted, but today she felt hungry too.

'Let's go to the Blue Danube,' he continued, eager for goulash, spatzel and soup.

'Uh-uh, Dog's Bar. I don't feel like an Eastern Bloc girl today.'

'You want booze, you lush.'

'Just a glass of wine with lunch, is that a crime?'

'Let's go then.'

'Fifteen minutes, lippy *etcetera*.'

Doc and Claude both loved eating and they both loved wine. They also loved their mid-week lunches together. There were no crowds. They didn't have to worry about conversation because they'd known each other since school. Claude gave a small sigh of pleasure, and smiled at the man sitting across the table from her. He looked all pumped up, coiffed. A perfect expression of the modern marketing directed at cashed-up male homosexuals. He created the body, used all the products and drove the European car, albeit a slightly eccentric one. He wore conservative, smart clothes and was handsome though not particularly striking. He could, and did, blend into a dance party perfectly. Claudette had secretly come to admit he was a bit try-hard, his earnest attempts at macho a constant apology for his illicit sexuality. Once a Catholic always a Catholic, she thought.

Doc thought Claude incomplete because she hadn't got herself a man. He'd suggested she try lesbianism, which showed how little he understood her and women in general. Like her mother, he still traced everything back to that one event in her teens, failing to see how much more complex things had become. Claude argued that she was simply more discreet about her love life, unlike Doc, who seemed compelled to share every gory detail. Still, they loved each other like an old married couple, usually too tired to fight.

'I'm getting a houseboy,' announced Doc as their food arrived.

'You're not! Haven't you got enough stinky old boys in there?'

'We just want one more.'

'What *sort* are you getting this time?'

'A needy one, I guess.'

'The poor thing, he won't stand a chance. Is he going to keep house for you all?'

'That's the idea. Do you know what our combined annual income is?'

'No, and I don't want to know, thank you.'

Doc often said things like this in an excited way, reminding

Claude of a kid with a million dollars. He still didn't seem to understand how vulgar that sort of talk was once you'd grown up. Claude knew his family, she knew where it came from, but she'd always hoped he'd leave that sort of thing behind.

'What do the others think?' she asked, ordering their second drink.

'They've come around to the idea. We've got our first interviews tonight. You can come over if you want, see what you think of them.'

'I couldn't think of anything more dull. Besides, I'm otherwise engaged, and Dix already thinks I'm a fag hag as it is.'

'Who says?'

'Dũng.'

'Don't believe everything Dũng says, he's a trouble-maker.'

'I like Dũng.'

'So do I, but he lies. He likes to say things to see what happens. Dix would never say something like that even if he thought it, he's too ... too proper. Even when he's drug-fucked and looks like he's ready to kill someone, he'd never say anything so outwardly vile.'

'Oh, bullshit, he's evil and I love him for it. I just can't believe that here we are in our thirties, educated, everything, and we're still behaving like bitchy teenagers.'

'It's fun, isn't it?'

'Mmmm.'

Flames crackled in the corner fireplace. Claudette felt the warmth and colour from the red wine leak into her cheeks. She looked at the empty glass and wondered whether Doc would go three glasses at lunch. Dixon would, she thought. He'd go three bottles.

Doc, Dũng and Dix had interviewed two disappointing residential prospects by the time Murray arrived. He wore a pair of tracksuit pants that buttoned up the side, trainers and a 'Better Red Than

Dead' wind-breaker which had cost him heaps. All the same, he looked more promising than the earnest Malaysian student and the junkie who'd kept nodding out during his audition. Dix had rolled his eyes. 'You did say cook, not cook-up, in the ad, didn't you Doc?'

Murray walked in and was immediately in awe. 'Man, this place is rad, totally berserk.'

He took in the huge living room with its masterfully restored Deco suite, and the adjoining dining room beyond. The D3 – as they affectionately called themselves – were lounging around with coffees like nothing mattered in the world, relaxed but intimidating to one as green as Murray. He was still very sore from the previous night. He no longer felt like he was going to die, but it was hard to focus on winning over new people when your stinging arsehole was placing itself at the centre of your universe.

Dũng offered him some coffee which revived his chilly white hands. The three were quite awe-struck themselves because (fashion-sense aside) Murray was hot on the eye. He was moderately tall – taller than everyone there, except for Dixon. His cheeks seemed to carry a low blush, but he was otherwise English-pale. His dark wavy hair swept back in abundant, youthful locks and his clear, finely featured face harboured glistening, quick, slate-grey eyes.

'You do have eyes rather like a fox,' said Dix, lighting a cigarette under Doc's direct glower of disapproval. 'You don't smoke do you? I'm the only one who does and it's not allowed, you understand.' Dix grinned wickedly, and produced a theatrical cough. 'Doc, coincidentally, is a doctor and a Catholic, but no priest. Poverty, chastity and obedience. Fails on all counts, don't you, love? Dũng, here, is an artist, and I'm a bad journalist.'

'You're not so bad.' Dũng gave Dix a smile.

'I am bad, working for the rag I do.'

'What paper?' asked Murray, finally finding a crack in the banter.

'Oh, I do a garden-slash-lifestyle column and home page for the *Toorak Courier*.'

'Toorak's really posh, isn't it?'

'Yes, but posh isn't all it's cracked up to be.'

'I love gardening, at home I grew all our vegies – corn, tomatoes, you name it.'

The boys were shocked at the wholesome miracle of this, a nineteen-year-old who loved gardens. Their hearts softened to butter.

'You'll get on well with Claudette then,' said Doc.

'Oh, great, there's a girl here too?'

'No, she lives next door but she loves her garden. This house is huge, but you can barely hang the laundry in the yard, it's so small.'

'If you can be bothered putting it out at all, this time of year. I put all mine in the dryer like God intended,' added Dix with a dramatic outpouring of smoke.

'So you're a cook, Murray?' asked Doc.

'Well, I don't have a certificate, never went to trade school or nothing, but I've been cooking for three years. I can make heaps of stuff. Lasagne, loads of different casseroles, chicken Kiev, shepherd's pie. I can do pavlova, apple pie, even lemon meringue pie, whatever you want.'

There was a pause as they all digested the items on his bill of fare. Each interviewer was struck by the poignant bucolic dignity of his out-dated culinary repertoire.

'Where did you work?' asked Dũng in the pause.

'Oh, this place called Vienna World. It's on the Hume Highway just as you cross the border into New South Wales. You get a lot of truck-stops and coaches.'

'I know it,' said Doc. 'I've eaten there myself. Blister-packed curried-egg sandwiches and bain-maries full of lukewarm stew everywhere.'

'Oh, they've got heat lamps now, keeps the stuff hotter for

longer but dries it out to the shit, you've got to stir it all the time. The food's heaps better if you go to the RSL – it's just down the road. They've got a smorgasbord for twelve bucks which is way better than what you'd get at Vienna World for the same money. But I don't go there because one of the cooks got sacked for being gay – that really sucks.' Murray tossed back a stray clump of hair from his face. He felt like he was rabbiting on, but they didn't seem bored.

'One of the biggest culinary crimes of the century, those heat lamps,' Dũng mused.

'But they're great for growing dope plants.' Murray quickly looked around to see what the reaction to his daring revelation would be.

'Mmm, we actually grew some like that last summer,' agreed Doc. 'Dixon smoked it all.'

'Oh, blame me. Claudette's still got a bag if you want some.'

'So that's where you've been getting it,' said Doc.

Murray heaved an inward sigh of relief. These guys were cool with that sort of stuff. The house was unreal and they even seemed to like him.

They did like him. Murray was like a new puppy, his eyes dewy with a need for acceptance. His nasty encounter had knocked the wind from his sails, but he needed to show his bright side, the unbruised petals of a wild young flower. 'Have you guys ever had, like, ecstasy at raves and shit?'

The three turned to look at each other mischievously.

'On special occasions and in strict, medically controlled moderation,' said Dix, deadpan, as all three tried not to laugh.

Each remembered the same thing, simultaneously. The sound of three mouths kissing, as Dũng had called it in his painting. The work depicted all of them, mouths locked. Doc, with his lasciviousness, Dix's bemused detachment and Dũng's own fresh permissiveness. Asian culture was always toey about odd numbers but Dũng hadn't thought it unlucky or uncomfortable. Their mouths had come together as perfectly and deliciously as two ever could. Mouths seemed designed for three-way kisses, and ecstasy had made the desire to try it all the more urgent.

Dũng watched Doc eying Murray. Four could be a different story. A clumsy, dangerous and awkward dance.

Nacht Leben

The D3 were a little less than enthusiastic on Friday night. They'd all been roped into getting the junk out of the spare room. Murray was moving in on Sunday.

Dix was half-way to legless from *après*-work drinks at the Toorak Hotel, where he'd been dragged into office politics with Beverley who didn't know he was gay. Dix had hoped to convince her, by way of alcohol consumption, that he wasn't a good relationship prospect. He'd finally escaped, having sweet-talked some cab charges out of the receptionist. If anyone discovered his cab charge rort, he'd be out the door.

Dũng and Doc were hauling furniture while Dix bumped into walls, not helping at all.

'When this is done, we'll order pizzas and have a cocktail,' announced Doc. 'Head out to the Duke, what do you reckon?'

'I suppose,' said Dũng, 'but I don't want a big night.'

Doc was keen to go out. He'd spent all day treating the annual post-Winterdaze party gonorrhoea harvest. If he was going to look at cocks and arses, he'd prefer some that didn't have anything wrong with them.

Chores and dinner over, they showered, dressed and had a drink. 'If you're mixing us something, Doc, don't make it too trippy,' requested Dũng.

'Well, I'm not drinking any more,' said Dix. 'I've had enough.'

'No kidding.' Doc rolled his eyes. 'Speeeedy trippy tonight, me thinks. It's too cold to walk, we'll take the car.'

'Not mine,' said Dũng.

'As if Doc would be seen in a Toyota Starlet. I'm surprised an artist would.'

'Shut up, Dix, or you'll never borrow it again. I don't care about types of cars like you two wankers; besides, the Citroën forever needs something fixed.'

'Detailing, Dũng, detailing,' shouted Doc as he locked the windows in the next room.

The karaoke was particularly bad at the Duke.

'Drunken, novice drag queens should not attempt to lip-sync Celine Dion. The only thing they have in common with *Titanic* is tragedy,' yelled Dũng into Dix's ear.

'And disco twinkies should not try Morrisey impersonations even if there is the possibility of a free case of Stolichnaya,' Dix shouted back.

Doc was deeply involved in conversation with some gym-junkie friend of his. Watching him now, Dũng and Dix quietly agreed that he was definitely doing another course of steroids.

'You can tell from his moods,' said Dũng, sensing and regretting the presence of drugs in his own system.

'He usually does two courses a year,' agreed Dix knowingly. 'One before he goes up to Sleaze, and one before he goes to Mardi Gras. He knows his liver will be shot by the time he's fifty, but he's altogether too vain to give a damn.'

Dix saw a friend in the corner and went to say hi. Dũng decided he just wanted to go home. He felt queasy and alcohol was not going to improve the situation. He waved goodbye across the room and ventured out into the bitter night.

Outside his heart beat fast. Huge clouds of mist escaped with each hot breath. He pulled his black leather coat around him as he approached the highway. A tram wearily hauled itself past, dead-eyed passengers staring like zombies from the windows. He waited, his fur collar tickling his nose and face. The drugs made him think the straying pieces of fluff might be spiders, but otherwise the big coat protected him against the dismal night. His heavy boots felt all the more weighty for whatever it was Doc had slipped them. He felt as though LSD and Rohypnols were competing fiercely in his brain – neither was winning.

He started off down Blessington Street and wondered why the street lights were out. He moved onto the path that ran beside the gardens and was alone with nothing but the sound of his own footfalls for company. The gardens, customarily shut by the ranger at dusk, were pitch black. The only sounds coming from behind their rusty iron gates were from bats or strange, eerie night-birds – big, evil fuckers too fat, or lazy, to fly north for winter.

Two blocks away, Dixon too was over the Duke. He went across to Doc and interrupted the pec talk. 'Let's go home, have some wizz and visit the Commercial Road establishments.'

'Yeah yeah, get me another drink first, will you?'

'One more and then we go, alright?'

Claudette sat with Bella at the Absolut Yoof fashion finals held in a draughty dockside warehouse.

'At least they got a vodka to sponsor them, it's colder than Russia in here,' whispered Claude.

'I know, they should have pushed Absolut for more than just vodka on arrival though. I'm cold and thirsty,' Bella answered.

Claude fidgeted with her program, unable to believe heroin-chic could make a comeback only ten years after its last dismal attempt.

'Don't these designers know this has all been done before?' she whispered to Bella.

'Claude, these designers were still pestering their mothers for Little Golden Books at the check-out when that was going on.'

Claude shut up and watched her life flash before her, again.

Midway home, Dũng heard a car coming from behind with the dull thrum of a hotted-up eight cylinder engine. He felt his neck-hairs bristle but refused to look back. His heart began to race when he realised the car was moving at a snail's pace. Within seconds it was alongside him. The window wound down as it idled along at walking speed. 'It's a bum-fucking faggot boy – you wanna suck some cocks, queer boy?'

Dũng looked at them defiantly.

'Well, looky-look, a chink faggot.'

There were five boys in an old white Commodore – boys of Arabic extraction, he assumed. He could smell cigarette smoke and some sort of fragrant Middle Eastern spice emanating from the open window. Dũng looked at these hulking guys who'd driven in from the suburbs to flex muscle and do harm. He thought of their mothers – timid Muslim wives, cooking and cleaning all day, feeding these boys up, pumping them full of food to make them big and strong. Big enough to hold down the girls they would marry themselves one day, strong enough to bash faggots.

Fucked over by masculinity, these guys, thought Dũng. One racial minority victimising another one.

They couldn't believe their luck, a chink and a faggot – all rolled into one. 'We're gonna make you bleed, faggot. We're gonna tear you open and see what you had for dinner, you piece of slopehead faggot scum.'

Dũng shuddered with fear and rage. He looked into their faces. All he could see was the smouldering glow of malevolent desires as they sniggered and growled in low, almost seductive voices. He walked on, feeling vaguely hypnotised by the sound as they muttered something else in their own language, some dark cultural incantation.

'Why don't you just fucking leave me alone,' he said, aware of how pathetic he sounded.

'Oh, faggot's scared. Whatsa matter ching-chong faggy boy? You no like girlie pussy? You not even like slopehead girlie pussy?'

Suddenly they accelerated, and in three seconds they were gone, leaving only the echoey boom of Metallica. Dũng gasped for breath and began to run. What if they came back? He was tripping quite badly but thought he could see two people getting into a car up ahead. He ran towards them, wanting just to be near other people. As he approached, something made him wary and he slowed down.

'Run, poof, run,' he heard from one of the men getting into the car. His terror returned two-fold. A cold sweat crawled along his skin. He was in a worse spot now than before, with park on either side of the street. The car pulled out and screeched the fifty metres towards him. This time there were two white guys and a girl in the back. Surely not with a girl, they wouldn't, he thought as the men jumped out.

'We're cleaning up the streets, you filthy jip fag.' The bigger of the two grabbed Dũng by the arms and twisted him into a headlock. The other, weedier guy came over and hesitantly delivered a few blows to his stomach.

'Punch him harder, Robbo. Punch him hard for being a poof and fuckin' double-hard for being a slit-eye Asian cunt.' The big one was wild, a crazy, aggro yob.

Dũng could see the girl watching out the window. She was sipping her alcoholic soft drink, giggling and biting her bottom lip. 'Fuckin' Asians,' she yelled as Dũng's captor began to shout fresh orders to his mate.

'Get the crowbar from the boot, Robbo.'

'I dunno, Mitch.'

'Get the bloody crowbar from the boot like I tell ya, let's make it worth our fuckin' while.' Mitch smiled down at Dũng and squeezed his face between his hands. 'May as well be hung for a sheep as a lamb, hey? We'll fix you up real good mate, you'll be one sorry fuck when we've finished with ya. But don't worry, we'll try not to kill ya – even though I'd fuckin' love ta.'

Hesitantly Robbo walked over and opened the boot.

All of a sudden headlights beamed down the street.

'Shit,' said Mitch, still holding Dũng. The car accelerated closer and Dũng recognised the sound. It was Doc's Citroën, lumbering to a stop.

The girl, who'd been biting her bottom lip with the thrill of the violence, cried, 'Look out!' as Robbo laboured over what to do with the crowbar.

'What the fuck!' screamed Doc as he leapt from the car. Dix was close behind.

Crowbar Robbo dropped his tool, slammed the boot shut and bolted to the driver's seat. He revved the car and took off without a word to his mate. Mitch had released Dũng only to receive his first blow from Doc, who was a man possessed.

Mitch sprawled on the ground at Doc's mercy. 'Who the fuck do you think you are, you piece of shit?' growled Doc in a shocked state of hyper-reality.

Dũng staggered to the kerb. He was shaking but soon had his breath back. Suddenly he was suffused with rage. Fierce mindless bloodlust overtook him like a new drug coming on. 'Fuck you,' he murmured, slamming his heavy boot into the guy's stomach. He looked at Dix who seemed unsure what to do. 'Hold his legs – apart!' Dix did as he was told and Dũng delivered a kick to the crotch, so heavy and forceful the scream registered at a pitch only a dog could hear.

Doc pulled off his belt and bound the basher's arms behind his back. 'What are you doing?' Dix asked.

'We're taking him to the cops. Take off your belt, Dix, quick, we need to strap his feet together.'

Mitch was moaning loudly as beads of sweat formed on his forehead. His face was white. Dũng had struck quite a blow to his oh-so-fucking-superior breeding apparatus. Maybe it wouldn't even work any more, Dũng thought with relish.

Dix handed Doc his belt, and grabbing a demisting rag from the floor of the car he gagged Mitch to muffle the increasingly loud moans that were rising to a crescendo.

Nothing like this had ever happened before, to any of them. Doc had been punched once in a bar fight and Dũng had survived all kinds of taunting and schoolyard brawls, but tonight the odds had been stacked against him.

'C'mon, let's get him in the car.' Doc motioned to Dũng and together they dragged Mitch into the back seat where he twisted and turned, his face flushing crimson.

'Who do bastards like you think you are?' snarled Doc, still wild with rage as he walked over to the driver's seat. Dũng was trying to keep the guy's legs still. Dix pulled a bottle of amyl from his pocket and reached over from the passenger seat. He doused the gag with it, spilling some right up the guy's nose. 'That should knock him out a bit.'

'Knock him out? It'll send him fucking wild, you dickhead,' yelled Doc as he took off with them in the car. As if on cue, the prisoner made a last-ditch effort to free himself. He manoeuvred himself frantically, trying to disengage his legs from Dũng's grasp. They flew up kicking the roof. He was writhing like a freshly snagged trout. 'Grab his legs, quick,' shouted Doc, swerving to a halt.

'I can't, he's flipping out.'

'Keep still, arsehole.' Doc leaned over, grabbing the prisoner by the neck.

Mitch's kicks had managed to loosen the belt that was restraining his legs and the back seat had turned into a kicking gallery. Dũng, pummelled by the guy's trainers, felt his head thump against the glass. Doc squeezed tightly, his fingers on Mitch's throat, but he struggled all the more. His legs were firing like loose cannons, threatening to break the side windows. Dix wondered if this crazy bastard would defeat them all.

Doc was in a rage, worse than anything they'd ever seen from the steroids. 'Keep still, you fucker, keep still!' But the more he choked him, the more his legs kicked out. Mitch was going blue in the face. He tried to swivel around and escape the strangling grip, but Doc just squeezed even harder. Finally, he felt he was winning. Choking this bastard was the only way they'd quieten him. Raging and tripping, Doc focussed on the hard ridge of thyroid cartilage that pressed up against his thumbs. He had declared war on Mitch's Adam's apple and began to wilfully push down on it, determined to bring it into line with the rest of the throat. The thrashing was easing, there was less movement. It seemed the harder he pressed, the safer they were.

'Doc! Doc!' Dũng was screaming. 'What are you doing? You'll kill him.'

At that moment, something deep in Mitch's throat popped, rasped and sighed. Doc heard the pop and knew at once he'd punctured the trachea. 'Fuck, fuck!' he said as the flailing legs slowed to a gentle, rhythmic motion. Their captive was convulsing, his eyes wide with terror, his face blue for want of oxygen. 'I've punctured the windpipe – he's fucked.'

'Can we get him to the hospital?' asked Dũng, still recovering from the kicks. He wiped the blood from where his own teeth had punctured his pummelled lips.

'It's too late,' said Doc to the hideous, whistling tune of Mitch's last breaths. Dying, hopeless breaths which never reached the lungs. Doc observed the vanishing vital signs, and his rage subsided with them. He watched the last remnants of life vacate the boy's face and, suddenly, that's all he appeared to be. An angel-faced boy of about eighteen.

'Jesus, you've really killed him,' moaned Dix as they shared, in silence, the realisation of their crime. Their heads throbbed. Amyl vapours pervaded the car. The chemical fumes almost rendered the horror scene surreal.

'Get that amyl rag out of the car,' said Dũng at last. 'It's making me crazy.'

'Don't throw anything out of the car,' warned Doc. 'We've got to figure this out.'

'We've got to go to the cops.' Dũng opened the window to let some cold night air in. 'It was self-defence.'

'Yeah, right,' answered Doc. 'His ankles and wrists'll be bruised from the belt, he's probably nearly had a seizure from the amyl – why the fuck did you put amyl on that rag, Dix, you bloody idiot? And there are three of us and only one of him. He's fucked but we're even more fucked.'

'How was I to know you'd kill him for Christ's sake,' protested Dix.

'He wouldn't have kicked so crazy if he hadn't been breathing poppers constantly – he nearly put Dũng's head through the window.'

'H-e-l-l-o guys,' interrupted Dũng. 'I have a dead guy lying across my lap. He's a piece of shit but I wish for our sake he was still breathing – only because it would have been easier to deal with. I'm fucking glad he's dead. He wanted to kill me. We just turned the tables on him – they don't expect that. We've got to look after ourselves now.' He began to cry.

'This is not a good situation for me,' said Doc. 'C'mon guys, what'll we do? What'll we do? I can't think straight from these drugs.'

'Oh, and I suppose we can.' Dix leaned across and turned off the lights so as not to attract the attention of an oncoming car.

'Fuck!' said Dũng. 'That's their car. They've come back to search for him.'

'Did they see us?' Doc asked.

'I expect so, they drove right past.' Dix nearly lit a fag then abstained, remembering the fumes. 'Let's get this car home, it's too obvious. And let's think, gentlemen. Let's think very fast indeed.'

Sheol

Dũng was in shock, shaking all over as they pulled up in front of the house. Juliette didn't possess a garage so the car could not be hidden. Doc looked over the fence at Claudette's. The lights were out. Missy was nowhere in sight.

'Dix, I'm going to open the boot. Help me drag his body in. We've got to do it quickly and quietly.'

They struggled with the limp bulk, looking over their shoulders for any prying eyes. The corpse must have weighed one hundred kilos, and both Dix and Doc realised what was implicit in the term 'dead weight'. Dũng tried to help, but he was still a mess. They closed the boot just as an elderly dog-walker passed by, his eyes straining over the dark patch of lawn to see what all the activity was about. The dog stopped for a slash on their front fence, then moved on. They were thankful for once that the sensor light was on the blink.

Inside, they collapsed onto the lounge suite. Doc put a blanket around Dũng and Dix poured them all a Scotch. Dũng needed his grazes tended to, but for the moment they just sat.

'You know what we have to do?' Doc broke the silence at last.

Dix closed his eyes slowly, too scared to think what might be coming next.

'We have to go to the cop shop and report the incident.'

'I don't want to,' said Dũng. He started shaking again, exhausted by the thought of such a venture. Courage, he thought to himself, 'Dũng' means courage. 'What will I say happened?'

'We'll say everything happened as it happened, except we'll

say that when the others drove off, the dead guy scaled the fence into the garden and did a runner.'

'I can't go up there,' said Dix.

'Well if you won't come, I'll take Dũng in his car. We can't take the DS.'

'Why not? They're hardly going to search your car for the basher,' Dix pointed out.

Dũng almost smiled at the thought of Doc driving his car, but fear kicked in again.

'We'll say we didn't get the registration of the car. It was a blue Magna, about ten years old, and we'll both stick to the same story. Dix, you can stay here and think about how to get rid of the you-know-what.'

'Why me? I didn't kill the bastard. Can't you use your medical connections to smuggle him into a hospital morgue or something?'

'Believe me, I'm thinking of every possibility.'

Dũng interrupted, his brow furrowed in thought. 'I'll have to say he kicked me in the face to explain all this.' He pointed to his face and Doc went to get some antiseptic.

'Be brave, baby.' Doc gently dabbed the blood away. For once he gave no thought to the dangers it might conceal. 'All done. It's time to go. We'll think about the body when we get back.'

He put his arm around Dũng and they climbed into the freezing little Toyota. Dũng's teeth chattered all the way to the police station.

Dixon curled on the couch, his head fit to explode. He was an illegal alien and now an accessory to murder or manslaughter – who knows what it would end up as. If he hadn't cashed his ticket in, he could just leave the country, but he didn't have the money and his Barclaycard was frighteningly overdrawn. He got some old CDs out. He wanted to escape into the past, not because it had been so good but at least it was intact, he'd survived it. Blue Nile's

'Tinsel Town in the Rain' drizzled from the speakers and he noticed it was raining outside. Rain is good, he thought, it washes things away: blood, saliva, semen, DNA.

He fixed another drink and went to pull the curtains closed. A light was on at Claudette's, and he shuddered at the sight of the Citroën. A perverse desire to peek at the corpse seized him, but he dismissed it at once. He stretched out to contemplate where they could put the body. They could take it up into the forest or mountains and dump it in the scrub, or, God forbid, dig a hole for it. Perhaps they could chop it into bundles and disperse it all over the place. He remembered the man who'd murdered his wife for running up ten thousand pounds on her Barclaycard. He'd sent a packaged piece of her to every branch of Barclays bank in England.

The whisky was making him feel quite mellow despite it all. Then as he drifted off on his drugs and music, it came to him. 'The well. Old Penny Asquith's well.' He raced to get the street directory and looked at the map of Toorak until he worked out what road Riverside Drive came off. If they could get the body down there, they only had to haul it over the fence, get it past that corrugated seal on the top of the well, and bombs away – hopefully, never to surface again. 'To fester and writhe with the rotten globs of her daughter's ill-fated cat.' He raised a toast to his own brilliance.

Still, Dixon was in rather a pickle. It was a year since he'd left the silent disapproval of his parents, eighteen months since he'd buried his best friend Soren. He still felt his stomach go when he thought of Soren, he still couldn't believe he was dead. He had guiltily wished for a family like Soren's, so much more fun than his own. Now he wondered why he felt that guilt. Perhaps this new guilt might obscure it but as he lay there he realised he felt no guilt whatsoever about this latest misdemeanour. No guilt, just fear of being captured. 'It's like drinking and driving: one never fears an accident, one just fears getting done.'

The front door slammed and Dix nearly jumped out of his skin. He'd dozed off.

'Fuck,' Dũng was saying. 'I wasn't the only one bashed tonight – it was like a soup kitchen in there.'

'What happened?'

'It was all pretty straightforward. They were happy to leave Dũng in my capable hands,' Doc smirked.

'I'll never sleep without drugs tonight, that's for sure.' Dũng collapsed onto the couch.

'Hear, hear,' seconded Doc.

'I have a brilliant plan for the body,' slurred Dix, forcing himself into a sitting position. He explained the miracle of the well to his astonished cohabitants.

'It'll have to wait until tomorrow night now,' Doc muttered.

'Oh no,' moaned Dũng.

'Well can either of you honestly say you have the strength or wits to do the deed tonight? We are exhausted and drug-fucked.' They all had to agree.

'Tomorrow night, late,' confirmed Dix.

Doc administered Normisons to himself and his patients.

'Can I sleep with one of you guys?' asked Dũng.

'Yes.' They answered in unison.

'Perhaps we can both sleep with you tonight, Doc?' suggested Dixon. Sure he wouldn't try anything too twisted or strenuous on such a stressful night.

The pills were making them all feel very messy, but Dũng was determined to shower while he could still stand. Doc too offered himself to the scalding waters in the sanctuary of his ensuite, and prayed forgiveness for a sin he could never confess. Dix went around the house, checking the locks with unusual paranoia. Suddenly the big house seemed exposed, vulnerable and dangerous. They collapsed together in the king-sized bed, snuggling up like gumnut babies, each looking uncertainly to the other for paternal protection. They felt an extraordinary bond that night as if their predicament had stripped them, momentarily, of all other agendas.

Dũng curled between them and Dixon stroked his hair. Dũng smelt of soap, Dix of liquor and Doc of secreted steroids. Dũng liked having Dix flank him from behind and the Doc's protection in front. It reminded him of the migrant camp he'd stayed in as a child. The children used to cram into the bunks together and play *hang otộng bi mật* – secret cavern. He'd always sought to be at the centre, buried deep in a throng, safe from harm.

He thought about those guys in the Commodore, remembering his grandmother's tales of how cobras would hypnotise their prey, their heads swaying back and forth until the victim was transfixed. Then they'd strike, and strike again, sending their victims into the wildest hallucinations, then fatal, breathless paroxysms. He remembered how if a cobra crawled into a baby's crib and left it unharmed, it was good luck – a blessing on the child. Perhaps Dũng was that allegorical baby; he'd walked the highwire of his worst fears, floated on adrenalin with nothing but luck between him and the hospital or grave.

The heating noisily resonated its sombre warmth through the hollow vents and Dũng felt Dix's large hand place itself firmly on his hip. His heart fluttered. He knew he'd never stop Dixon from touching him anywhere. He longed for it. And however much of a fuck-up Dix was, it just didn't matter. Sometime during the previous months, Dũng had lost his heart to that moody, pompous Englishman.

The Morning After

A very handsome cigar waiter with serious attitude was showing his wares to Claudette as she sat in Mink or some similar vodka bar. Claude was looking at the obscenely large cigars in his wooden case and laughing, 'They won't do – they're not big enough!' She looked over toward Bella to see if she agreed but Bella had gone. Everyone had gone. It was just her and the waiter. She looked down, realising she was stark naked. She felt herself flushing and when she looked at the open case in front of her it had turned into a mirror. She confronted her own image, her face powdered and rouged like a nineteenth-century tart. The phone beside her on the bar began to ring and she panicked. What would she say? What could they want? Thank God, she thought, it's a dream.

'Hello, darling, it's me.'

'Mum, why do you always ring me at nine on a Saturday morning?'

'I want you to come tile shopping with me, you've got such a good eye, darling.'

Claudette rolled her good eyes and tried to clear her head. She knew that if she went, her mum would toy with her suggestions. They'd look at samples, catalogues and magazines. Her mum would get excited for a few moments about something 'bright' or 'modern'. Then she'd decide, 'Oh, I think it'd be a bit too lairish for your dad,' and all their excitement would dissipate to an agonised decision between a lighter or darker beige.

'I need at least two more hours' sleep, Mum. Doc and his boys kept me awake last night with a lot of car moving and thumping. God knows what they were up to.'

'How many has he got in there these days?'

'Two, but there's another one coming. A "houseboy" is moving in tomorrow.'

'A servant?'

'Well, a student or something from the country. Apparently he's quite a gardener, I might try and poach him.'

'Isn't that English one a gardener too?'

'No, he just writes about gardens, never turned a sod in his life – though he got me some nice rose cuttings for the trellis.'

'He's quite handsome that one isn't he? It's a shame he's, well . . . you know.'

'They're all "you know", Mum.'

'I sometimes think if it wasn't for that . . . monster you might spend a bit more time seeing some regular fellows.' Her mother's voice adopted that hardness women use when they are speaking of the heinous things men do.

'Mum, don't.'

Claudette knew her mother was desperate for grandchildren and time was running out. There was still an evil man out there somewhere who was blamed by Claudette's mum for every questionable action or varied path she had taken since 1979.

Not that she'd ever forget walking through the back door into her mother's Beaumaris kitchen that hot February evening with dirt all over her and blood running from her nose. Her one-piece bathing suit had been cut open at the crotch with a swift slash from the same knife that had threatened her throat. He'd threatened both vital regions and she'd never felt such terror.

When he'd finally released her, alive but red raw and dripping with the residues of his savage invasion, she hadn't known what to do. She'd scanned the area in a stupor. She'd lost her towel and bag somewhere in the bushes but couldn't find them so she'd simply made her way home, back to her house, two blocks away.

She had stood, waiting to cross Beach Road, the gusset of her bathers flapping like a cartoon parody of a mini-skirt. She had thought cars might have stopped at the shocking sight of her, but they hadn't. She'd walked all the way home, trying to cover herself with a swimming costume that seemed to ride up with every step.

The kitchen had just been done up then. Now, all these years later, her mum was renovating it again. How many kitchens to a lifetime she wondered.

The doorbell chimed its way into the waking reality of the sleeping knot of men as they lay at strange, contorted angles in Doc's bed. He was the first to heed its cruel, incessant chime. He donned a robe and answered it, with a dawning trepidation of what might be waiting in the outside world. It was Claude.

'What were you boys up to last night, all that thumping and banging and moving of cars?'

'Oh, Claude, you've no idea what happened to us. Dũng got attacked and we came past in the car while it was happening.'

'Oh Christ, no.' Claude's eyes took on a teary shine. 'Is he okay?'

Doc filled her in on the public version of events. 'We didn't get to bed until three.'

Dix wandered out, scratching his head, looking like fresh Hell.

'I could still hear you at four when I looked at the clock.'

'We'd taken Normi's by then, we were out cold.'

'That's weird. I could have sworn I heard someone in the drive thumping on the boot of the car when I woke up.'

Dixon's blood ran cold. What if he was still alive in there? Doc kept a poker face even as all colour drained from it. 'It wasn't us.'

'Oh boys, I'm sorry. I should leave you to sleep. I was going to get those paint charts from you. Mum wants me to go out interior designing with her, but it doesn't matter – it seems obscenely puerile in the light of this.'

'It's alright, they're just here by the phone.' Dix handed her the charts.

'Give Dũng a kiss for me, I'll bring him some flowers and stuff later.'

Claudette departed. She never walked all the way around to her gate, she just hopped over the fence where a low topiary hedge offered a handy break. Her driveway took up most of her front yard and her old BMW was a white flag, forever indicating whether she was in or out.

Doc and Dixon nervously barefooted it out onto the cold gravel of the driveway.

'You're not going to open the boot, are you?' asked Dix, hanging back.

'It's alright, he's dead – I know I killed him. That pop is not something anyone survives.' Doc rounded the back of the car. 'Oh fuck, oh fuck, fuck, fuck.'

Dix rushed to his side and his jaw dropped. 'What will we do? What the fuck will we do?'

They stared down at the boot. There were scratches in the paintwork. It looked as if someone had tried to pry it open. They stood speechless for a minute. Suddenly Dũng was at the door, complaining of a headache. He surveyed the scene and his hand shot up to his mouth. 'What's happened?'

'Go back inside,' ordered Doc with startling alacrity. Dũng went, more out of helplessness than obedience. Doc tried to open the boot, but the lock had been damaged.

'At least they didn't get in,' he said as he jiggered around with the key and the button.

'How do you know they didn't? Maybe it's empty – maybe he's gone,' said Dix in a deathly whisper.

'Shut up,' cursed Doc through clenched teeth. Suddenly something gave, and the boot creaked open. Doc nearly jumped clear with fright. Despite his medical certainty that the boy was dead, he still had a fear, nourished by horror movies, of the body springing out at him – a crazed zombie baying for blood.

He allowed the boot to open a little and Dixon edged closer. Nervously, they both peered at the crumpled grey figure that lay within. A faecal whiff hit their nostrils and they both fell on the boot to slam it shut. But now it wouldn't close. The catch was buggered.

They looked at each other in horror.

'What now?' No sooner had Dix posed the question than Claudette's mum pulled up, right in front of them, all smiles and cheerful greetings.

'Look at you two in your dressing gowns – aren't you freezing?'

They both forced ridiculous smiles and leant on the boot.

'We are a bit,' said Doc. 'We're just looking at the car. Someone tried to break into the boot and they've wrecked the paintwork.'

'What the dickens would they want in the boot for heaven's sake?'

Doc was momentarily lost for words. Dix flew to the rescue.

'The CD player is in there. I mean, honestly, you try to hide these things and the drug addicts just seem to sniff them out.' He sniffed theatrically himself, aware that a faint, unpleasant odour still lingered.

'Well, that's what I say to Claudette, you know. She's always lording it over me about property values here but no matter what you say, it's still virtually St Kilda and I've never thought it a particularly safe area, especially for a single girl. Even down our way a woman was held up at knife-point right in front of Coles. She only had five dollars in her purse so they took her shopping as well – six cans of dog food, can you believe? It was in the local paper. I think when the police catch up with hooligans like that, they should be sat down and made to eat all six cans.'

They nodded idiotically at her with their last reserves of teenage–parent respect.

'Well,' Claude's mum smiled busily. 'If you can't fix that lock, give my Vic a call, he's always good with that sort of thing. Now, I must go and see if my daughter has dragged herself out of bed yet. You should put something on your feet . . .'

'I know, we'll catch our deaths,' said Dix with his most radiant farewell smile as she vanished next door. Dũng peered from the front window, biting his lip. They quickly turned their attention back to the boot while Doc fiddled frantically with the key as they pushed, and pushed again, to get it closed. Finally, as if by divine or Satanic intervention, it stuck. They sighed with relief.

'What if it just springs open again of its own free will?' asked Dix with his usual pessimism.

'I'll stay here and hold it down while you grab that sack of potting mix from the backyard. And get some rakes and shit. Then we can put the potting mix against it and leave the other stuff leaning against the car as if we're gardening. C'mon, quick, before Claude and her mum come back out.'

At three in the afternoon it began to pour with rain. It had been a spectacularly miserable day and by five, it was almost dark.

'Why don't we just go at six?' suggested Dũng, desperate to have the whole thing over and done with.

'We can't,' snapped Doc. 'There'll be football traffic, everyone will still be awake. We'll go when we said. Midnight.'

Claudette had turned up an hour earlier with flowers, chocolates and Homer Hudson ice-cream. She hadn't pressed them for any more information than they'd offered. She respected the trauma something like this could cause. They'd finished all her gifts. The ice-cream container sat on the floor with a spoon sticking out of it. Some had dribbled onto the polished wood, but a heavy all-pervading ennui prevented anyone from cleaning it up.

'I feel sick,' said Dũng.

'You're probably a little concussed from his kicks – you're staying in bed tomorrow,' commanded Doc over the rim of his too-manyth cup of coffee. Dix had filled an ashtray to overflowing and the room seemed far less civilised than usual.

'Your slave's arriving tomorrow too,' Dũng reminded Doc.

'Well, that's why we want to do this right tonight.'

'What if someone's spying on us?'

'Obviously they are. We'll just have to watch out and hope they don't follow us on this evening's errand.'

'I just hope *she* doesn't hear anything,' Dũng pointed towards Claude's house.

'Well, she said she was going to some interior-design-awards-dinner with Bella. With any luck they'll hit the piss, end up at Mink or the Gin Palace, and won't be home until three or four.'

The twilight dragged on as they waited for the appointed hour.

Midnight Vagabonds

Dũng and Dix wore beanies; Doc, a baseball cap. The rain hadn't let up all evening which would make their task a very muddy one. The car still smelt of amyl from the previous night. They all prayed the boot wouldn't fly open during the journey.

At twelve-fifteen, the Citroën made its way onto Punt Road. There didn't seem to be the usual Saturday-night traffic. 'Who but the desperate or the damned would venture out on such a night?' observed Dix.

They turned down Toorak Road, past the optimistic glimmer of brightly lit cafés. So keen were they to be done with their task, they nearly went through the changing lights at Chapel Street. As they lurched to a dangerous stop, almost sliding into the cluster of crossing pedestrians, they heard their grim cargo heave in the boot. Dũng gave a little squeal of horror as it thumped against the back seat.

A police car pulled up on their right. Nervously, Doc played the 'don't look at them, but don't not look at them either' game. The last thing he wanted was to be breathalysed. The police turned right at Chapel Street and the Citroën cruised along until they reached Orrong Road, where they took a left. Dix had the street directory on his lap and was trying to navigate. 'Doc, you should have looked at this before we left.'

'I do know my way around Toorak, thank-you-very-much.'

'Don't you two start.' Dũng opened the window an inch so a breath of air could demist the back windows.

When they arrived, the street wasn't nearly as empty of cars as it had been when Dix had visited. Someone was having a do at one of the other houses that backed onto the river. Pulling up at Lady Asquith's side gate, they heard the exuberant murmurs of a party in full swing and the unmistakable sounds of M People.

'Is this going to work?' asked Doc, turning the engine and lights off.

'We'll make it work,' said Dix, deciding at that point to take over. 'We must all grab the body and haul it over the fence together. If no one arrives or leaves that party, we'll be okay, and the body can just lie in the drive until we get over there. Doc, you take the car to this park.' He pointed at a small patch of green in the directory, 300 metres away. Doc would need to navigate around several blocks to reach it by car. 'We'll exit the other side of the property and meet you there.'

A couple of party-goers left the neighbouring house. A drunk boy in a dinner suit was making indecent lunges at a giggling girl in a cream cocktail dress. 'Stop it, Garth, this is a Bettina Liano, cost me a fortune.' They climbed into a nearby Alfa and piss-farted about in there for another five minutes before the car launched off down the road. It was now or never.

'Please let the boot open this time,' prayed Doc as they leapt from the car. He jiggered with the key for a second and it released.

'Fuck!' exclaimed Dũng as the fetid smell of excrement made its way into the frosty night air.

'Just don't think about it,' said Dix, trying to work out the best way to get the now-stiff cargo of meat from its resting place.

'Is it still all clear, Dũng?' asked Doc.

'Yep.'

'Okay, Dix, grab the legs, I'll take the shoulders.'

'You grab the ankles, I'll grab the wrists,' sang Dix. No one laughed.

'Dũng, you grab his belt. Help us to lift him clear of the boot.'

'I don't want to touch any of the shit,' said Dũng, doing as he was told but reminding them he was still a princess at heart.

They looked at the fence they had to haul the body over, each realising it was going to be harder than they'd thought. Had the body been floppier they could have fed it over until it fell to the ground on the other side. As it was, their victim now resembled a very heavy, curled-up store mannequin. His shape seemed a deliberate last act of defiance against his hapless killers.

They stood at the fence, drenched with rain and exposed to all the world.

'What the fuck do we do now?' sighed Doc with tired resignation.

'We'll put your bloody steroids to good use, my dear.' Dix handed his share of the burden to Dũng and began scaling the fence with a vigour he hadn't shown for decades. At the top, he swung onto a large adjoining oak tree. Standing in its fork, he lent back over the fence.

Suddenly they could hear people from the party talking on the front porch, people who would be able to see them once they reached the street. Dix felt a flood of adrenalin give him strength. 'Now! Quick, Doc.'

Doc heaved the body high enough for Dix to grab an arm. The effort on his face reminded Dix of the expression he wore when he was being fucked. Dũng was trying to help Doc by taking some of the strain. With all the strength he could muster in his normally sedentary physique, Dix hauled the body up to that crucial point where the balance of weight was enough to topple it over. With a crash it fell onto the leaves and shrubs below. The tree on which Dix stood was so wet and slippery he almost plummeted after it.

'Quick, boys, get back into the car until those people are gone.'

Dix hung from the tree like a monkey. He watched from his darkened vantage point as four people made a dash for their car. One of the girls held her handbag over her head in a futile attempt to stay dry, as she and another woman ran ahead. 'Veronica's driving, not me and definitely not you, Stewart,' she yelled. She clambered into the car and after a couple of failed starts, the engine turned over and they were gone.

Doc and Dũng raced back to the fence. Dũng was boosted to a height where he could grab Dix's hand and scrabble over the fence.

'Okay, Doc, you piss off. We'll see you soon,' ordered Dix, through a seam in the fence.

The Citroën slunk away into the night, leaving them with the sound of the KLF from the party and the constant, cold dripping of rain.

Dix told Dũng to wait with the body as he went on a reconnaissance mission to re-acquaint himself with the well's whereabouts. Dũng stayed on guard, his senses on red alert. His gloves were soaked through and his beanie felt as if he was wearing a wet flannel.

Dix soon returned with the news that they only had to drag or carry the body sixty metres or so. Dũng grabbed the legs while Dix kept hold of the armpits. Breathlessly they squelched their way to Mitch's secret, waiting grave. Dix noticed the iron cover was still unfastened, though the gap wasn't as wide as he remembered. He felt Mitch's pockets, making sure they were empty. They seemed to be.

'Dũng, you're going to have to get up there and hold that piece of metal for me. There should be just enough space to get him down the hole.' He began to feed the rigidly curved body into the musty well. It caught on something almost immediately.

'Shit.' He pushed harder, and the hefty shoulders went through. Suddenly the body began to pull away from him, the hips being the last thing that needed help past the corrugated iron.

'Bombs away,' whispered Dũng as they heard the echoing splash beneath them.

'Sanctus Christus homophobus nomorus,' chanted Dix with High Church grandiosity.

Dũng climbed down, his gloves in tatters, his fingers red and cut.

'You better get a tetanus shot from Doc.'

'It's okay, I had one last year.' Dũng's face was smeared with mud. He tried to wipe it away with a shredded glove, but that only made it worse. He felt Dix's thumb and forefinger stroke the back of his neck, and a shiver passed through him.

'What are you playing at?' he asked. 'I never know how to read you, Dixon.'

Dix laughed. 'Like a book, my dear.'

'What sort of book? A romance, a porno or an accounting textbook?'

'Never an accounting textbook.' Dix was staring into Dũng's coffee-coloured eyes.

Without further thought, Dũng pushed him against the well and kissed him long, hard and deep.

Dix gave himself over to the feel of Dũng's lips. His tongue wasn't frantic and confused like Doc's. It was languid and thorough, easy and supremely sensual. It searched and investigated each corner of Dix's mouth. Dix knew if he accepted its invitation, he would be truly adored. He luxuriated in its promise a moment longer, then softly pulled away. His cock was hardening. An erection would prove most uncomfortable in the tight old jeans he was wearing.

Their hearts beating fast, they battled their way silently through the undergrowth. Ten minutes later, they reached the last fence they needed to scale for the night. Dũng went first and, as he cleared the top of the wooden palings, Dix noticed how much more limber he was. Only five years difference and I creak and crack like an old man compared to him, he thought. Then he found his footing on the palings and was over.

They briskly walked the two blocks to the car. The houses they passed were in darkness, just the occasional sensor light acknowledging their presence. Doc started the engine on their approach and they collapsed, breathless and sodden, into the waiting car.

Dix flopped onto the back seat, and stared at the ceiling. He could still make out the kick marks from last night's fatal struggle. He let out an exhausted breath. 'Just drive, she said.'

Country Fresh

Murray arrived at midday with two suitcases containing all he owned. Dũng was watching a *Star Trek Voyager* tape in the lounge but found it hard to sustain his usual level of engagement. Doc was in the dining room doing something on the computer. Dixon lay on his bed and attempted to read a book, a virtual impossibility given how sensational the plot of his own life had become in the last forty-eight hours.

'We should have told him not to move in,' said Dũng. 'God knows what's likely to happen next. I don't like it.'

'Well, he's at the door, case in hand,' answered Doc from the hall as he went to answer it.

'Hi, Doc,' said Murray chirpily, a gorgeous grin engulfing his face. 'Is that what everyone calls you – Doc?'

'Everyone except my mother.'

'What does she call you?'

'The prodigal son and an assortment of other expletives,' answered Dixon, emerging from his room. Murray smiled but had no idea what prodigal or expletive meant.

Doc grabbed one of the cases and ushered the novice down the hall to his room. Murray hadn't seen this part of the house. He glanced into Doc's room as they went past. 'Where's the kitchen?'

'We don't have one, didn't we mention that?' answered Dixon.

For a minute Murray almost believed him. 'How'm I supposed to cook?'

'You see, you should have asked more questions the other day.

Rule one, never accept an appointment without first assessing the facilities.'

'Shut up, Dix – he's winding you up, Murray. We have a fantastic kitchen which I'll show you in a minute. This is your room. You get the little stairway to the turret which is haunted.'

'Don't say that,' said Dũng, who had paused the video and half-heartedly joined the welcoming party.

'Can I check it out?'

'Of course, I'll get the key. It needs some work. It's the last bit of renovation I'm yet to complete, but it's too small to use for anything except spying on Claudette when she sunbakes nude in her back garden.'

Murray laughed.

'We should get you a draught-stopper for under that stairway door – it can be a bit cold and windy this time of year.'

Murray surveyed the room. The boys had furnished it with Doc's old futon, a chest of drawers and a full-length cheval mirror. 'This is great! I reckon I'll get some of those black and white photographs by famous photographers. I saw 'em in Chapel Street, only about forty bucks, framed and everything.'

Dixon caught Dũng's eye and tried not to smile.

'It's your room, Murray, put up whatever you like,' said Doc, refusing to be drawn into their conspiracy of aesthetic bitchiness.

It all seemed too easy to Murray. Cook dinner, make sure there was always stuff in the fridge that could be heated up, do the washing, gardening and cleaning. They'd pay for all the shopping and Doc was going to give him $100 a week on top. Murray figured he could probably get a bar job a couple of nights a week and he'd be laughing, he wouldn't even spend his savings. His new employers didn't seem like they'd be too demanding, in fact it wasn't like a job at all.

Doc showed him a pad he'd put on the kitchen wall. 'We'll

just mark the pad if we're going to be home for dinner.'

'Not that we ever know,' added Dix off-handedly.

'I'll work out a cleaning list which shouldn't take more than an hour or so a day. We'll dump all the washing, including bedding, in the laundry, and if we need anything ironed we'll let you know.'

'Sure,' said Murray with a shrug.

'Anyway, we're all taking it extra easy today. We had a very nasty experience the other night, as you can see from Dũng's cuts and bruises. He's still getting over the shock.' Doc recounted the standard-issue story.

'I'm never leaving the house again,' muttered Dũng, unpausing the video in a bid to end the discussion.

'Is this *4.1*?' asked Murray.

'Yeah.' Dũng grinned.

'Excellent. It's a Borg episode, isn't it? "We are Borg, you will be assimilated – resistance is futile," chanted Murray.

Dixon walked in. 'We are D3, you will be assignated – resistance is Zeuxian.'

'You'll have to get used to Dix, he speaks in tongues and we haven't been to Cambridge like him,' said Dũng, noticing Murray's blank expression.

Dix wagged his tongue suggestively. 'I think I'll go to JC's, if it hasn't been petrol-bombed again, with my favourite fag hag, if she'll have me.'

'I wish you wouldn't call her that,' said Dũng with a pout of political correctness.

'Dũng, if I can call myself a fag – and love myself for it – why then can't I extend that love to fag-haggery, the noblest of women on the Brearly scale of human worthiness? We must seize back derogatory terms and make them ours. Moreover, what other woman is there who will match me drink for drink, witty comeback for witty comeback? I'll go fetch her. She can come and meet Murray.' He was out the door.

'Don't worry, Murray, Dixon's showing off. He's quite sweet really, in a moody, alcoholic, drug-fucked, English sort of way.'

'Are you two boyfriends?'

Dũng lowered his voice so Doc couldn't hear. 'No, he was sort of on with Doc but it seems to have petered out. We're good friends.' Dũng thought about the kiss from the previous night. It had been like something from *The Living End*.

Murray nodded. He was beginning to see how very different life in the city could be. He looked at Dũng, who was wearing some really groovy track pants and a long-sleeved T-shirt with motifs all over it. Dũng's clothes could have come straight out of a fashion mag.

'Dũng?'

'Yo.'

'Do you reckon, maybe, you could come shopping with me some time?'

'Sure, but don't worry. We'll always leave a list of what you should get. The supermarket's just up the road and you can take my car when you go – if you can drive that is.'

'No, I mean for clothes and shit. I reckon I look like a bit of a bush pig compared to all those Commercial Road queens.' Murray blushed and tried not to meet Dũng's eyes.

'Well, I wouldn't worry too much about all those Saturday-night nobodies. Tear away the Dolce & Gabbana and you'll find a lot of nervy little knee-knockers. But hey, I'd love to take you shopping, and I'll make sure you get stuff cheap too. I know all the good joints.'

'Cool . . . Dũng? . . . Are you freaked out about those poofter bashers?'

'More than you can ever know . . .'

'Something pretty bad happened to me the other night.'

'What?'

'Oh, I just picked up this guy who, like, did stuff to me I didn't want him to do.'

Dũng thought back to Reg, his sugar daddy and nemesis from a decade ago. In particular, a barbecue he'd had when Dũng had been living with him. Dũng had drunk too much and flirted with some of Reg's fifty-year-old cronies, though God knows he hadn't fancied any of them. Reg had decided that if the Saigon princess wanted to tempt her minions then she should put her pussy where her mouth was. Three of them had come in. One after the other. Each one flabby and foul-breathed from beer. Finally, Reg had called a halt. 'Perhaps her highness will show a little more respect now,' he'd said as his finger investigated the greasy, dilated passage the others had established. 'Well come on, Reg,' Dũng had replied with all the venom in his heart. 'Me all greasy for number one husband. You try, you like.' Reg had slapped him.

Dũng looked away from Murray now. 'Shit happens, you survive.'

Murray felt a flush of embarrassment. He changed the subject. 'Is that turret really haunted?'

'Nah.' Dũng shrugged. He certainly wasn't going to freak Murray out with ghostly tales.

The front door opened. It was Dix and Claudette. Claudette had obviously been tempted to visit 'Fag Alley' as she called JC's, although there were usually plenty of straights – too many, if you asked for Doc's opinion. Claudette, like Dix, still enjoyed strutting her stuff despite advancing age. Her stuff tonight consisted of a clingy silver-grey dress which went down to her ankles but was split to the thigh. 'I can't believe I've been sucked back into wearing this retro synthetic stuff,' she said as she smoothed down the waist panel.

'Do a turn for us, darling,' commanded Dix.

'I love those boots, Claude. Where'd you get them?' asked Dũng.

'Prada – for a song when I did that ad for them in *HQ*.'

'This is our new tenant, Murray,' pronounced Dix with a flourish.

'*Enchanté.*' Claude held out her hand. Murray shook it clumsily as he stood, and Claudette knew she was looking at the most handsome of Doc's houseboy applicants.

'Murray's been *Trek*ing with Dũng this afternoon.'

'How are you, hon?' Claude bent down to kiss Dũng, carefully touching his abrasions with lavish fingers.

'Alright, I guess. I'll probably drive everywhere from now on. Arseholes.'

'No word from the police?'

'Nah.' Dũng shuddered inwardly at the thought.

'So, Murray, you're a gardener too I hear?'

'Just vegies and that.'

'But that's super. I want to grow some things to eat this summer, maybe you can help me out?'

'Cool with me.'

'Come on, old girl,' Dix interrupted. 'Let's get out of here before afternoon turns to night. I've got work tomorrow.'

'Nursing a hangover is a full-time job for Dixon,' said Claude to Murray. 'Perhaps next week you can come with us?'

'That'd be cool.'

'Have you noticed how everything is "cool"?' Dixon said to Claude as they climbed into the cab. 'Who'd ever have thought that sentiment would have been revived so thoroughly?'

'Who'd have thought man-made fibres'd be back with such a vengeance either?' Claude giggled, her hair crackling against the polyester sleeve of her frock.

Dixon pulled something from his pocket. 'What's that?' she whispered so the driver couldn't hear.

'A present from Yul in Amsterdam.' He handed her a tiny orange tablet.

Yul's illicit generosity humbled Dix. While others in the world had stockbrokers, accountants or agents, Dix had Yul – his fearless drug *providore*. Yul had been a trusty pal to both Dix and Soren, and even now his arms still reached around the world to tempt him with the newest, freshest chemical sensations.

'Go on, take the bloody thing. I won't offer again.'

'Dix, not on Sunday arvo.'

'It's okay, they're really mild and cruisy.' He neglected to tell her that their effects endured for about ten hours.

'What are they?' she urged with some petulance.

'E's – the newest sort. Yul sent them to me on a Jeff Koons' Puppy card. These are the eyes. The nose is already gone.'

'I don't need to ask where that went,' she huffed.

Dixon was fidgeting and undoing his belt.

'What are you doing?'

'Sticking it up my rear passage, dear,' he whispered.

'My God.' She turned away, nearly gagging as she tried to swallow without water. The bitter taste filled her mouth and she ordered the cab to pull into a service station. She raced in and bought some water, sculling half of it. As they resumed their trip, Dixon turned to her.

'Do you think if I were a girl, I could stick it up my – you know?'

'Cunt,' retorted Claude in the harshest whisper. 'Well I am a girl and I'd say definitely *not.* At best you'd get some nasty yeast infection, at worst, Toxic Shock Syndrome. You'd be dead before you got to the hospital.'

'Can you imagine the headlines?' whispered Dix. ' "Miss Placed Eccie – Thrushed to Hospital – Girl Flies, Dies".'

The two started giggling uncontrollably while the cab driver shot them constant disapproving glances in the rear-vision mirror.

Vidiots

The remainder of the household ate pizzas and watched videos until their heads ached. The dry air from the heating and their day-long, adolescent lack of activity made them feel stupid. This was made even worse by the joint Murray rolled. Dũng finally took himself to bed at about ten-thirty.

Murray sat up for a while talking to Doc. He seemed like the boss, if this was, in fact, a job that Murray had taken on.

Doc had put a Cafe del Mar CD on – he'd noticed it was one of Dix's less retro favourites. Now he looked over at Murray and longed to touch him. He dreamt of being able to focus his desire on one person only, to look at a crowd of gorgeous men and have one in particular stand out. Someone who would be the one, who would offer him peace. A heavy weight descended because he knew it would never happen.

Dũng maintained that everyone chose their path before they were born, and that lust, greed, beauty and love were preordained commodities in any given lifetime. Doc shared his fatalism yet balked at the personal responsibility that lay behind it.

Doc had tried to talk to Dixon about things, to confide in him, but Dix seemed to reduce everything to a glib platitude. Doc felt he'd loved Dixon at one point. He still cared for him. It was possible he'd return tonight, wizzing off his dial, in need of sedatives, and visit Doc in his bed. Doc knew he'd lie awake in the hope of it.

He also knew he could make a move on the beautiful boy sprawled unselfconsciously on his couch and it might be reciprocated. But he knew Dixon and Dũng would take a dim view of it and that was enough to stop his hands from straying. Such dilemmas, and all on top of a dead body that could surface at any time. A chill ran through him at the thought.

He bade Murray good night and told him not to worry about breakfast. 'No one should be subjected to Dixon or myself at eight in the morning,' he added gravely.

Murray sat on his futon and thought how excellently warm the room was from the heating, though Doc had been right – there was a distinct draught from beneath the stairway door. He still hadn't been up to the turret room; he'd do that tomorrow. He looked out the cold glass of his window which faced Claudette's fence, and opened one pane a fraction. There was a leafless tree outside – a Japanese maple, Murray guessed.

He pulled his shirt off, his body skinny and tight in the mirror's shadowy reflection. He dropped his trousers and kicked the shoes off his feet, running his fingers over the muscular ridges of his tummy. Then he shed his boxer shorts. His hands ran up his chest, pausing for a moment at the meaty red nipples. Bold and chunky, they shocked people a little on first sighting. Even girls had grabbed them excitedly on intimate occasions. He surveyed his body and felt happy. He was happy with his cock, a decent size even on the droop. He liked the way its pendulous softness contrasted with his tight skinniness. He felt his arse to see if it still stung to the touch. It seemed to have recovered from the savage intrusion of a few days ago. He thought about having a wank, his mind scrolling through a few snapshots of the people he'd met in the last few days. He thought about Doc and how fidgety he'd seemed on the couch. Then he thought of Claudette and the cloud of perfume she'd brought into the house. He couldn't settle on anything for long, so he flopped onto the bed and doodled with his forefinger on his stomach.

He heard the front door open. Dix returning home, he guessed. He got under his doona and listened while Dix went into the bathroom. The toilet flushed, taps ran and Dixon coughed up some shit. As Murray began to doze off, he heard Dix shuffle back up the hall to Doc's room. There was the sound of a door closing and the heating blasting on again.

The river beckoned him, its deep swirls and willowed banks. His sister pushed out a frail wooden boat from a muddy shallow, offering it to him. Murray knew the river was deep and swift but sunlight sparkled on it, disguising the perils. He sat in the boat and glided out into the gathering currents realising, too late, he had no oars. As he rounded the first corner, it became evident the craft was too feeble to brave such a swift and turbulent flow, but he was incapable of turning back. The sun receded, leaving a fast, grey river. Jagged, dead gum trees hung over the banks, their sharp, accusing fingers ready to take out his eyes if he wasn't careful.

As he approached another bend, he saw his mum trying to force her way into what looked like a deserted hut. 'Mum,' he yelled. 'Mum, help! Mum, please help.'

She didn't hear him and he knew there'd be trouble around the next corner. She was yelling herself – yelling at someone inside – oblivious to his passing.

'I know he's in there. I know you've got him in there. I'll be back.' As she turned to look at Murray it was no longer his mum but a girl.

He gasped for breath and woke, sure that the voice was real. His bleary eyes looked to the window which seemed more open than before. He squinted into the darkness, his heart racing as he noticed the branches on the maple shuddering. Suddenly, something moved. A gust of icy wind washed over him. A flash of white, a grey hand, a face in motion. He went to scream but his voice failed him. Finally, when he felt he possessed the strength, he lurched from the bed, pulled the window closed and glanced fearfully into the darkness. There was no movement but the wind, no sounds but the heating vents.

He waited until his heart had slowed to something reasonable. Then he headed to the bathroom to take a piss. As he was returning to his room, he came upon Dixon who seemed to be sleepwalking back to his. He was armed with his clothes but bone naked. Murray was momentarily stunned. They regarded each other through the gloom.

'We must stop meeting like this,' Dix cackled. Murray noticed Dixon's cock was still shiny with lube and its proportions forced him to re-evaluate his earlier moment of pride.

'Hey, Dixon, is this place really haunted? Something weird just happened.'

Dixon's eyes looked whacked. 'This is the home of weird things.' He adopted Vincent Price's most goulish intonations. 'Time that passed and guests who stayed, too long on the turret played . . .'

'What do you mean?' Murray whispered urgently. 'Did something happen in there?'

'I'll tell you tomorrow.' A wave of drugged mischief came over him. 'Come and sleep with me if you're scared.'

Murray actually thought about it but was dissuaded by the gleaming cock before him. He could smell sex on Dixon and didn't feel like beating off those sorts of advances.

'I've closed the window, I'll be alright.' He went back to his room, this time closing the blinds as well. He shivered quietly and kept his eyes clenched shut like a child. Oh boy, he thought, oh fucking boy. Then it occurred to him that it hadn't seemed like a boy at all. It had seemed like a girl, some pale waif of a girl. A hopeless, lost figure peering into darkened windows on the coldest of nights.

Doc stirred restlessly in his bed; he could still taste Dixon in his mouth. He felt a little like crying. He'd returned from the bathroom to find Dixon gone. 'I should say no to him, he can't just come in here for sex when he's drug-fucked,' he whispered as a melancholy sandman began to molest him.

But, of course, Dixon could. It seemed Dix could do just about whatever he liked as far as Doc was concerned. 'He could have stayed though, slept with me all night instead of slinking away into the gloom like some shoddy 4 a.m. pick-up.' Dixon could be arrogant and cruel as Doc knew. Wasn't that half his charm?

Home Duties

Doc and Dix were both gone by the time Murray got up the next morning. Dũng was already painting in his room, slightly niggled by the fact he no longer had the house to himself five days a week. Still, he could lock himself away and listen to his music – it was greedy to want the entire place to himself.

Murray had never met a real artist before. He wondered whether Dũng was the type who'd go crazy if you knocked on his door. After acquainting himself with the kitchen, he meandered into the laundry, put on some washing and went to make coffee. There didn't seem to be any instant so he made a plunger full. Nervously, he tapped on Dũng's door.

'Come in.' Dũng was engaged in some small brush detail on *Tiếng lầm bầm*.

'Wow,' said Murray as he surveyed the huge canvas mounted at one end of the room. He studied the figures, then noticed the turret. 'That's our roof, isn't it? Why's that guy hanging himself?'

'Oh, it's just part of a story,' muttered Dũng, still focussing on his work.

'What does "too long on the turret played" mean?'

'Where'd you hear that?'

'Dixon, last night.'

'Did he come into your room and try to spook you?' asked Dũng with an approximation of disinterest.

'No, he didn't need to. I saw him in the hall when he was going back to his room.' Suddenly Murray wondered if he'd been indiscreet. Going back to his room could only mean he'd been in another bedroom.

Dũng swallowed his response to Murray's inadvertent news. 'It's from a silly poem Dixon wrote, or started writing. I only know that because I saw it on his desk when I was getting my e-mail. He's usually very shy, ashamed even, of stuff he writes. He reckons he's no poet but he still keeps writing like a fool. He wants to be like Byron, but always ends up sounding more like Neil Tennant. I'm surprised he mentioned it – he must have been drug-fucked or drunk last night.'

'I think he was a bit,' agreed Murray. 'What did he mean? He said he'd explain it but he's gone to work already.'

'I may as well tell you, and it's no big deal – more of a house joke, you know.' Dũng looked at Murray. 'That Jewish man in the painting, and Dix's poem, both refer to the man who built this house back in the twenties. His name was Franz Zultman and he designed a number of flats and houses around here. He was a developer really, but he went broke in the Depression and supposedly hung himself up there.' Dũng skipped the full story. There was no need to tell Murray that Zultman had thrown himself off the turret with several metres of picture wire tied around his neck. Or that his body was found almost, but not quite, in two pieces. 'I mean no one even knows if it's true, it's just one of those stories you hear.'

'Something weird happened last night. I tried to tell Dix but he was too out of it to listen.' Murray was nervous about sharing too much with Dũng. He'd felt rebuked by him the previous evening when he'd tried to confide.

'You shouldn't worry about the junk up there. The wind gets in and rattles stuff around.'

'It wasn't up there,' said Murray with a pregnant pause. 'It was outside. I had this horrible dream and when I woke up, someone was outside my window. I'm sure they said something to me as well, but I can't remember what it was.'

'Someone was outside your window?' Dũng looked up, a slightly haunted expression on his face.

'Yes!' said Murray with a hint of impatience.

'Did you see what he looked like?'

'No, it was just like a flash. But there is one thing . . .'

'What?'

'I'm not sure it was a "he".'

'A girl?'

'Maybe.'

Dũng went back to his painting. He seemed agitated, biting his bottom lip.

'What are you thinking? It's not Claudette is it?'

'No,' said Dũng with a dismissive wave of the paintbrush.

'Who?'

'I've no idea, it's just . . .'

'Just what?'

'Well, it's just that someone tried to break into Doc's car the other night and . . .'

'And?'

'Well, we're a bit freaked out since the bashing.'

'You think those bashers might still be after you?'

'Something like that.'

'Fucking spin-out. Why don't you call the police then?'

'I've reported the bashing and believe me, the police won't be any help with this. Come and get one of us if anything else happens, alright?' He changed the subject. 'Do you want to go shopping this arvo?'

'Sure,' said Murray, allowing himself to be diverted.

'Okay. Let me work until two and then we'll hit Chapel Street.'

Murray put on a Smashing Pumpkins CD and rattled happily around the house, checking out gear. He worked out how to use the dishwasher and cleaned the rest of the kitchen. He made some more coffee, lay down on the big Art Deco lounge and phoned his mum. Mondays were her day off.

'Hey, Mum.'

'How are ya, Shane?'

'Good, but I've got to tell you, Mum – it's Murray now. No offence, but you know I was never that keen on Shane.'

'Well, la-di-da, I suppose Tree'll be changing her name to Scary or Posh next.' She laughed. 'So what's happening? Where are ya living? Are ya keeping your nose clean?'

'Mum, I'm not a criminal, you know. In fact I reckon I've done pretty good.' He explained his new situation to her.

'These blokes: the artist, the doctor and the Pommy bloke. Are they . . .'

'Gay? Yeah, Mum. The house is huge, four bedrooms. Mine's got this stairway up to a tower thingy.'

'And what about girls? I thought you were more keen on girls?'

'I'm only living here, Mum, you know – I have to run the joint: do all the shopping. There's even a car I can use – cool, hey?'

'Well, you watch yourself, love. God, next you'll be off to Mardi Gras the way you're going.'

'Hey, and guess what else, there's this girl, well woman, next door. Her name's Claudette and she wants me to do her gardening. She's like thirty-four but you wouldn't think so.' Murray suddenly remembered his mum still wasn't quite forty and he thought about how different the two women were. His mum was still a bit of a girl but years of working and bringing up two kids single-handedly had tired her out. Claudette seemed like some glamorous TV personality by comparison. Murray felt ashamed for thinking like that about his mum, whom he adored. 'How's Tree?'

'Oh, you know, never off the phone to that Russel boy or Stacy. God knows what they talk about. That girl from Vienna World was asking after you. I'm not keen on her. She told me to tell you that she's going out with that Cal Wotsisname. Quite huffy she was. "You don't waste any time, do you?" I told her, and she said, "There are plenty of other fish in the sea." "Most of them carp," I said. She was showing off her new car down at the service station. I felt like saying, "That'll keep you in hock for the next five years".'

'Well, Mum, it's good to be away from all that small-town friction.'

'I'll bet.'

'Dũng – he's the artist – is taking me shopping for clothes this arvo. I need to get a new image, I reckon.' Bush pig no more, he thought with a flutter of excitement. Drug-fucked disco pig instead.

'There's nothing wrong with the country, love. Just don't forget you can come back whenever you get tired of living in mansions and buying other people's groceries.'

'Yeah, Mum. I love you.'

'I love you too and we miss you. It's not the same without you. I thought I'd drive down with Tree one weekend, take her to one of the shows for her birthday. You can come too, if you'll still be seen out with us.'

Dũng and Murray spent a couple of hours trying on clothes. Murray spent a good chunk of his savings on shoes, shirts and trousers. One pair of pants Dũng insisted he buy had zips all the way up the outside of both legs. They were tight and Murray's bum looked enticingly gorgeous. Dũng felt quite jealous as he watched Murray revolve in the fitting-room mirrors.

'Cute arse,' said the shop assistant to Dũng. 'Is he yours?'

'Nope, he doesn't belong to anyone.'

'He will soon,' smirked the assistant as he collected discarded items.

Murray just smiled. 'Why are these queens so forward?'

'I don't know, but he's probably right.'

'It might not be a boy though, hey?'

Dũng looked at Murray in surprise. 'Aren't you queer?'

'Sure, I guess, but I'm not full-on gay.'

Dũng, suddenly fascinated, smiled to himself. Doc had broadened his social horizons without even knowing it. Wouldn't it be funny if Murray brought a girl home? Dũng was always keen to see Doc's boys-only existence challenged.

'Well, darling, maybe we find you a pretty girl.'

They shopped at the supermarket, had a drink at the Duke – 'Our local,' advised Dũng – and headed home. It was five o'clock, and almost dark. As they rounded the corner into their street, Murray noticed someone standing by the phone box. She was a pasty-faced girl with lots of black eye make-up and tight jeans. Her eyes seemed to lock onto the car as it passed and she saw Murray watching her.

'Is she a prostitute?' asked Murray.

'Who?'

'That chick on the corner.'

'I didn't see her.'

'She was just hanging out on the corner. Looked like a real scrubber.'

'No one's written their names on the dinner board. Does that mean you're all out?'

'Nah, it's Monday. Dix doesn't get paid for a few more days, so he'll be broke and won't be going anywhere. Doc's usually here for dinner, and I'm here.'

Murray set about making a lasagne and a salad. An Italian kitchen-hand had taught him how to make it '*bellisima*' and he thought it was his best thing. A look through the pantry had already revealed Vietnamese rice paper, exotic noodles and strange herbs that signified a much fancier level of cuisine than he was used to cooking. He made up his mind to get adventurous – gradually. There were cookbooks on a shelf: Stephanie Alexander, Jill Dupleix, Charmaine Solomon and Dix's favourite, Delia Smith. He poured over these books while the lasagne baked and realised how dumb his culinary resumé must have sounded. Still, they'd picked him, and the kitchen was fantastic.

There was a knock at the door. It was Claudette, all rugged up in a coat and gloves.

'Come in,' he said a little nervously. 'I'm cooking and Dũng's still painting.'

Claudette went straight to the freezer and pulled out a bottle of gin. 'Would you like a martini?'

'I don't know. I've never had one, and I don't like gin much.'

She waved her hand at him imperiously. 'Martinis are nothing like gin.' She began pulling jugs and glasses out of cupboards. 'Cambridge should be home any minute and I intend to be waiting for him. After last night I can't imagine he'd be working back late – not that I can imagine *him* ever doing that anyway.'

Murray watched her, bemused.

'It was his drugs that kept me out until six this morning, so it can be his gin that kicks them back in tonight. What are you making?'

'Lasagne.'

'Can I stay for dinner?'

'I guess,' said Murray. 'I've made a big one.' Murray sipped his martini and his face contorted. 'It still tastes like gin to me.'

'That's because I haven't put the olive in yet.'

The front door slammed and Dixon stormed in. 'I nearly picked up trade on the tram tonight. Men are so made that they can resist sound argument, and yet yield to a glance. Claude, my darling. And a martini on my homecoming. Perhaps I do need a wife.'

'I'm sure "wifey" could do without you. Didn't you get enough trade last night? In the toilets?'

'Claude, the idea, and in front of the boy. No, I returned to my lonely bed at four this morning.' He shot a glance at Murray. 'Not a word from you, cherub.'

Murray flushed, sure that Claudette would think Dix had slept with him. He went about cooking, quite unable to compete with the two lushes on the bar stools who whispered and giggled raucously as they sipped their drinks. Eventually they realised they were being rude. Dixon looked over at Murray.

'I think we should introduce Murray to the joys of JC's cocktail hour when he's older. One week older.'

'I'm not sure I can be doing you-know-whats as a matter of course on Sunday afternoons, Cambridge.' Claude slipped off her coat.

'Me thinks the lady doth protest too much,' taunted Dix.

'I got new clothes today,' interjected Murray, immediately feeling self-deprecating and stupid.

'What did you get?' asked Claude over the rim of her glass.

'Heaps of stuff.'

'You must model something for us,' added Dix.

Murray flicked his hair back and went all coy. 'I'm cooking now, maybe later.'

'Nonsense, I'll make the salad dressing. Go and model something.' Claude eagerly took over the kitchen. Murray vanished to his room.

'You know, Dix, I could probably get him some work, modelling.'

'Why not? He'd probably be keen. I feel a bit awful, I've hardly spoken to him and I'm sure he thinks I'm a pompous – what is it you say here? – up-myself dickhead.'

'We all do, why wouldn't he?'

They heard the Citroën pull up, and Dũng emerged from his room.

'Are you two still going?'

'We're just starting. Have a martini – you've been off the booze quite long enough for one dose of concussion.' Dix shuddered at the memory he'd been suppressing quite successfully for two days.

Doc wandered in with a dozen mixed reds he'd picked up to cellar.

'Where's Murray?' he asked as the bottles clinked to the floor.

'About to take to the catwalk,' said Claude. 'Tonight we're getting dinner and a show.'

Murray entered wearing the zip-up trousers, a blue body shirt, some clunky-funky shoes and a vinyl jacket with a black fur trim on the collar. He attempted a shy run-way turn, and they all whooped and applauded. Dũng beamed paternally.

'How would you like me to be your agent, Murray?' said Claudette. 'I think we've got waif-cum-Schenkenberg here.' The D3 were all very impressed.

Murray basked in their approval for a minute. 'I've still got to get your teas on the table.'

'You make it sound like a counter meal,' said Doc.

Murray felt the gin rising to his brain and giggled. 'Number 54, youse teas are ready.'

They all moved into the dining room and Dũng set the table. Murray followed bearing his lasagne. 'Perhaps you could teach me to cook some of that Vietnamese food, Dũng?'

'That's *my* speciality. Don't you worry, *em yêu ơi*.'

'What's that mean?'

Dũng touched him on the nose. 'Darling, of course.'

'Cool,' said Murray.

Once they were seated, Dixon toasted his arrival.

'As Wilde himself said, "It is only shallow people who do not judge by appearances". '

Murray felt half flattered. He realised that was probably as good as it got with someone like Dixon. Suddenly he felt as if he'd always been here, and it was merely for him to relax a little and enjoy it. He realised no one was going to stand over him – it was obviously only Doc who'd wanted a houseboy. The others would eat his cooking and hopefully like it. The only thing he was nervous about was the night-time, alone in his room. He didn't want another night like the last.

He didn't mention the spectre at dinner, though he didn't like the thought of the house being under the watchful eye of queer bashers. Still, he wondered to himself, surely the basher wasn't a chick.

two

'No man can guess in cold blood
what he may do in passion.'

Old proverb

Cuisine Extra

'So Bert, a lot of people think they're going to feel hungry but the calorie controlled program allows you delicious snacks throughout the day. And what's great is you can even enjoy a glass of wine with dinner.'

Claudette clicked the TV off. 'A glass of wine! Stupid cow, doesn't she know it's only the second and third glass that do anything?' Claude put her hands around her own waist. 'Four kilos, if I could lose just four kilos I'd be happy.' The fax began to ring and she stood over it, the eager midwife of possibility.

'Yes!' she cried as an acceptance on her quote for Daimaru's Christmas catalogue printed itself out. 'Fifty grand. Joy to the world!' She'd be able to cream twenty grand off the top if she budgeted on models and photographers correctly.

She'd have to get herself into gear though. She only had two weeks before shooting if she was going to meet the six-week deadline. This was the first time she'd scored such a huge contract. She went out to the car to grab her Filofax and noticed a scrawny girl with too much eye make-up loitering near her front gate. Their eyes met and the girl shuffled off down the street. Strange, thought Claudette.

'Bert, the recipes are not only great value for the budget-conscious housewife, but the kids won't even know they're eating food that's good for them.'

Murray felt like one of the housewives in question as he ironed

Dixon's shirts in the kitchen, his eyes fixed on the screen. He hadn't worked out how to get cable on the kitchen TV yet. He switched it off and put the radio on. He had the house to himself today but needed to get out. He stacked last night's lasagne plates and the breakfast dishes into the dishwasher, took out the wine bottles and breathed in some cold air. He looked out at the street, quiet now with everyone at work. Then he noticed that girl again, down by the phone box.

Dũng sat at the traffic lights, en route to see his mum. Trân, his sister, had been on the phone hassling him for not having been over there for weeks. And Mum had been ill and off work. He was going to do her shopping for her, cook her some soup, and give her some money.

Dũng wondered why even though she never appeared more happy herself, her kids had achieved the better life she'd sacrificed so much to give them. She still clung to her role as a living martyr. In part he knew that she still suffered the shame of no longer being a member of the bourgeoisie – of being a peasant in another world. But all that was so long ago and plenty of Vietnamese families had built themselves up again over the last twenty-five years.

The small ancestral shrine in the corner of the lounge, where once they had left oranges and tea, had now taken over the whole back end of the room. Gradually, in the ten years since his grandmother had died, his mother had receded into a haze of Buddhist obsession, claiming that her life was merely a vehicle for accruing merits for a better life next time.

Dũng missed Bà nội. She'd made an effort to enjoy life as an old woman and had found moments of joy in Australia. He smiled, remembering the old Greek woman from two doors down, Mrs Tsolazedis, who used to spend hours in the kitchen with his grandmother. God knows what they had talked about. The two possessed only a handful of English words each. There were always lots of hand and head gestures. Sons, daughters and television all seemed to surface in their conversations. War came up too, inevitably resulting in much hand-wringing, handkerchief-twisting, sighing and head-shaking.

They'd sit in the kitchen, Bà nọi drinking tea from a flask, Mrs Tsolazedis drinking Greek coffee which she brought with her in a thermos. They sat with parcels of home-made Greek and Vietnamese cakes strategically placed on the table in what looked like a culinary chess game. Dũng and Trân used to joke about it. 'I'll eat one of yours, if you eat one of mine.'

The old women went on coach trips together, to Albury and other border-towns, where they played the pokies with bus-loads of other Australian pensioners. They always took their own lunches, wrapped in foil and string. They spoke only to each other, and Bà nọi, who had the 'lucky touch', would bail Mrs Tsolazedis out when she lost more money than she should have. Mrs Tsolazedis would get in trouble from her son if she spent too much on the pokies.

'Vietnamese is lucky, Greek not same-same.' Bà nọi would shake her head at the dire locklessness of the old Greek woman. She'd hold up her 'lucky finger' and pour a bag of gold and silver coins onto the kitchen table. She'd count them into even ten-dollar lots, then catch the bus to the bank. Dũng and Trân always got their share of coins.

Dũng smiled as he drove through his old stamping ground. His grandmother had come out to Australia on a boat which ended up having no water. The dead were thrown into the sea, and he and his family had arrived in Darwin half-dead themselves. Dũng, thankfully, was too young to really remember that trip. Mrs Tsolazedis, on the other hand, had come as a legal migrant to her waiting family on a comfortable aeroplane. Yet Bà nọi still thought herself the lucky one. Crazy old crones, he thought. He decided he would do a painting of ancient migrants playing pokies. He'd call it *Thư hai sư xà chi phia nào kiẽn (Second Chance to Win).*

As he pulled into his mother's drive, fake red candles glowed ominously on the lounge-room sill.

Murray turned the key in the lock and the small, wooden door creaked open onto a staircase so petite it looked like something from a fairytale. It was steep and took a sharp right-angled turn to the tiny glassed-in turret at the top. A built-in seat went all the way around the two-metre enclosure. Dũng had been right, it was piled so high with junk, it obscured the view in some spots. Off in the distance he could see the grey shimmer of Port Phillip Bay.

He looked down to see Claudette feeding her cat. She was wearing a Japanese kimono and Murray noticed the way she held her hair back from her face. There was always something exciting about watching people who couldn't see you. She was bashing the cat food into a Willow pattern bowl, her expression pinched and slightly revolted.

Claudette's garden stretched back in an orderly fashion. He could see lavenders and scrawny bare deciduous trees on the lawn. One was a Japanese maple, just like the one outside his window; the other, some sort of miniature oak or elm. He could see a herb patch and a trellis which hid a compost bin. Claude was scuffing around the garden in her slippers, looking for any stray, ripe lemons on a small tree by the fence.

Suddenly she seemed to sense someone was watching her. She looked up to the turret. Murray waved at her but she was squinting, unable to see beyond flaking paintwork and the sun's bright reflections on the weathered glass. She went back inside. It was cold despite the sun.

Murray cleared a spot on the window seat. He beat the dust out of the cushion and sat down. He lit a joint and pondered how the turret would make an excellent smoking room if it was cleaned up. On mornings like this, it captured all the sunshine you craved for living in Melbourne. As he drifted off to the whims of the weed, he fancied he could hear a piano somewhere.

A doorbell interrupted his sunny daydream. Head spinning, he descended the stairs and went to answer it. It was the girl he'd seen on the corner.

'Yeah?' he said.

'That guy, the one in that weird blue car, 'e's a doctor, isn't he?'

'What's it to you?' asked Murray in his most unbutlerly tone.

'I jus' wanna know 's all. I've got something he might be interested in.'

Murray looked into her quick, sharp eyes and doubted it.

'Not just him neither, them others as well.' She opened her hand to reveal a Zippo lighter with a Sydney Swans emblem on it. 'I've got something else too, but I'm not showing you.'

Murray stood dumbfounded. She had clearly escaped from a mental asylum and he felt altogether too stoned to deal with her.

'He doesn't smoke and I don't think anyone here barracks for the Swans,' said Murray in the cautious and patronising tone usually reserved for the ill or half-witted.

'Oh, he'll be interested, I reckon. You just tell him Angel was here and I'll be back.' She waved her finger at him. 'Got that?'

Murray nodded idiotically as the demented girl walked off up the driveway. 'I'll be back,' she repeated in a querulous voice of nervous bravado.

He closed the door and locked the house carefully. He wanted to go down to Acland Street but felt cautious, what with her out there peering in windows.

Then he rallied. Whatever it was she was after, it wasn't his problem. He donned his new coat and stepped out for the remains of the day.

The Whole Story

Crest-fallen or fêted? The Crest hotel sits like a forlorn Titanic. *Stripped of her original Deco fittings she waits impatiently for an eager investor to uncover nostalgic gold mines where previous owners have failed to yield profits . . .*

'What the fuck do you think you're doing, Brearly?' shouted Brian as he slammed the page on Dix's desk. 'We're trying to sell the fucking joint – you know that. I told you before you went up there, or has this article been done from looking at the picture? We need lines like "years of financial mismanagement have been the undoing of this powerful and profitable hotel". If we can editorialise a sale for that hotel, Bryson & Davis will contract the back two pages for twelve months. They're even offering two grand to the journo who writes the selling copy.'

'Two thousand dollars,' said Dixon. 'You never told me that.'

'I shouldn't have to, you get paid too much already. But if you can't do better than this, I might write it myself. Hell knows I could use the money.'

'Can I take a photographer up and have a full page, with four-colour process shots in the glossy section?'

'Use our archival stuff. The place has been empty for years and with all the fittings gone, we'll have to rely on shots from its glory days. Believe me, Dixon, it's been on the market for years. We'll be pushing shit uphill to sell it. B&D reckon they want 3.5 million but I reckon they'd sell it for 2.5 – it's listed with the National Trust so there's fuck-all can be done with it structurally. Punters with that much money know a white elephant when they see one.' Brian slammed a bulging file on Dixon's desk.

'Such wisdom, Brian. You're a comfort to us all I'm sure.'

Dix waded through various articles from the past seventy years. The two-thousand-dollar bonus sounded dodgy. How could they ever claim credit for the sale?

He looked at some large photocopied sepias from the twenties. A trio of flappers sipped champagne on the Overlook Balcony with a lone man who looked uncannily familiar. His eyes fell to the copy which listed left to right: 'Miss Florence Enright, Mrs Lila Coventry, Miss Penelope Foyle and Mr Franz Zultman enjoying spring sunshine at a Fleur de Lys charity luncheon'. A shiver ran down his spine because he'd never seen a picture of Franz Zultman before. He stared at the face. Zultman had that classically inscrutable, pale visage of the period: handsome, moustached, but somehow insipid. All his fire and personality were probably trapped in eyes that were now washed-out pixels, corrupted by time and Xeroxing. Dix fancied he saw the face liven for a moment as sometimes happens when one stares at a picture for a long time, but dismissed it as a chemical kick-back from the weekend. His eyes scanned the picture and caption again, and recognised something else. Surely not, he thought, as he looked at the ring on Penelope Foyle's finger, there couldn't be two of those rings.

He called Beverley over – she always knew the more intriguing aspects of Toorak's society history.

'Bev, what family was Lady Penelope Asquith from?'

'Asquith nee Foyle. Big department store chain bought out by Georges in the fifties. Of course, the old Georges doesn't exist any more. You would have loved it, terribly smart, all those Pringle jumpers and Hunting pinks . . .'

'Please, darling, I'm twenty years away from a Pringle cardigan and I don't hunt.'

'Most of Penny's fortune now rests in that Toorak property you covered. God knows why she hasn't sold it and moved into one of those Como apartments with all the other heiresses and war-brides who frittered away their family fortunes. I wouldn't feel safe living in that Toorak cash-palace all alone.'

'Nor I,' said Dixon with a shiver.

'Of course, Penny was quite a girl in her day, you know. Didn't marry until she was in her thirties, and old Lord Asquith was nearly fifty then. Apparently he'd never 'felt the need for a wife', if you get my drift, but he had to carry on the name, what-what, as you do. Penny's daughter didn't look a thing like him – she'd be in her fifties now too.'

Dixon found her jaunty, private-school earnestness a little over-powering but kept silent. It was good to let Bev, font of the profane, to gurgle away once in a while.

'Shocked society terribly our Penny did. Had an affair with a Jewish property developer, the one who designed the Crest, incidentally – remember this is before World War Two. Dreadful scandal. Her father nearly disinherited her. He was a Grand Poobah – Melbourne Club and all that. Well, anyway, the Jew killed himself, or so they say, and she vanished for two years to God knows where. Europe I expect, that seemed to be the place for money and shame.'

Dixon felt fresh shivers course down his spine. It was too much, these events all colliding. He'd always wanted to discover intrigue, and this sounded just his cup of tea. But could he bear going back to that house? Quietly, he gathered up the files, and went and told Brian he'd be visiting the Crest the following morning. He needed to get the feel of the deserted hotel. He could pick up a set of keys from the estate agent. He hoped Dũng would loan him the car. Perhaps Dũng would even come with him. It might be scary alone.

Murray was cooking Cajun Chicken with sweet and pontiac potato fries. There were also corn and broad beans in his bag. A woman in the supermarket had been demonstrating the Cajun blackening powder in a little frying-pan. The recipe was on the side of the packet so he thought he'd give it a whirl.

His trip to Acland Street had taken hours, each shop offering all sorts of temptations. He'd bought some soothing aromatic oil to burn in his room and a tatty paperback about an Amsterdam prostitute called Nina H from a second-hand book store where the owner smoked a cigarette through a hole in his neck. He'd seen sex shops he was too shy to go into, and been told by the Hungarian lady in the butcher shop that he was too thin. She'd let him try some home-made salami, but he'd bought the chicken breasts instead.

By the time he'd got back, it was getting dark and the sensor light was working again. He put his silverchair CD on, which he suspected the others wouldn't like, and set about getting dinner ready. Dixon was the first one home and he went straight for the dregs of the gin in the freezer.

'Shit, that guzzling alcoholic bitch drank it all.'

'Who?' asked Murray.

'All of you guzzling bitches. Never mind. I need a booze break.' He propped a hip against one of the bench-tops. 'Off to the mountains tomorrow.'

'For work?'

'Yes, there's an old hotel that's for sale. Designed by the same architect who created our very own Juliette.'

'Wow!'

'I've only been up there once. It's terribly pretty. Perhaps you'd like to come too? I'm going to ask Dũng as well. We'd need his car in any event.'

Murray signed up enthusiastically. Later, during a momentary silence at dinner, he broached the subject of the girl.

'She asked if I was a doctor?' Doc looked at the other two. 'And she showed you a Sydney Swans Zippo?'

'Yeah, and she reckoned she had something else you'd be interested in, but she wouldn't show me. Her name's Angel, but you wouldn't guess it from looking at her. Do you guys know her or something, 'cos if you do I wish you'd tell me who the fuck she is. She kinda freaks me out a bit.'

There was a moment of edgy, conspiratorial silence. Finally Dũng spoke.

'We don't really know who she is, but we think she might be the girl who was in the car with the bashers. You see, she pissed off with the other guy and we were left with the one who'd grabbed me. Then he scaled the fence. She must have stalked us or something.'

'But I don't get why you'd be interested in a lighter.'

'Either do I,' said Dix in a firm bid to close the conversation.

'Anyway, she reckons she'll be back – so you'll probably get to meet her yourselves.'

'Lucky us.' Doc gave a nervous cough.

Murray cleared the dishes away and rinsed them off. As he approached the dining room he heard Doc say worriedly, '. . . I hosed it out with disinfectant and it still smelt of shit.'

Dixon looked up as Murray entered. 'Doc, I wish you wouldn't talk about proctoscopes at the dinner table. It's an insult to Murray's fine repast.'

Murray was no Einstein but he knew bullshit when he smelt it. They weren't telling him the whole story.

Bella stretched out on the couch, her glass of red wine precariously balanced on its plush arm. Claudette tried not to think about the potential stain on the cream upholstery – she had vowed not to turn into her mother for at least twenty more years. Wolf, Bella's German Shepherd, lay by the fire with Missy. They still remembered each other from the days when Wolf and Bella had lived in the house too. Bella looked up through the window at the gloomy turret. 'Have you decided if that house is haunted yet?'

'I don't know,' said Claudette. 'It has some strange vibes and

I could swear someone was watching me from the turret today.'

'Were they?'

'I don't know, the sun was in my eyes and I couldn't see.'

Bella shrugged. Her once long hair was cropped quite short these days, but she still hadn't adjusted to it and continued to move her head in sudden ways as if a weight of hair was getting in her eyes.

'Do you think I look like a dyke?' she asked abruptly.

'With those nails?' Claude grinned. 'I don't think so.'

Bella had boutique porcelain nails, more like pricey jewellery than part of her body. They made an expensive sound when she tapped things. Claudette broke hers all the time, and went every month to have them fixed. But she knew, for a fact, that Bella went every week. Bella's nails were one of her trademarks.

'Not even the femmiest of lipstick lezzies gets her nails done every week.'

'I don't go every week.'

'Liar, I looked in the book last time I was there, and you were booked in for two months ahead.'

'Sprung.' Bella picked up her glass. 'All the better to scratch you with.'

'You'd think married men would give you a wide berth – it would be so easy for those talons to tell on them.'

'It would be easier sometimes if I was more like you and hated men.'

'Hate men? What do you mean?'

'I don't know . . . hate the way they are. The impossible alchemy of male and female.'

'I don't hate them. I know they're here to stay. Hating men would be as futile as hating existence.'

'Well that's easy enough to do, I often hate existing.'

'Existing and fucking are two different things,' murmured Claude. 'I haven't had a fuck for three years, Bell.'

'I know.'

'I just can't be bothered with all the dynamics and communication. Erica Jong was right about the ideal of the zipperless fuck, but it doesn't exist. I look at the boys next door and their lives seem like one big orgy. If they're not fucking each other they're picking up trade. If they're not doing that they're at sex venues. And if they're out drinking and get a sudden wave of uncontrollable lust, they can get a quick blow job from some troll lurking in the toilets. It just doesn't seem fair and it's certainly not decent. I'm simultaneously envious and disgusted.'

'Not all men are faggots, Claude.'

'I know, but when you see how gay boys behave it makes you wonder if straight men wouldn't prefer endless interchangeable partners. It makes me nervous.'

'Ah, but pussy's different. They know they have to work harder to get pussy.'

'And they hate us for it. It's like dragging a piece of steak along on an elastic string to tease a starving lion. I just want to put them out of their misery but when I do, I feel contempt for their weakness.'

'You just don't value yourself enough. Maybe because of . . .'

'Don't go there, sister, that is *not* the case. When I got raped – I've never told you this – I was grateful when he started fucking me. Grateful because up till then I was sure he was going to murder me. It's amazing how your values change in a life-threatening situation. And you know how they tell you to vomit because it puts them off? Well, I could remember having been told that by a self-defence woman who came to my school, but I couldn't do it. You know why? Because I would have been too embarrassed. There I was, a knife at my throat and cunt, and I couldn't spew because it was unladylike. Never mind the fact that my vomiting might have made him angry enough to kill me.'

'Yeah, well, who can chuck up on call, in public anyway? I've always wondered about that bit of advice. I bet a man made it up.'

'Then I went back to school and everyone knew. "Psst, psst,

psst, she's the one . . . on the beach . . . it was in the paper." And everyone was ever-so-nice, the way teachers and mothers and girls at school are, but of course dates were out of the question. Boys were too scared to try their luck in my rape-ravaged puss. It had lost its high school charm, its "I might just let you" enigma.

'Thank God I'd already done it with a couple of boys prior to the attack, at least I knew I liked it. By the time I got to uni I knew I'd have to be sexually aggressive if I wanted a fuck. So then I was a slut. That, apparently, was because I had no self-esteem. Even when I started hanging out with Doc and all his gay friends, it was assumed I was so screwed up that I needed to be with "non-threatening males". Never mind that some of those "non-threatening" males got me so messy on drugs I'd have fucked anything that moved and once or twice did.'

'Go girl,' said Bella, 'you're on a roll now.'

'But it just shits me. I mean the hideous joke of it all is that the beach I got raped on was a gay beat. There were poofs there all the time, even caught them at it a few times. Mum used to think it was a disgrace and the area needed cleaning up. I used to feel safer because they were there.'

'Didn't any of them see you?'

'From a distance perhaps and when they saw, they quickly avoided coming closer. By then I was being raped and they either didn't care or thought I was with my boyfriend. Who knows what they thought.'

'Well I don't imagine beats would be hot-seats of homo-chivalry.'

'After the attack, the cops spent weeks patrolling all the beach-fronts. All they managed to do was arrest dozens of gays – or "odd-bods" as Mum used to call them. The PC brigade tell you that you've got to report rape for the benefit of all women *etcetera, etcetera*, but I would have been better off in the long run if I'd gone home, cleaned myself up and said I'd tripped on a ti-tree root.'

'You don't know that. It might have turned you crazy – all that suppressed rage and stuff.'

'Maybe, but I never knew where to direct that rage anyway. Who should pay for what happened to me and millions of other girls? I certainly wouldn't tell any guy about it now. The worst part is when you get them in the sack they treat you like you're made of glass, and all you wanted was a hot, sexy fuck.'

Bella giggled and kicked her legs. 'What do you do?'

'Nothing, Bell, that's the way it is. I'd rather have my one savage teenage rape than years of beatings at the hands of an alcoholic husband.'

'Claude, it shouldn't be a case of either–or.'

Claudette shrugged and Bella dropped it. 'So what's Doc's houseboy twinkie like?'

'Oh guess . . . Gorgeous, of course.'

'How old?'

'Nineteen, twenty, or something.'

'A screamer?'

'No, not at all. Quite butch and country actually – still smells of hay bales and the milk shed. He's not only a cook, but a gardener. Wants to grow vegies in my yard.'

'How sweet.'

'I tell you what though, if you've got some spare time I'd love you to do some shots of him. I think with a little bit of cultivated attitude he could be quite a find.'

'It seems sad to have to drag the boy from barnyard bumpkin to arrogant attitude.'

'If we don't, worse people will.'

'Too true,' said Bella.

The Crest

'Whether one is motoring up from town for a secluded weekend or simply a day-tripper in search of a Sunday roast, the Crest offers the service of yesteryear in the surroundings of the future . . .'

Dix glanced up from the moth-eaten brochure he held. 'That, me dears, is what they said about it in 1932 when it was struggling to keep its doors open through the Depression.'

Dix's fellow voyagers were only half-interested in the Crest's chequered history. Dũng was preoccupied with thoughts of his mother and Murray was thinking about the girl, Angel. They were well into their hour-long drive, and had motored beyond the fast-food restaurants and car-yards that marked Melbourne's city limits. Now they were passing lots of mock-Tudor Devonshire tea shops and Austrian-style schnitzel palaces. Busty neon wenches winked cheekily at them from beneath their flashing fluorescent yokes and pails.

'Yodel, odel, eh hi hi,' sang Murray as he stretched out on the back seat and made his ears pop.

The car was hot and filled with rugs, coats, boys and food. Its demister was working overtime as the outside temperature dropped. Soon they were buzzing along neat winding roads which cut through dense fern forest and towering gums.

'There's some snow,' shrieked Murray as they rounded a bend and changed down for further ascent – but it was only a white shopping bag caught in the gutter.

After twenty minutes of scenic driving they turned off the Sassafras Road and into the garden kingdom of a fallen lady. The Crest loomed like a failed World Fair attraction, a cyclone fence her only protection against vandals and fornicating delinquents. Dixon unlocked the padlock and they entered the property.

The carpark was empty, weeds breaking through the gravel. Unseen birds warned of their arrival while brightly coloured rosellas scattered in a panic of plumage. Clambering out, they followed a pot-holed path directly to the front door. Murray hauled a backpack full of food and wine which Dix had decided should be eaten on the Overlook Balcony.

'It'll be freezing,' moaned Dũng as Dixon tried out his keys in the regal front door.

'Well dear, I didn't phone ahead to have the concierge put the heating on.'

The door swung open and they entered cautiously. They wandered past a desolate reception desk and a deserted bell-boy counter.

'Can you imagine how much it would cost to heat?' asked Murray, passing a fireplace that could happily accommodate a small house.

It seemed to Dix as if they'd stumbled upon a setting worthy of the Famous Five. 'Aren't we supposed to split up to go exploring at this point?'

'It's not a movie,' said Dũng.

'It fucking could be, this is *sick.*' Murray dropped the pack by the reception desk, handed Dix the wine and gazed at the central stairway, marvelling at the sheer size of it all. 'Cooee!' he yelled, his voice reverberating through four floors of neglected splendour.

'You can see elements of Juliette's design here, can't you?' Dix was looking at the cornices. Each had moulded plaster images depicting the icons of 1920s progress, leisure and style. Trains hurtled towards the future in dramatic perspective, ships steamed by on chalky alabaster waves, dapper angular gents lounged by grand automobiles and Erté-inspired female figures lolled in furs and tightly fitted gowns. 'This detailing is just superb.' He shook his head in wonder.

Murray was fiddling with some servant bells which could be heard ringing faintly in other parts of the hotel. Meanwhile, Dũng was trying the balcony doors with each of the hotel's dozen keys.

'I'm going to find the staff quarters, where I belong,' said Murray, excited as a gun dog.

'Off you go then. We'll ring for you if we need anything, won't we, Sir Dũng?'

'Indeed . . . Ah, gotcha!' The balcony door slid sideways on a track hampered by grit and chipped paint. Dix lugged the pack out onto the huge paved plateau.

'I think we need some of that wine. Dũng, would you do the honours?'

'Isn't that what we brought the butler for?' But Murray had long since disappeared.

They stood silently for a while, gazing out on the overgrown garden, the grounds dropping away into the gorge that lay beyond.

Dũng poured some red wine into Doc's best glasses. 'I'm sure he'd understand. We couldn't have paper cups, not here on top of the world.'

'Cheers!' They smiled at each other conspiratorially.

'Look how quickly everything gets taken over by nature,' said Dũng, turning away and pulling creepers and grass from the masonry cracks.

'Ah, nature is a hanging judge.'

'So are we,' said Dũng with a look of faraway consternation.

'No. The fox condemns himself, not the trap.'

They heard Murray plodding through a room above them.

'What will we do about that girl?' said Dũng, finally voicing a shared, suppressed anxiety.

'There's room enough for two in that there well. A family plot perhaps?'

'I'm serious, Dix. What will we do?'

'How should I know? Nothing, until she comes back. We don't even know what she wants.'

'I just feel sick with worry all the time.'

'That, luvvie, is because you don't drink enough.'

Suddenly Murray was standing right by them, an old soda siphon he'd discovered in his hand. 'Drinks, suh?'

'How'd you get down here so quick?' Dũng gasped.

'You mean up. I've been downstairs in the kitchen. It's huge.'

'But we just heard . . .' Dũng looked at Dixon and they both pulled silent screams.

'I think we'll take luncheon in the grounds, chaps,' Dix said briskly, and led them from the balcony into the deep, dank gardens.

'That Franz Zultman really left some creepy shit behind in his buildings, didn't he?' mused Dũng. No one answered.

'I wish you guys would tell me what's with that girl.' Murray pouted a little.

'Don't worry about her, Murray.' Dix's voice took on a warm paternal tone he never knew he possessed. He put his hand on Murray's shoulder. 'She was probably the girlfriend of the basher who got left behind. No doubt he's given her the flick and is shagging some new piece of trailer trash as we speak. I bet she hasn't seen him since that night and thinks we've got something to do with him pissing off. But why should we bother ourselves with the sordid ins and outs of barbaric, beer-swilling thugs and their attendant gutter slags?'

'Yeah, well, I've seen that type of chick before,' nodded Murray, flattered at last to be privy to some theory about the girl.

'When, and if, she finds the nerve to come back, we'll set her straight. As straight as it's possible for us to set anyone.'

They carried on down the zig-zagging path and felt the temperature drop as they trudged to the bottom of the gully. A lake came into sight, and a wooden boathouse, oozing with dilapidated rustic charm. Rhododendrons, willows and ferns battled for space on the crowded banks and the trio wished they'd brought a rug.

Instead they sat on a wooden seat, drank the wine and ate left-over chicken with pide bread.

'It's not really picnic weather, is it?' observed Dũng as he disappeared into his jacket.

'Whose idea was it to bring this second bottle?' Murray filled his glass with a devilish grin. He gulped half of it and went off exploring again. Dũng looked at Dix and was struck by his expression. It was the same one he'd seen at the well. It suggested a sly lasciviousness – a carnal portentousness.

'What do you think is in there, Dũng?' Dix pointed towards what appeared to be a large storage facility built under the steep hillside.

'I dunno, probably where they keep rakes and things.' Dũng's voice flirted in a schoolyard sing-song.

'Let's look.'

'Haven't you had enough scares for one day – for one lifetime?' Suddenly Dũng was serious again. It didn't look an ideal location for exploring his desire for Dixon.

'The wine has lent me courage. Come on.'

They went up to the dark entrance and found there was no door, just a gloomy cavern that seemed to emit a reptilian breath of cold and damp.

'Oh my god, Dix, I'm not going in. Who knows what's in there!'

'You'll never, never know if you never, never go.' Dixon grabbed Dũng's reluctant hand and dragged him into the pitch-black space. 'Your tiny hand is frozen,' he whispered.

A drop of something icy struck Dũng on the forehead and he yelped.

They ventured three or four metres inside. Still they found no back wall. 'I've gone far enough, Dix. Stop, this is awful.'

'What's awful?' asked Dix as he grabbed Dũng, cupping his face in his hands.

Dũng smelt the wine and tobacco on Dix's breath, then felt his tongue licking the inside of his ear – a hot-blooded slug in the cold darkness. 'What are you doing?'

All at once they were kissing, just like the other night. Dũng felt tension flee his body. Had he been this rigid with nerves since then?

Their breath echoed in sudden savage gasps through the bizarre grotto. Neither could see a thing.

Dũng's cock hardened painfully in his trousers and, as a hand came to rest on it, he knew he wouldn't be able to save himself, or the situation, this time.

Dixon undid his trousers, and Dũng's eyes, visionless in the black, rolled back in anticipation. He felt Dixon lowering himself to his knees, heard them crack, and groaned – heavenwards as pleasure engulfed him. A cauldron mouth had taken his cock. Long, hot, greedy mouthfuls made him achingly aware of the tangible cold around them. 'Oh fuck, Dix, *hàn-động*.'

Pulling him up, he wrestled Dix's trousers down, lamenting his own loss of sensation. He'd been dying to taste this, and as he slipped his tongue under the generous foreskin he found delicious closure to his longing.

Dix leaned back against a steel drum and groaned. Releasing his weight and relaxing, he felt the drum shift. It rolled over with a resounding boom. Losing his footing, he reached for Dũng and they abandoned themselves to the icy concrete floor.

'More,' cried Dix with a fervour that startled them both.

They fed on each other in a breathless, animal frenzy – each stopping just short of spilling their charges. For some reason, they couldn't entirely relinquish control.

Suddenly they heard footsteps.

'Shshshsh,' said Dũng.

They stood up, both dizzy with lust. Slowly their delicious fug subsided, leaving them as nothing more than naughty children about to be caught by an authority figure. All sniggers and mock fear.

Someone had entered.

'Are you guys in here?' They heard Murray's shuffle as he entered their newly claimed domain.

'C'mon . . . Dix . . . Dũng . . . you're freakin' me out.'

Murray tripped on the drum that had fallen sideways and fell forward against Dixon's rigid member. He gasped in fright and surprise. 'Fucking hell, are you two bonking in here? I can't see a thing.'

Dũng was pulling his trousers on. He too tripped, his limbs entangling with the others. It was a blind bungle, and no amount of laughter could conceal the embarrassment of it all.

'You blokes are too rad.'

'Tell us about it,' said Dũng, endeavouring to sound cool instead of flustered. They struggled towards the light, trying to compose themselves.

'Didn't mean to frighten the horses, Murray,' quipped Dix.

'Fucking *horse* is right. You two are fucking *off*, you know that?'

Dix and Dũng guffawed like drunks as their eyes became accustomed to daylight.

'Totally fucking crazy,' said Murray with a stern head shake that belied his youth.

A Message

Claudette stood in the kitchen, washing up, the French doors open to the garden. She was thinking about work, which graphic designers to use, which models. She hated doing mundane things like the dishes, but she had the ability to mentally absent herself. Missy wove frantically around her legs.

'Are you possessed by the devil today, Missy, or what?' she asked as the cat rubbed its pale fur against her skin.

She heard something rattling outside the house and her brow furrowed as she listened. She heard it again. It was coming from Doc's.

'Murray, is that you?' She knew both cars were gone, so it could only be him. 'Murray?'

Claude heard someone scurry away and raced back through the house, intent on getting to the front door to see who it was. But the front door was deadlocked, and it took her precious minutes to find the keys. By the time she reached the front fence all she could see was a girl vanishing around the corner. She was sure it was the same girl she'd seen in the street earlier.

She checked the passageway between the two houses for any signs of a break-in. There weren't any. She wondered if Murray had heard anything and traipsed round to Juliette's front door to ring the bell. There was no answer. Turning to leave, she noticed an old lottery ticket stuck under the doormat with a note scrawled on it.

You tell that doctor that I want to see him.
It's hard for me to come at night and I'm in
trouble and I reckon when you know what
I've found you'll have to help me.
Angel

Claude took the note in case it blew away. What had Doc got himself into this time? She wondered if this girl was like the vile Ricky. Surely he hadn't started selling scripts to junkies? He didn't need money. She wondered if she should phone the police, but decided to wait until Doc got home. There was certainly nothing dull about living next door to that lot.

Dũng said he would make dinner when they returned from their curious adventure. He felt like some old-fashioned comfort food. Murray hid away in his room, overcome by the newness of it all. He lit a joint and began reading about Nina H. She had this room where men could see her from the street and sometimes, if she liked the look of them, she would show them her fanny. If she really liked the look of them she would put one of her fingers in there and lick it. Sometimes it worked, sometimes it didn't, but she didn't care because she was just as happy to have sex with women, except for this one guy, Detlev, who she had some sort of spiritual connection with.

Murray was starting to wonder if perhaps this book wasn't the true life story it purported to be. The way Nina talked about it all suggested she knew she was giving you a fat. He imagined he might give her a go if she did the finger thing to him. He looked at her picture on the cover. She looked a bit like Agnetha from Abba, and the book dated from back then as well. She'd be too old now, he thought.

He put Nina down and thought about the huge cock he'd felt that afternoon. He remembered Claudette boasting the other night about how she could fill a bra and Doc saying something about Dixon filling a spa.

They were weird, all these relationships around him – if that's what they were. Murray's own dick was getting sort of hard but he knew dinner would be soon and he was having trouble focussing on anything specific. He wondered if Nina ever had that problem, but as the subheading of her book said, 'I'm a whore and so much more . . .' Murray thought that was pretty cool. He also liked the poetry she wrote at the start of each chapter, and wondered what someone like Dix would think of it. 'You call me slut, you call me tart, but I bring pleasure and that is art.' Dix would probably just laugh. Murray was a little scared of people like Dixon who always had something fancy to say about everything, and who acted like they knew it all.

In a way, Doc and Dũng were more approachable, warmer. He wouldn't be at all surprised if Doc wanted to have sex with him and after what he saw today, it didn't look like he'd be stepping on anyone's toes if he did. He'd never fucked a bloke and he reckoned it was about time he knew what it felt like.

He heard Dũng calling everyone to the table so he sucked the joint down and joined the family, his eyes as red as firecrackers.

At the table Doc was given an edited version of the day's events. Murray already knew that some things weren't going to be disclosed. 'Doc, dear to our hearts though he is, doesn't need to know everything, you understand,' Dix had drawled as they'd sped home, and Murray had just nodded.

'Don't be patronising, Dix.' Dũng had briefly lifted his eyes from the road to glance at Murray. 'There are no secret codes here, Murray. The rules get made up as we go along.' He eyed Dix. 'You make it sound like some sort of secret fraternity – we don't know what we're doing.'

Now they all chomped their way through Dũng's exotic fare as

Dix lectured on the architectural parallels between the Crest and Juliette. Murray switched off and concentrated on his food. The dishes had names that he couldn't pronounce, but which Dũng rattled off in the perfunctory sing-song of his first language. Murray liked the food, although he was a little apprehensive about the chilli. The other flavours – coconut, coriander and lemongrass – presented him with exciting olfactory revelations. They reminded him that his culinary repertoire had many roads yet to traverse.

He looked up as he took a swig of wine and caught Doc eying him, a tell-tale glint in his hazel eyes. Murray grinned back, feeling mischievous. He'd drunk a few glasses of wine, and he still couldn't work out what was going on between the other two. The doorbell chimed and Doc rose to get it.

He returned to the table with Claudette. 'Apparently we've had another visit from our little friend. She left a note this time.'

Dũng and Dix exchanged glances, and Doc passed Dix the note.

'She gives me the creeps, that chick,' muttered Murray.

'Why would we give a damn if she's in trouble?' asked Dix of no one in particular.

'Trouble couldn't have found a more deserving home,' added Dũng, taking the crumpled note and scanning it briefly. Still, a worried silence fell over the dinner table. Murray took the dishes into the kitchen and turned to find Claude at his shoulder.

'What are you doing the day after tomorrow, Murray?'

'Nothing much.'

'Want to come to my friend Bella's studio with me and get some photos done?'

'Cool with me.'

'I'll give you a call around midday. I've got something on in the morning.'

Claudette accepted a glass of red from Doc and quizzed him a bit more about Angel. Murray told her about their meeting, trying to make Angel sound as spooky and menacing as possible. 'Fuckin' crazy bitch,' he concluded.

Several drinks later, Claude wandered home, aware there was something Doc still wasn't telling her. It just didn't make sense. Why would Angel hold them responsible for her boyfriend disappearing after he'd bashed Dũng? She shuddered. What could Angel have that the boys would want? And why was everyone except Murray pretending to be so bloody disinterested? There'd been some weird energies at the table, she reflected.

Juliette's inhabitants were all a little on edge. They felt haunted by this world and the next. It wasn't a night anyone felt like spending alone in their beds.

Midnight Snacks

Precinct sauna was having a circus night, at least that's how Dix interpreted it. The usually dingy establishment was lit up, adorned with tents, and a girl in an old-fashioned party dress was doing a tap-dance routine on a make-shift stage. They're letting girls in, he thought without surprise. Then the tents caught his notice. What wickedness might therein lie? No sooner had the thought escaped him when a tiny midget emerged from under a flap, wearing nothing but a Tarzan-style lap-lap.

'Here, come here!' He spoke in one of those squeaky voices, just as Dix had expected. There was something irresistible about him, and Dix felt himself harden as he followed him into the tent. Suddenly, he realised that he was, himself, stark naked, his excitement quite evident. He flushed with embarrassment.

The midget was waiting for him. 'That's quite something you've got there, quite something I reckon, I beckon.' He tried to reach the meaty flagpole that swung like a divining rod above his head, but couldn't. Dix found himself marvelling at his own size – it had never been like this before. The midget looked up. 'You want some midget boy pussy?' he asked. 'It'll be tight alright. Every night, midget sex is out of sight.'

The midget danced about, Rumpelstiltskin-style, and despite the art-house absurdity of the scenario, Dix was raging with lust. The midget didn't even reach his knee and it didn't take a mathematician to realise the proportions of this mating were obscenely improbable. The midget didn't mind. 'Pick me up, make me swoon,' his arms were outstretched. 'Fly me to the fucking moon.'

Dix obeyed and the midget swung from his greasy cock like a monkey, singing softly. Dix, entering further, could feel himself passing through what must have been vital organs. The further he went, the more the midget seemed to relax. He looked down at the fleshy bundle fixed onto him and listened to its song. 'I want to see what drugs are like on Jupiter and Mars.'

Dix could feel something happening around him, something moving in and closing. A cervix, he thought, though it couldn't be. It locked onto the shaft of his cock with an engineered precision. It wasn't a nice feeling any more – if ever it had been. He was trapped, something was going to cut him off and there was nothing he could do.

'UUHGGG, get it off,' he mumbled as he woke, heart racing, sheets drenched. The house audibly sighing with his return to consciousness.

'Bloody dope and red wine,' he murmured. The heating seemed to be on too high and he could hear music, the same song from his dream sung by Astrud Gilberto. The clock glowed 12.30 a.m. He dragged himself out of bed to turn the heating down, and opened his bedroom window. Doc kept the place sealed like a vault in winter.

As he padded down the hall he could see the light on in Doc's room and hear murmurs emanating from within. Nearing the door, he smelt dope smoke and realised who was inside. He pushed it open a fraction and there they were, Doc and Murray. Murray was in the driver's seat and Doc was backed up onto country boy's equipment, his face aglow. Their eyes met. Dix quickly eased the door shut and wandered back down the hall. He peeked into Dũng's room where the object of his earlier affection now slept like a baby. Then he walked through the kitchen and adjusted the heating control. 'Fifteen degrees is quite warm enough at night.' Looking out the front window he saw Claudette's light was on, and picked up the phone.

The Gingham Girl was just one of Claudette's dateline identities. She was a mixture of barnyard naivety and whorish salacity.

I'm the gingham girl with eyes of blue, curly blonde hair, milky full breasts and a whistle-white pussy with a red-hot cherry pie smack bang-bang in the middle. Ask me to pull back my layers of sweet, pouting pastry and I'll tell you about the hot fruit inside.

She hit the return key and knew she'd get replies. Gingham Girl was popular in the Salon *de* Singles: 'the world's busiest cyber dating chat-line'. She wasn't sure what she meant by 'whistle-white' but no correspondent had ever pulled her up on it, so it stuck.

Hey Miss Gingham, pull back your pastry, I'd like to snout me some of that pie. I'd lick that sweet fruit and drink every drop you could make of that there pie juice.

Claude considered her reply. Food as a metaphor for genitalia was a trap that was hard to escape sometimes. She could go all night comparing clits to cherries, vulvas to ripe figs, and end up eating everything in the fridge without so much as a tremble of an orgasm. Miss Gingham usually attracted Yankee respondents when she went on-line. It was nice, but she always pictured some obese guy with a baseball cap and a can of Budd.

All at once, the line dropped out. She'd forgotten to turn off call-waiting and the intrusive beeping had ruined the connection. Who would call at this hour, she wondered, picking up the phone. 'What?'

'Hello dear,' whispered Dixon with obscene huskiness.

'Hello Cambridge. That accent, at this hour, could bring a girl unstuck.'

'Are you entertaining Mr Buzzbee?'

'No, he's fresh out of batteries. I was talking to Mr Middle

America in the cyber salon – sipping a virtual cocktail while getting ready for some farmyard foreplay. Your phone call dropped me out, you bastard. What about in there?'

'We've got one angel and two devils, three if you count my dream.'

'Tell Mumma.'

'Oh, the usual sort of thing, Diane Arbus meets *Eraserhead* – toothed sphincters, a visit to the circus, sex-crazed dwarfs. With the images floating around my head, I don't need half-price Tuesdays to get my cinematic jollies, especially not after the snapshot I just got of a certain doctor and his houseboy. Surprise, surprise. What have you got in there?'

'A half-finished *boteille de vin rouge*, an unopened picnic hamper from David Jones, and a Black Forest cake from Glick's. Also a roaring open fire.'

'I wasn't asking about your fanny, Love.'

'Arsehole.'

Dix peered out the window and saw a shadowy wisp of smoke emerge from the chimney. It seemed to be writing something in a filigree script across the moon.

'Sounds cosy. I can smell the wood smoke from here.'

'Come over.'

'In my dressing gown and slippers?'

'Why not?'

'Can I smoke?'

'You know I don't mind.'

'Doc does.'

'I know, he's mean and anal.'

Dix's mind flashed to the image of homosexual males *in extremis*. 'He certainly is tonight.'

'See ya soon, Cambridge.'

Poor Dix, thought Claude. Out in the cold, superseded by a younger model. At least it happened to men too and not just women.

Claudette liked the fact that Dixon was relatively new. He didn't have preconceptions about her, and it seemed as if Doc had been professionally discreet about the more problematic aspects of her past.

'Here, Cambridge, get this into you.'

'It looks positively disgusting.' He eyeballed the wedge of Black Forest cake – the cream, the glacé cherries and the chocolate – as if it were Mount Everest and he, a mountaineer. 'And I'm to wash it all down with a glass of your finest red, is that right?'

'I don't know about finest. I think this bottle cost about seven dollars, but I'm not opening another until it's empty.'

'I have to work tomorrow, Claude, you witch.'

'You're the one who intruded on my romantic solitude . . . So Doc's done the deed with Murray?'

'Doing, dear. Perhaps it's finished now, who can say?' Dix swallowed a mouthful of cake and guzzled the wine. 'Dreadful stuff. Give me some more at once.'

'So you and Doc, it's not "on" any more?'

'Questions, questions . . .'

'Give me no answers . . .' They began to sing a Spandau Ballet song.

'Stop!' cried Claude. 'We're too young to be so retro.'

'We are not,' said Dix. 'If twenty-year-olds aren't too young I don't see why those of us who were actually there should be. I mean we lived through "The Lebanon" and "I Ran", we know the answer to "Love + 1".'

Claude giggled. 'That's exactly why. We're the most lazy and jaded generation ever. We thought a weird haircut, a designer beer and prance around the floor to Stephen tin-tin Duffy singing "Kiss Me With Your Mouth" was tantamount to revolution. Now we're supposedly in positions of creative power, we just repackage everything from our childhood and sell it to an equally jaded youth culture who wear a lot of nasty synthetic clothes which we hoped would never come back.'

'I suppose in the seventies they were repackaging shit from the fifties, though I'm sure not on the same scale. What was that line in the eighties about the seventies? "They got peace and revolution, we got AIDS and Whitney Houston". Perhaps the nineties can be "We got crack and Massive Attack".'

'No, it won't work. The nineties, thankfully, are too eclectic to package.' Claude stole a drag from Dixon's ciggie.

'Don't, you fool!' He snatched it back.

They turned on a music video show and Dannii Minogue was on. They looked up from their cake and watched as she drove across the Nevada desert in some sixties American convertible, lip-syncing. Then she took one finger up to her face and delicately pulled a strand of hair from her baby-doll eyes.

'It shits me. How does she do that and manage to look so cute and sexy? She's been marketed within an inch of her life . . . Oh, yes, jump into the pool! That's right, show us how thin you are . . . We can't miss that!'

'You sound bitter, Claude, my dear.'

'Me? Never. I've just had too much to drink, which won't help my midriff any.'

'Sometimes you look a lot like Miranda Richardson, you know?'

'Do you really think so? Oh, Dixon, that's the nicest thing anyone's said to me in ages. I hope you're not lying – I'm too insecure at the moment to bear it if you are.'

'Nonsense, you just got a huge commission.'

She shrugged. 'I didn't get that on my looks. I'm not opening any more wine, you can have some brandy.'

'Perfect for in front of the fire. Why, Claude, must we be constantly bombarded with youth? I mean God knows most of the population is over thirty.'

'Well it's obvious, isn't it? Youth is the time of greatest

possibility. At twenty we haven't failed to achieve our dreams. At thirty-five half the people in the world have. Possibility is what makes the world go round. Why do you think Russia and China and communism didn't work? Because people would rather spend their lives in poverty and failure as long as they know there is the possibility that they could one day become famous like Dannii or Kylie, or get rich from Tattslotto, or morph into a notable politician like Pauline Hanson. It's a trick of the world that the most ordinary people can attain the most extraordinary positions – and people want to keep that dream alive at any cost. I mean, what sells more copies, *New Weekly* or *Green Left*? I rest my case.'

'You sound like the next Ayn Rand.'

'Surely we don't need another. Besides, we're actively engaged in marketing all these things: tits, bums, houses and chocolate cakes. You, Dixon Brearly, just long to be running down the steps of a Viennese opera house in a dinner suit, a smoking gun in your hand, Midge Ure sideburns on your face. You can't bear to be hurtling towards forty, no longer the model, just the end consumer, poor love.'

'So shoot me. And I'd prefer "hurtling towards thirty-five", thank-you-very-much. Nothing is ever enough to the man for whom enough is too little.'

'Hear, hear,' chanted Claude as she raised her glass.

Murray lay in Doc's bed while Doc washed in his bathroom. It was certainly weird being there and he doubted it would happen again. He felt almost embarrassed now that it was over. He was also surprised at how into it Doc had got. There was something about this whole butt-fucking thing that didn't gel with Murray. It felt okay and everything, but why would you fuck a guy up the arse when there were women with cunts walking around? He switched on the TV and watched Dannii pull a strand of hair from her eyes.

'She is so sexy, the way she does that, don't you think?' Murray asked as Doc climbed back onto the bed and joined him.

'Who? Dannii?'

'Who else?'

'She's alright, if you like that sort of thing.'

Murray thought about 'that sort of thing'. Pretty girls and women lolling about on motel beds, painting their toe-nails or touching-up their lippie. 'I suppose it must be hard getting into sex when you know how all the bits work, when you've seen them in operating theatres and hospitals.'

'I don't think about it.'

'I bet'cha do. I would – all those tubes and passages. I can't bear thinking about medical shit.'

'It's a dirty job, but someone's got to do it.'

'Yeah, yeah.'

Murray had his chin resting in his hands at the foot of the bed; Doc leant against the pillows, his knees to his chest. A condom lay on the polished floor where Murray had tossed it. He seemed to have lost interest very quickly, Doc reflected. He thought about Dix looking in on them. 'Dix saw us before, Murray, when we were . . .'

Murray blushed. 'I thought you closed the door.'

'I did. I think we might have upset him a bit, he can get quite jealous.'

Murray, still stoned, let out a cynical guffaw.

'What was that for?'

'Nothing.'

'No, what was it for, Murray?'

'Well, he's hardly an angel himself, if you know what I mean . . .' Murray looked hard at the TV. 'She's quite something, I reckon.' Dannii, swimming underwater, suddenly burst out of the pool into the desert sun, all smiles and 'come hither' sexiness.

Doc regarded her suspiciously. 'She's supposed to have had a lot of plastic surgery. I know someone who saw her up close at Mardi Gras and they said you could tell.'

Murray rolled on to his back and lit the half-finished joint from the ashtray. He turned back to Dannii who was deliberating over two different micro-dresses.

'Who cares if it's all fake? You can get into some very hot business with chicks, y'know.' He didn't say it but he was beginning to think that pussy and babes might be a lot more inspiring than arseholes and doctors.

Social Pages

'Hello, Lady Asquith? This is Dixon Brearly. You might remember me – I interviewed you for the *Courier* the other week about your splendid garden.'

'Of course, dear. I thought you made great sense of my ramblings.'

'Well, Lady Asquith, I was rather hoping you might be able to help me out with some other research I'm doing into Melbourne's social and cultural history.'

'I'd be happy to if I can, dear.'

'Would you mind if I popped by later this afternoon then?'

'That would be fine. Not too late though. I find I'm very tired in the evenings these days.'

Dixon's visit to the Crest had fed his desire to know more about its builder. He had not mentioned his research plans to the other boys, however. He imagined that they would be nervous about him revisiting the place where they'd off-loaded their terrible cargo. Dix had some strange notions himself about murderers always returning to the scene of the crime, but he refused to be superstitious about it.

He rang the doorbell but it wasn't Lady Penny who answered it. It was her daughter, Caroline. She had a traditional Toorak blonde bob, a weak, socialite smile and a face that was too smooth for a woman in her fifties. She ushered him into her mother's day room.

'I can't let you stay for very long. Mother's had a bit of a turn and she's rather fragile at present. Mother, Mr Brearly is here to see you.'

Lady Penny lay on a day-bed, lit by the sun's fading glow through one of the leadlight windows. She appeared almost transparent, her frailty much more in evidence than it had been on his first visit.

'See that tree, Dixon?' He followed the direction of her gnarled finger to an immense conifer beyond the driveway. 'I planted that myself when I was no more than ten years old. It's incredible to think something so small can grow so large and overshadowing in one's lifetime, don't you think? I never thought it would come to block out the sun when I most long to feel it.'

'Indeed,' answered Dixon.

'So what part of the property have you come to report on this time, dear?'

'Well, Lady Asquith, I'd hoped to ask you about some other history actually. You see I'm writing an article about the Crest Hotel.'

'Goodness, is that place still going?'

'Well, it's not going, but it is still there, soon to be sold.' Dixon handed her the photograph.

'For goodness' sake,' she murmured as she glanced at it. 'Where did you find this?'

'I imagine the paper keeps all sorts of things in their archives. It's not really the hotel I'm interested in so much as Franz Zultman.'

Her expression hardened perceptibly when he mentioned the name. 'He's been dead for donkey's years.'

'I know, but you see I live in a house he designed in Elwood.'

'Which one, dear?' Her voice was raspy now, and her curiosity somewhat trepidant.

'Juliette.'

'Oh my Lord.' Her hand came to rest on her heart.

'Are you all right, Lady Asquith?'

'Yes dear. Juliette was his pride and joy, you know.'

'And his downfall.'

'What do you know about that?' Her eyes seemed to blink away the years momentarily.

'Just that he couldn't cope when the Depression hit and killed himself.'

Lady Penny issued a single, unhappy laugh. A darkness had crept into her voice. 'The Depression, was it?'

Dixon's interest was sparked. 'Wasn't it? I believe you were friends, weren't you?'

'Friends.' She laughed again and began to cough. 'I suppose you could say that.'

'Well that's what people did say, didn't they?'

'My dear, people have said a good many things about me and a good many more things about Franz.'

'Was he a nice man?'

'Nice, what a dreadful word. Didn't they beat that out of you in the university? When I knew Franz I was no more than a girl. He was rich, a talented architect, a fine pianist and weak in the same way as most men.' She tapped the photo emphatically. 'I would have been about eighteen when this was taken, only a year or two after my début.'

'And Franz?'

'A good ten years older.'

Dixon took a deep breath and a big gamble. 'I've heard it said there was a scandal?'

'A scandal there was indeed . . .' She gazed out towards her tree. 'Franz Zultman was a . . . Jew, dear.'

'I know.'

'I wonder if you do. I wonder if you can imagine what it was like for me to *befriend* a Jew in the twenties? Even a Catholic would have been unforgivable as far as Father was concerned.'

Dix gambled again. 'Was he a friend or a lover?'

Lady Asquith didn't seem to hear the question. 'When I was young, Dixon, people . . . kind people . . . might have referred to me as a free spirit. Sadly there were too few kind people about then. You see, I was quite a beauty in my day. I know it sounds vain to talk of oneself in such a way, but when one is as old as I am, one can look back at oneself when young and see a completely different person. We never feel we are beautiful at the time that we are. I suspect that's why they say youth is wasted on the young. Our faults seem too obvious for us to enjoy youth's splendour. It is only much later that you can see yourself for what you really were. Pass me that box over there.' She pointed to a miniature Victorian trunk which sat on a doily-covered table.

Dixon silently complied and she opened it, rummaging through a bunch of snapshots from various eras.

'There.' She handed a tiny sepia shot to him. Dix looked and saw a young lady being helped from a Daimler by a gentleman. She was smartly dressed, even for the time, as was he. Dix felt a shiver of excitement. It was clearly Franz and Penny. Then he noticed the background and his hand trembled with something verging on anticipation. It was Juliette as a new house, the garden nothing more than small shrubs.

'Is that the two of you?'

'Yes, dear, but look a little closer.'

He looked at the front windows, then followed the lines of the house up to the turret. There seemed to be a dark figure there and a snaky line coming from the window.

'It looks like someone's in the turret,' said Dixon.

She passed him a magnifying glass and he took another look. A chill passed through him. The line from the window looked like a ghostly piece of rope. The figure, although more clearly defined, was still too dark to make out.

'Who is it?' asked Dix.

'No one. It wasn't there when I originally got the picture back.

I never even noticed it until I returned from travelling abroad in 1933. He was already . . . gone . . . then. I'm sure it's just a light stain or something, but when you know the story as I do, it's a menace, and quite distressing to see.'

'I can imagine.'

'I wonder if you can, Dixon. My father was a very wealthy and powerful man. I may have been privileged in some ways, but I was still a woman. Franz was a Jew. Before the war Jews were regarded with the utmost suspicion and my father despised them. Neither Jews nor women were trusted at that time, and in those days a social disease was more than his reputation could stand.'

'A social disease?' asked Dixon, floundering slightly.

'A disease, Dixon,' she said, somewhat impatiently. She looked him straight in the eye. 'The kind anyone might catch if they aren't careful.'

Dix felt his jaw drop. He couldn't believe this frail, carefully spoken woman was actually talking about the clap. To his horror, he felt a blush creep over his cheeks.

'Shame has many names, dear,' Lady Penny continued unperturbed. 'Don't look so worried. You don't really think your generation was the first to have them, do you? I suppose I was lucky I wasn't pregnant.' She shivered. 'Dealing with that was a nasty butcher's business in those days.'

'So Franz was your lover, Lady Asquith?'

'As I've said, Dixon, I was very young, a free spirit. I also fancied myself a sophisticate in all sorts of ways. He was a Jew and it would never have done for anything to come of it. Far too much was at stake, you understand.' Her words hung eerily in the darkened corners of the room. 'I'm afraid I'm tired, dear. I really will need to have my rest now.'

The afternoon sunlight had vanished and the harsh glow of a single Victorian reading lamp rendered Lady Penny, prematurely, a corpse. As if on cue, Caroline appeared to see him out.

'Do you think I might borrow that picture, Lady Asquith?'

'Oh no, Dixon, that must never leave the house. I must always be reminded.'

He had no idea what she meant and no time to ask. Caroline was guiding him firmly towards the door. Old people could be infuriatingly obscure at times.

'Well, thank you for your time, ladies.'

Dix stumbled from the musty mansion onto the badly lit drive and began the long trek towards Toorak Road. Fog was beginning to descend and the cold seemed to get into his bones. Unseen dogs barked at him, their wet snouts poking beneath security gates. The strange sepia picture with its dark figure stayed grimly in his mind. He longed for a taxi and a drink.

While he waited for his tram, Dix thought about how jealous he'd been the previous night of Doc and Murray. It wasn't as if he had anything even vaguely approaching a relationship with Doc – nor did he want one. And he'd been just as faithless himself. He thought briefly of his ongoing little flirtation with Dũng and smiled at his quick rush of desire.

Then he felt, again, a pang of loss for Soren. If Soren had lived he would never have needed a relationship; theirs had been perfect. They'd talked about everything together. Done everything together. Except sex. But even that they'd shared, comparing notes on their respective conquests, sometimes even trying out the same partners. They had roomed together, holidayed together and gone clubbing together. They were soulmates and Dixon still found himself talking to Soren inside his head sometimes. He knew he had to stop doing this because Soren was somewhere else, not caught up in Dixon's current adventures and deceits. He felt a wave of grief and loss.

A tram approached and Dix swung on. A nostalgic sentimentality had overtaken him; he even spared a thought for his parents, back in Bath. He must ring them, it had been a month now and it was his turn. They never said as much, but they were wounded that he'd chosen to live so far away, and they abided strictly by a routine of 'turns', as if daring their one line of communication to drop out completely.

As the tram trundled along Chapel Street, Dix realised dinner would be waiting for him at home. He salivated at the thought. Murray wasn't half bad in the kitchen, and not at all unpleasant on the eye. How supremely decadent it seemed to be living in a staffed house. He could never have afforded that in London.

About Last Night

'Where's Dũng?' asked Doc, plonking his case on the kitchen floor.

'He won't be home till later. He's at his mum's.'

'Look, Murray, about last night . . .'

'It's alright, Doc. I know it didn't mean anything.'

That wasn't exactly what Doc had been going to say, but he nodded his head as he listened to Murray extricate himself from the situation.

'You know, I'm kind of, like, only half into guys, if you know what I mean.'

Doc continued to nod, almost mechanically now.

'Hey, I'm cooking chicken parmigiana. I know it's not, ummm, Stephanie Alexander, but it's good winter food, right?'

'Delicious,' said Doc, as he opened the wine for which he now had a desperate thirst.

'Doc, do you know Claudette's friend, Bella?' Doc's head nodded yet again. 'Well she's going to do some photos of me. Claudette's lined it up – reckons you can get great money from modelling.'

'Bella can be a bit trying but she's an excellent photographer. And if you make it, you can earn a fortune.'

The front door slammed and Dixon pranced in. 'I hope I'm not interrupting anything.' He'd tried to make it sound like a jovial, light-hearted dig but feared it sounded sarcastic. He looked over Murray's shoulder at the food preparation. 'Yum, yum! I think we're very lucky to have you here, Murray. You're too talented.'

He plucked a potato wedge from the baking tray Murray had pulled from the oven. 'I fear we'll lose you to greener, more lucrative pastures.'

'Like the catwalk and the pages of *Studio*,' said Doc. 'Bella's doing a session with him . . .'

'Tomorrow,' supplied Murray.

'I think "Fox" should be your modelling name. Short, but stays in one's mind,' Dix suggested.

They laughed. 'Your first shoot could be Fox in Winter,' he added.

'Or Fox Hunting,' said Doc.

At dinner, Dixon couldn't resist recounting his interview with Lady Penny. They discussed her cryptic recollections.

'It would seem that our dear departed predecessor, Franz Zultman, gave the young Lady Penny a filthy dose of the pox,' Dix smirked.

'God,' said Doc, 'in those days it's a wonder someone like Foyle let her near a Jew.'

'I don't think he did. But nothing throws disparates together like polite society and cold hard cash. Who was it who said that refinement is merely the degree to which one conceals his greed? The real horror is . . . Oh, no, I shouldn't, it might freak Murray out.'

'What?' whined Murray, determined not to be the reason for anything remaining undisclosed.

'It's just about the turret, that's all . . .' Dix hesitated.

'Look, I know the story, alright? Nothing could freak me out more than that chick at my window the other night.'

'Well,' Dixon lowered his voice. 'She showed me a picture that made my blood run cold . . .'

He recounted the story as dramatically as he could, keeping the other two poised for a full five minutes with fork-loads of food at their mouths. As the tale approached its terrible climax Murray felt almost sick with fear. He wondered if perhaps he hadn't dismissed the musky, masculine protection of Doc too soon.

The macabre silence that ensued was broken only by the chime of the doorbell. All three jumped in unison.

'That fucking Claudette, I'll kill her,' snarled Doc as he went to answer it.

'You're the doctor, are'n'cha?' On the door mat was a pale scrawny girl.

Doc gave a mute nod.

'You work in that clinic, up Carlisle Street, don'cha? I know you do, 'cos I've seen you go in there.'

'I, er, go there every day,' confirmed Doc, knowing this – at last – was Angel.

'Well, I've got something you might be interested in.'

By this time, Murray and Dix had appeared behind him. Seeing them gather she asked, 'Where's the Chinese one?'

'Vietnamese,' corrected Doc, scratching his head.

'Whatever.' She shrugged. 'Maybe you should let me in, I've got something you'll wanna see.'

She moved past him towards the lounge. 'I've already shown him.' She pointed accusingly at Murray as she passed.

Reaching into her coat pocket, Angel pulled out the Zippo lighter, carefully wrapped in a handkerchief.

'This belonged to Mitch, the guy you bashed near the park.'

'*We* bashed?' exclaimed Dixon. 'We rescued our friend from him.'

'That's what you reckon. How come that night I found this and his keys then, out by your blue car when I came round later?'

Doc's mouth gaped, but Dixon chimed in like the Devil's own barrister. 'Because, when Mitch hightailed it away from us, and jumped over the fence, he dropped them. They probably fell out of his pocket. Naturally I picked them up to take them to the police for fingerprints. But when I got home, they were missing from my jacket pocket. They must have fallen out. Probably when we carried our friend in from the car – he was still in a state of shock from your boyfriend's brutal, unprovoked attack and couldn't even stand. Now I know why I couldn't find them again, that night or since. Still, better late than never. I'm sure the police will find them helpful. Will you hand them to us now?'

'I don't think so.' Angel put the lighter quickly back in her pocket. Realising she was surrounded by three men and that the door was closed, she added, 'And you better not try anything neither 'cos I didn't bring the keys – I left 'em with a girlfriend in case you tried anything on. I still reckon you done something to him,' she concluded, but she sounded defeated.

'What do you want?' asked Doc, attempting his best bedside manner.

Angel looked down and stared at the floor. She sighed. 'I haven't seen him since . . . and I'm pregnant. It's his baby. I'd just told him that day.'

'Well look . . . Angel . . .' Doc found it a difficult name to call her. 'It's not really our concern . . .'

Her nerve returned. 'It is if you did something to him.'

'Perhaps he's done a runner,' said Dixon, incredulous at the situation. 'Perhaps he doesn't want the baby?'

Suddenly Angel looked tired. She exhaled heavily.

'Well, that's kind of what I've been thinking. That's why I wanted to see *you*.' She pointed at Doc.

'Me!' he said, taken aback. 'Why me?'

''Cos you're a doctor, of course, and if Mitch's pissed off back to Queensland, I don't wanna have the kid. I want an abortion, and I reckon *you* don't want me makin' trouble with the cops.'

'Angel,' said Doc in his most professional tone. 'I'm a GP. I've never performed an abortion in my life.'

'But'cha know about them, right?'

'Angel, you could get one done through Medicare. For free. In a proper hospital.'

'No I can't.'

'Why?'

''Cos I'm living at the fucking Little Sisters of Charity women's shelter and them nuns wouldn't let me stay if I did.'

'Surely they don't have to know?'

'Oh, they have to know bloody everything. I'm on remand and they have to look after me till I'm sixteen.'

They all looked at each other, shocked by her age.

'It's worse than that. I'm only allowed to stay there if I don't see Mitch. They'd blow the whistle on me for sure if they knew I'd been with him, they reckon he's nothing but trouble. He's been in the nick, you see.'

'You wouldn't have to say it was his child.'

Angel looked at Doc in horror. 'What, and have them think I'm a slut?'

'She's got a point, Doc – an erroneous one, but a point, nonetheless. What about that other man, the one in the car that night?' asked Dix in an attempt to get a few more facts.

'Fuckin' Robbo, he's a dickhead. We met him at the pub. He's scum, he is. After we drove off, he tried to get a root out of me. I made him go back to where we'd left you but Mitch had already gone. I wouldn't put out so he dumped me, down near that phone box. That's when I saw your car. I knew it was the same one.'

'And the next night you looked in my window?' asked Murray.

'Well, I had to find out if it was you guys. I was going pretty crazy about Mitch and being pregnant and that.' Angel pulled a folded page from her pocket. 'I want to go to this place, you know, for the operation.'

She handed the page to Doc. It was a glossy list of private hospitals, photographed as if they were smart B&Bs. The one she'd marked was in East Melbourne.

'That's an expensive hospital, Angel.' Doc felt his complex

feelings of guilt and sin begin to surface when faced with the issue of abortion. He made an executive decision. 'Angel, I want you to come and see me tomorrow so we can talk about this and see what can be organised. Right now I want to drive you back to the shelter myself because you shouldn't be traipsing about in this cold.'

'Just you, right?' Angel eyed the others suspiciously. 'I don't trust all of you together.'

'Just me. Now, will you do that? Come in tomorrow?'

'S'pose.'

Doc nodded to the others and led her outside to the car.

As he turned the engine over he explained a few other things. 'Now, I can organise everything for you. I can tell the nuns that I've found a cyst which needs to be removed immediately, and I can pay for a decent hospital for you. We'll say we've had to put you in a private bed because of the public shortages at the moment. Will you let me tell them the details?'

She nodded.

'How many weeks are you?'

'Seven.'

'Okay. All I want you to do is bring those keys and that lighter with you so we can give them to the police, though you've probably rubbed off all the prints on them.'

She shrugged. 'It's just up here, on Grey Street.'

'Alright, Angel, I'll see you tomorrow, at the clinic, yeah?'

'Yeah.' She got out of the car and didn't look back.

Doc cruised home slowly along Shakespeare Grove, surprised to see the number of boys hovering in the shadows. They sat on fences or huddled in carparks and driveways. Like animated Disney attractions they waited, coming to life only when illuminated by the beams of headlights.

Doc needn't have driven home that way but he couldn't help himself. A melancholy trance track played on the radio as his lights picked out the boyish faces in the dark; pale, plaster of Paris mannequins, somewhat shabby on closer inspection but strikingly seductive in the momentary glare. He recognised Ricky Drouin's pinched face and shuddered.

Accelerating, he continued on, reaching the relative safety of Poets Corner. As he continued along Mitford Street he noticed a religious maniac – someone who regularly wandered the streets pushing a shopping trolley plastered with placards. 'Jesus can save the Babylonian whores' and 'Thou shalt not lie with a man as a woman' he read. Others seemed to be written in a foreign language, for they were indecipherable. As he passed, the man waved, thrusting one placard specifically in his direction and smiling hideously.

Sin is
in
your
blood
brother

It made no sense until Doc caught sight of it in his rear-vision mirror. The message conjured up all his darkest, frozen fears.

Nightcap

Dũng's car arrived only minutes after Angel's departure. Dixon was greatly relieved he'd missed the event.

'Murray, can you get Dũng some supper? Dũng, sit down and I'll fill you in on this evening's dramas.'

Dũng did as he was told and Dixon gave him the Angel spiel, right through to the abortion.

'Good thing I wasn't here, I'd have found a knitting needle and done the job myself.'

'Dũng, she's only fifteen years old. She wanted to have the baby, but of course now that Mitch has shot through *back to Queensland*, she's changed her mind.'

'Only a fifteen-year-old delinquent could possess enough misguided romance to want a baby like that.' Dũng shrugged. 'So what's going to happen?'

'Well, she's going to see Doc tomorrow.' Dix lowered his voice. 'I'm sure old money bags will be able to negotiate his way out of this with his trusty cheque book and old school tie.' His voice turned into a barely audible whisper. 'After all, he is the one who orphaned the poor child.'

Dũng gave a shudder. 'It's like a nightmare, only it's not the turret for once.'

'Do you have turret nightmares too?' asked Dixon, gulping down some more red.

'Oh, just this dream I have sometimes. I s'pose it's the curse of being a tortured artist, neither my conscious nor unconscious give me any rest.'

'Tell him about the picture and that old woman stuff,' urged Murray, who'd walked in with Dũng's food.

'I think I'll let him eat first.' Dix ruffled Dũng's hair.

Murray shrugged. 'Scared the shit out of me.'

He went back to the kitchen and thought about Angel. Dixon had never said anything about that lighter before. He'd made that up on the spot. Murray wasn't stupid. If Mitch really had disappeared then they'd definitely had a hand in it. Perhaps they'd even killed him, Murray speculated with ghoulish relish. Not that he cared one way or the other. Those bruises on Dũng's face had been real enough. But what if the body was somewhere nearby, in the house? He shuddered and tried not to think about it. Unfortunately, the only other thought that came to mind was Dix's story about the turret.

'Too much crazy shit,' he muttered, placing the last of the cooking pans in the drying rack. He needed to get out for a while. He decided to visit Claude and find out about tomorrow's photo shoot.

Claude was engrossed in her favourite TV show when Murray arrived at her door so she was somewhat distracted. It was not a show she liked interrupting, but she had to admit that, lately, life next door was providing even more gripping viewing. Nor was she disappointed by Murray's latest installment.

'What? She wants Doc to abort her baby?'

'Well, maybe not Doc himself – he's never done one, apparently – but she wants to go to some posh hospital and have him pay.'

'And Doc agreed to it?' Claudette was incredulous.

Murray nodded tentatively. 'I think so.' Claude didn't go into the matter any further. She was beginning to speculate about all the same things as Murray. She wondered if she hadn't always been a little suspicious about the whole thing.

'Where's Bella's studio?' Murray interrupted her thoughts.

'Oh, in South Melbourne. Bring some of those clothes you bought the other day. She'll probably have some other stuff you can borrow. She's got some Fashion Council thing on at the moment.'

'Cool.'

'So, Murray, what's this I hear about you and Doc getting together?'

'Shit, you can't do anything around here, it's worse than home . . . Listen, we're not getting together. It was just something that happened. I'm more into chicks, I reckon. But I'm a little confused right now. I'll get over it.'

'I'm sure you will. I think you'll find it's far too complicated getting involved in household sex like that.'

'You mean don't shit where you eat?'

'More, don't plough the home paddock, but yes.'

'Yeah, I know. But I sort of had a bad experience when I first got to Melbourne, and I thought maybe I should, you know, get over it.'

'What sort of experience?'

'Oh, it's nothing really. It's kind of embarrassing.' Claude looked encouraging so he continued. 'I was sort of raped, I guess.'

'Oh, Murray.'

'I mean it was my own fault and everything, but . . .'

'What do you mean it was your own fault? You told someone to rape you?'

'Nah, it's just . . . Well, maybe it's sort of different from a guy raping a chick, you know? Like with girls, you've got to be extra cool and play with them really softly . . . gently until they're really hot and ready for it. Like you *know* when they're into it, right? You've got to be thinking about their feelings and stuff before you . . . well, you know.'

Claudette knew all right, and as Murray gave his short lesson on male–female sexual relations she began to feel some of the early signs of consent taking place herself. She reprimanded herself and retreated momentarily to safer ground. 'Look, Murray, much as I love those boys, you can do without being involved in their sex lives, if you know what I mean.'

'Yeah.'

'Doc and I had a fling once, when we were about twenty and he was still confused, but he seems to have sorted that out since.'

'You reckon? Did he wash his hands straight after?' Murray started giggling at his indiscretion.

'We shouldn't laugh about that, Murray, he's got a real problem there.'

'I know,' he answered, still smirking. 'I'm a bastard.'

'So this girl, where does she live? Is she a prostitute?'

'I dunno. Some Catholic doss house or something. She's a scrag.'

'Murray, you don't know what she might have been through. She might have been sexually abused, raped, anything.'

'Raped!' Murray laughed. 'I've seen chicks like her before. They'd be rooting you long before you ever got a chance to rape 'em.'

Claude let it go, and quietly returned to the subject of Murray's own recent trauma. 'Well, what about this rape thing that happened to you?'

'Oh, I was stupid and went back to this bastard's hotel room. I should've sussed him out better.' Murray shrugged. 'He just kept going on and on about how I wanted him to fuck me even when I said no.' He looked at Claudette. 'I mean even with guys you've got to have some, you know, foreplay, you shouldn't just whack it in, if you know what I mean.'

'Of course I do,' she said, shocked that he should think her so naive.

'Exactly,' said Murray with emphatic hand gestures, as if that wrapped the whole thing up.

'You could have reported it, you know,' Claude persevered.

'What? To the concierge or something?'

'No, to the police, of course.'

'Like, "Hi, I just went back to a hotel room with this married guy whose dick I sucked and who I was in bed with and who raped me".'

'That's right. Expose him for what he is.'

'And wreck his marriage?'

'Well, she ought to know what he's like, don't you think?'

'No way. When you come from a town like mine you know there are rules about that sort of thing. Even if you were stupid enough to tell someone's wife, those women'd never thank you for it. No way. It'd be Shame City for them.'

'Well, what about AIDS then?'

Murray shrugged. He didn't want to think about that. He remembered his raw fear at the sensation of the man's bare dick. 'I bet there are just as many girls getting stuck into each other behind closed doors.'

'What, you think they hang around supermarkets the way men hang around toilets?'

'Well, back home, the chick at Blockbuster Video was on with this nurse from the hospital. They were copping off in the park one night. I saw them. They reckoned they were reclaiming the space. Towns like that'd explode if there weren't parks there when-the-sun-goes-down.' Murray imitated an explosion with his mouth and hands that sent him sprawling across the couch. 'Bloody rape, it's a fuck of a thing.' He laughed at his joke, and Claudette found herself laughing at him, or was it with him? He had a raw social confidence she rather admired.

'I should go home, Claudette. I'll see ya tomorrow.'

'All right, hon. See you then.'

Murray gazed up at the turret as he negotiated his way back over the side fence. The glass windows looked like black ink. He'd wanted to tell Claude that story too, but he knew it'd spook him to do so. He decided he'd take one of the sleeping pills that proliferated in the bathroom medicine chest. Then the ghosts could come, go and hang themselves as they pleased, he thought as he approached the warm glow of Juliette's curved porch.

'Well, I told her I'd help her if she gives us the evidence,' Doc told the other two, arriving home shortly after Murray had left. The D3 sat round the dining table, Dũng's dinner untouched. 'Though whether I can get her into Winslow House remains to be seen.'

'I'm sure she couldn't really do anything with the evidence anyway,' sighed Dix.

'I know, but I'd rather play it safe. If I can get our Angel into this clinic, subconsciously, she too might be glad to be rid of all traces of Mitch.'

'I doubt it. Her subconscious'd be all car sex and single-mother's pensions,' sneered Dũng.

'Dũng, get over it. God knows what sort of upbringing she's had.' Doc suddenly became all righteous.

'Well, that's no fucking excuse as far as I'm concerned. I come from a single-parent family and a Housing Commission shack. You don't get poorer than we were. Mum didn't even speak English, but do you see me in some Vietnamese knife gang?'

'Ah, but you have your art as a means of expression,' said Dix with a raised brow. 'You got a ticket out.'

'That *ticket* didn't come cheap. As far as I'm concerned she's just evil. She might be dumb as shit, but there are plenty of dumb people who don't hurt anyone. I can't forgive them any more than Claudette could forgive that guy.'

'What guy?' asked Dixon.

'Dũng!' Doc looked daggers at him.

'What happened to Claudette?' pressed Dix.

Doc frowned. 'It's something that happened a very long time ago, Dix, and I'm sure Claude would rather it wasn't spread about.'

Dũng looked at the anger in Doc's face. 'Well I'm sorry, I thought he knew – sue me!'

He stormed out of the room.

'It's alright, I won't ask,' said Dix. 'So are you and the houseboy hard at it now?'

'Is that really any of your concern?'

Dixon shrugged. 'He who desires but acts not, breeds pestilence.'

Doc laughed. 'In my line of business, I find the opposite to be true. Anyway, you and Dũng seem to be getting matey.'

Dixon shrugged again.

'Don't tell me, Dũng can't take it.'

'Not everyone, Doc, is as obsessed as you about taking it. Nor about douching afterwards.'

Doc was hurt. It was just like Dixon to pick up on those things. Doc struggled daily not to wash unnecessarily but found he couldn't help it.

'It must be a fucking nightmare to be so promiscuous and so germ phobic at the same time.' Dix emptied his glass. He knew he was being unnecessarily cruel, but couldn't stop himself. He couldn't bear the way Doc rushed to the bathroom after sex.

Doc stayed silent, waiting for a parting shot that wasn't long in coming.

'Well, you're the Lord of the Manor, dear. You must take your pleasures as you find them. I can't imagine I'd ever be any good in a relationship anyway.'

Lying on his bed as midnight approached, Murray drifted happily, his mind floaty from the tranquilliser. He giggled at how cool it was that a pill could do that. Why didn't people take them all the time, he pondered, as a sweet wave of supine surf broke on the shores of his unconscious. It was almost as if he could see into the world of sleep.

He sat on his bed, no longer afraid of anything the night or turret might usher forth. He cast his bleary eyes over Nina's biography. He wondered what it would feel like being a chick. His fingers ran down his body and he tickled himself along the perineum as his dick hardened to his touch. He felt out of it and sexy. He'd probably even do it with Doc if he came in right now. 'I'm a poker not a taker,' he giggled.

There must be more to getting fucked than he'd experienced. Doc was full on into it, moaning the way chicks did. 'Fuck me, fuck me'.

Murray's woozy mind shifted to Claudette. There was something wise and seductive about her. His hand reached for his erection and as he surfed through the porno channels of his imagination he began to feel magic build up in his cock. He changed his tack, pushing now like he was trying to take a piss. He breathed deep – in and out – feeling the blood rush to his face, intensifying the heat in his cheeks. He tossed the doona off and arched his back, holding his breath until he almost passed out. Then came the searing rush, filled with flashing memories and images, all impossible to trace. He heaved his bum up further from the bed and felt the warm spatter of cum on his chest. He let the dizzying breath out with a long, noisy sigh and knew that, now, those pills could do the job he'd employed them for.

'Don't you want to, Dũng?' Dixon's finger tickled the down on the small of his back.

'Of course I fucking do. But it's problematic, don't you agree?' Dũng clenched his arse tight against the wandering digit. 'I mean I feel like a kid doing this in secret, and I don't want the situation where I live turning into a drama.'

'Well, if Doc's shagging Murray, isn't everything just perfect?'

'Dixon, you fuckwit, he's doing that to wind you up. You're the one he wants, and you know it. Besides, Murray likes girls, so

I don't think we can count on him to keep Doc entertained.'

'Oh, we all pretend we're interested in girls at his age.'

'No, I think you're wrong – maybe it was true when you were young.'

'It's not *that* long ago.'

'Long enough. Anyway, we both know you're deliberately misinterpreting things because just like your motherland, you've got expansionist policies. First you colonise Australia, now you want to invade Vietnam.'

Dix laughed. 'You're the first person whose ever tempted me into Asian regions, I have to say.'

'Well, lucky fucking me! Dixon, I don't want to be a thief in the night and fuck with you furtively after Doc's gone to bed. I'm not like you and him, I can't just switch on and off like an appliance, alright? And because I haven't had as much to drink as you I still have just enough self-control to send you back to your room. So, seeing as you've gone to all the trouble of sneaking in here, give me a tonguey, and then piss off back to your bed like a good boy!'

Dix did as he was told. He feigned good humour but felt the determined Don Juan within him definitely slipping. He closed Dũng's door quietly, avoiding the reckless, drunken evil that tempted him to try his luck in another chamber. He looked at the closed door of Doc's room and Murray's. Things were too sedate. Drugs had not been in evidence enough lately, he decided, remembering a solution was already on the way.

If he'd stopped to think, Dix would have realised he wasn't much different from Doc. He was simply dirtier because he seldom felt the urge to wash his hands afterwards.

Shoot

Murray decided he'd let them get out of the house well before he got up the next day. He still felt pleasantly dopey from the sleeping pill, and his bed seemed irresistibly cosy. Dixon stuck his head in at around eight.

'Murray, sorry to wake you, but I meant to say, if any mail arrives addressed to Soren Utsen, just put it in my room. It's for me, unless the postman asks about it, in which case we don't know anyone by that name.' He winked. 'Oh and don't mention it to Doc. There's no sense in making him needlessly paranoid.'

He was gone with a wave.

Doc left shortly afterwards, no doubt to tackle the details of Angel's predicament. With the coast clear, Murray slowly surfaced.

Sure enough, when the mail arrived, there was a parcel. He put it on Dix's unmade bed wondering what nefarious transactions it contained. Drugs, he decided, and hoped he'd get to try some.

He left the room and began to throw together a few clothes to take to his shoot. He went into the bathroom and played with some of Dixon's expensive moisturisers. He found some tinted ones, some sheer day-glo ones, and some Sunbase ones, which looked a bit like make-up. No wonder Dix always had such a healthy glow – it was all fake. Murray snuck into Doc's bathroom next and found a lot more of the same shit plus about a dozen bottles of expensive aftershave. He wondered what guys did with all this stuff. No wonder they all took so long in the bathroom.

Dixon sat in the State Library scrolling through stories from the *Argus* between 1929 and 1932. The place was filled with quiet, earnest people, the silence punctuated only by coughs. Mostly Dixon's cough, a hacking disco flu which winter was nurturing along very nicely. A front-page story caught his attention.

> *Angry investors stormed the offices of Zultman Holdings in Collins Street yesterday as work on two more building projects came to an unscheduled halt. Mr Franz Zultman, president of the company, says workers on Zultman sites have been lured away by competitors Gardner & Foyle, a subsidiary development arm of the Foyle department store chain.*
>
> *Many prominent industrial commentators ask why, in a time of vast unemployment, G&F would be offering above-award payment for building work, especially given the growing pool of unemployed builders prepared to take substantial drops in wages.*

Dix sighed and rubbed his eyes. The pages rolling across the microfilm projector had his vision swimming and his stomach nauseated.

Still, he persevered because the story that was unfolding before him was, with Lady Penny's helpful background, almost too good to be true. There was no doubt that the tide that had turned against Mr Zultman was more than just the Depression.

Franz Zultman had not only found himself the target of Foyle's manoeuvres but had been branded 'a self-interested Jewish money monarch' by the press and had faced numerous building delays from councils goaded by outraged community groups. His flagship development, a bachelor apartment building in South Yarra, had come unstuck after incurring the much-publicised wrath of local residents who had labelled it 'a haven for harlots, adulterers and non-Christian residents of low morals'. Dix recognised the half-completed apartments in question. He saw them every time he crossed the river on Punt Road. Clearly, they'd been finished at some time, despite all the furore.

Dix continued scrolling. One hour and a whole year later, he saw a quarter-page advertisement in the *Argus*.

> *Quality apartments at prices you can afford. Compact, modern apartments with smart appointments and river views. Ideal investments for bachelors or country gentlemen in need of a town residence.*

It was the same block of flats but in the small print he read, 'Gardener & Foyle Housing: Australia's future'.

Mmmm, thought Dix, flicking back. Zultman had taken his life ten months earlier. Young Penny, who had been seen waving from a boat in the social pages a year before, was now safely on the other side of the world. Something stunk in the Deco state.

Murray's nipples hardened from the cold in Bella's studio. She took advantage of this, zooming in close and capturing their coffee-and-milk contrasts. She hoped the photos would look like geographical studies of fresh flesh – the brown beacons thrown into sharp relief by the creamy acreage surrounding them.

Murray lay atop three pearly Swiss Balls, the type used in gyms, his clingy body shirt unbuttoned to his pants. The sprinkle of dark hair that once adorned his chest had been melted away by hair removal cream, and his face had been tinted to a light tan, the lips matted out.

'Okay, sweetie,' instructed Bella, 'roll back so we can peek at your bellybutton.'

They'd left him with a light train of hair from his bellybutton down to his trousers.

'Okay, now do something with a cigarette – Jake, can you give

Murray a cigarette – I don't usually like doing cigarette shots. Shouldn't really be getting the kids hooked on fags, but someone hooked me years ago, so fuck 'em.' She moved some props around. 'Now those bathers, let's try a few in those, Murray.' He went off to put them on.

Bella strolled over to Claude, who was scanning through a mess of contact sheets in search of future models to use.

'He's not bad, Claude. And they're so cute when they treat it like play, aren't they? I think we should use him in the Christmas catalogue instead of one of the other models.'

Claude agreed. 'He'll be heaps cheaper than the agency boys, and I didn't like that dark one they showed us – he looked a bit simpering and effete, I thought.'

Bella rummaged through the pile for a photo. 'This one?'

'Mmm. Nathaniel, isn't it? He's a nasty piece of work as I recall.' Claude turned up her nose.

'Can't remember his name. They're just items in a mail-order catalogue to me, Claude.'

They giggled.

'Murray could do sportswear, and the CBD stuff too – just send him to a decent hairdresser. Your's is good.' Bella tore open another roll of film with her teeth as the boy himself reappeared.

'These bathers are great, Bella! They've got these undie things inside so you don't get sand up your crack.'

'You can keep 'em if you want, darl. Someone left them here ages ago. Now let's get you down there, that's right, arch your back over the pretty beachball and let's see that nice little – well, not so little – package in your bathers. Now bend forward over the ball, roly-poly, legs practically apart. Lovely.' She turned to Claude. 'The fags love these shots – they can see his little pink arsehole straight through the Lycra. How to sell them cherries without the pornographic pip,' she whispered.

By five o'clock, Angel still hadn't shown up, and Doc had been twiddling his thumbs without a patient since three. As darkness gathered, he said good night to the departing receptionist and exited the building to the rear carpark. There she was, smoking a cigarette by his car.

'Why didn't you come in and see me?'

'Didn't want to.' She shrugged. 'Couldn't see the point, but then I got thinking . . .'

'Thinking what?' asked Doc, alarmed. Surely she hadn't changed her mind and decided to keep it?

'Well, it's about the baby and that.'

'And what?'

'And that there is no baby – not any more.'

'What? You had a period last night?' He tried not to sound too incredulous.

'Not last night.'

'Well, when for God's sake?'

'Last week.'

Doc felt a surge of anger. For a moment he forgot how young she was, and was overcome with an impulse to slap her. 'What on earth are you up to, you stupid girl?'

'Don't get aggro at me, it's not my fucking fault, all the shit that's happened to me. And I'd rather be with Mitch than those nuns. I thought now that I'm not pregnant, you know, that Mitch might get back with me. Anyways, I'm sixteen next month. They can't make me stay after that, and I'm not gunna.'

'But, Angel, you don't know where Mitch is.'

'Yeah I do.' Angel looked smug. Doc paled. 'I reckon he's gone back to Queensland so as not to get any hassles from the cops.' She shot Doc an accusing look. 'I'll surprise him. But I need money to get up there. Look, here's a letter he wrote me from jail, reckons he loves me. I just don't wanna give up what we had.'

Doc spared a brief, cynical thought for what they might

have had. Quick shags in parks and bus shelters, stolen nights in dirty squats, his thrill at her being virtually a child. What could she possibly find desirable about a jailbird like Mitch? He glanced at the letter, willing himself not to be moved, regardless of the message. Sighing impatiently, he brought it up to his eyes and his rough movement caused the thin paper to tear along the fold.

'Now look what you've fuckin' done,' Angel screeched as he stood with the two pieces in his hand. 'That's all I've got.'

'I'm sorry, Angel. Just give me two seconds and I'll fix it for you. Stay there.'

He strode back into the office, an idea forming as he looked again at Mitch's spidery script. Taping the pieces together, he fed the page gently through the fax machine and pocketed his copy. Flipping open the surgery diary, he scrawled NOT IN TODAY over the next day's appointments. Saturdays were usually busy but not tomorrow; the receptionist could rearrange the three patients who'd already booked.

Back outside, he returned the original to Angel.

'See, he did love me.' She folded it carefully.

'Not enough to hang around when you were pregnant,' Doc pointed out.

'I just want to find him and find out,' she moaned.

'I don't think that would be a good idea, Angel.'

'I don't give a fuck what you think. I wanna go!'

'And you want me to foot the bill?'

'I could make trouble if you don't . . .'

'Angel, you don't have anything to make trouble with.' Doc thought briefly of her performance the previous night when they'd all thought her pregnant. She'd seemed so convincingly in need of their help. Now he was being worked over again. He wouldn't back down, he decided. He wanted to be rid of her. 'Remember, you're the one who wasn't supposed to be seeing Mitch. And you're an accessory to his crime, which I'm sure won't do *your* remand situation any good. I simply wanted to help you with an unwanted pregnancy. Pretty decent of me considering what your boyfriend put us through.'

'Well, fuck you.' Angel stormed down the lane. Doc watched as she disappeared in the opposite direction to the nearby cop shop. What talents could Mitch have possessed to so obsess her? Perhaps they should have looked while they had the chance. He shuddered at the idea. A smell of shit seemed to linger in his nasal passages whenever the topic of Mitch came up.

Doc drove off to the gym, ready to pump some iron. En route he rang Qantas and booked an 8 a.m. flight to Brisbane for one Simon White. The man had left his Medicare card at the surgery months ago. It was all the ID Doc needed to pick up an electronic ticket, and he'd pay in cash.

He pondered his one-day outing as he made his way to the weights. He'd be in Brisbane by 10.30 a.m., have lunch with Richard if he was free, and then catch the 4 p.m. flight home. He'd be back in time for dinner and the usual Saturday night shenanigans. He'd bitten the bullet with Angel and it felt good. No more damned blackmail for me, he resolved, heaving the weights as high as his triceps allowed. He cried out as they came to rest back in their cradle. Dũng's calligraphic skills were going to give them all a welcome break from stress, just so long as that rotting carcass stayed right where it belonged.

Signing the Paper

The air was heavy with onions, chilli and garlic when Doc walked into the house. For a moment, he was transported to South East Asia, but as he entered the kitchen he knew he was fairly and squarely back in Elwood.

Dix and Dũng seemed to go strangely quiet at his arrival.

'Is Murray still out?' he asked.

'Yep,' said Dũng.

'Good. I need you to forge this handwriting for me.' Doc produced his copy of Mitch's letter and filled them in on his showdown with Angel. 'I'm quite sure she won't go to the cops, but there's nothing quite like a Dear John letter to set the girl on a new path. So our boy, Mitch, in Queensland, aka you, Dũng, is going to write it. And, at considerable, non tax-deductable expense, I'll fly up there tomorrow to post it.'

'That's a pricey postmark,' observed Dũng as he dug out a suitably grotty piece of paper to work on. 'Come on you two, help me compose this.'

'Now what words would one choose for some correspondence between an inveterate racist imbecile and a wiley slattern? Let me see . . .' Dix struck a pose.

'Angel, you were a grouse under-age root?' suggested Dũng.

'Come on, you two, read the letter and let's do this properly.' Doc didn't want Murray walking in on them.

In a surprising burst of solidarity, the three composed something they hoped would convince Angel of Mitch's continued existence while simultaneously dumping her, once and for all.

Angel
I know I shouldn't of pissed off on you like I did that night but I'm already in troubel from fucking cops and the parole bastards. I reckon the last thing I need is you and a baby screeming at me too so get rid of it if you can. I can't help you, got no money. I'm going further up north meself, maybe get a job or something so don't waste your time thinking about me alright.
Look after yourself
Mitch

Carefully, Dũng crafted the letter, duplicating the previous letter's spelling mistakes, and soon Doc had an equally authentic envelope in his bag.

Over one of Dũng's stir-fries, Dix recounted the details of Franz Zultman's downfall. 'It may interest you to know that those huge front bay windows used to house a very valuable Steinway baby grand, which took a year to arrive from Vienna.'

'I wonder who got that,' mused Doc idly, pondering whether it was just what the room was lacking.

'Strangely enough, I think it's the same one Lady Asquith has in her front room. It seems odd though that he would have left it to her after all that happened. Perhaps her old man bought it from the spoils of Zultman's estate? Don't suppose I'll ever know.'

'How can you spend your whole day researching this?' asked Dũng. 'What about your work? One day, Dix, they'll wise up and sack you.'

'Probably, but who cares? A tidy stock of eccies arrived today for which I paid a mere five pounds each.' Dix didn't admit it was an advance on his Barclaycard. 'My rough calculations lead me to believe they will yield nearly ten grand in profit.'

'You're not dealing from here,' said Doc with an emphatic wave of chopsticks.

'Of course not, dear, why do you think I spend my weekends . . .'

'. . . With your nose in the trough,' finished Doc.

'I like to think of it as facilitating recreational euphoria, but cheapen it if you must. Anyway, who are you to talk, Doctor Fill-me-up?'

'Did you say fill or feel?' asked Dũng.

'Does it make any difference? He answers to both.' They cackled.

'Just so long as you realise how much is at stake with all this illegal shit.'

'Said the murdering, sexually harassing doctor to the drug-smuggling, illegal immigrant.'

'You know bloody well that it was Ricky who harassed me, Dixon.'

'Temper, temper,' chided Dix unrepentantly. 'I knew that'd get a rise out of him,' he whispered to Dũng who was clearing the plates. 'Where's our chief cook and bottle-washer anyway? Cooks three bloody meals, does a load of washing, and before we know it he's a supermodel . . . Didn't I say we should get a plain one? The prettier they are, the more they expect. We'll be cooking for him before we know it.'

Murray sucked a wad of spaghetti into his mouth and washed it down with red wine. Claudette watched him feed with fascination. He was like a starving beggar, unsure of which gratification to indulge in first.

'This is yum.'

'Yeah, I like this place – it's usually packed on Fridays.'

Claude twirled her fork with a little more precision and grace, but showed no more restraint when it came to the wine. 'So Angel should be booked in for her abortion by now?'

'If she turned up. She'd be crazy if she had a baby at fifteen.

My mum reckons the last thing anyone needs when they're young is a brat. She had me when she was eighteen – got married to my dad because she was pregnant. Worst mistake she ever made, she reckons, but she always says me and my sister are the best thing about it.'

'That's sweet. Is your dad still around?'

'Nah. He went off with this chick who was a bit like Angel, a real slag.'

'You make it sound like the girl's fault.'

Murray shrugged. 'Mum always says blokes have no sense when it comes to chicks. A sniff of minge and they're no better than dogs down a lane.'

'Do you think that's true?'

'Dunno, maybe.'

Their eyes met across the table until Claude looked away. She couldn't shake the image of the two dogs. It unsettled her.

'I wonder if the guys were expecting me to make them dinner.'

'Call them on the mobile if you want. I'm sure they'll survive though.'

'Yeah, stuff 'em. So you really want me in this catalogue you're doing?'

Claude grinned. 'I'll even pay you. Not that much, of course – say $150 a day. But you've got to start somewhere, and why shouldn't she who discovered you benefit before your price goes up?'

'I like you, Claude, you've got style.' Murray punctuated his pronouncement with his fork, splattering the Italian street scene on the wall behind her with a lump of tomato.

Claude laughed. 'You nearly got me with that.'

'Sorry. I like Bella too. She's pretty cool.'

'Yeah, she's quite an operator. She used to share my house about a million years ago.'

'Is your place haunted like Doc's?'

'What makes you think Juliette is haunted?' Claudette remembered her sense of being watched from the turret the other week.

Murray shrugged. 'I dunno. I never believed in that sort of shit, but Dixon told this story last night, freaked me out big time . . .'

Doc took a Normie and went to bed early; he had to be up by six in the morning for his flight. Dũng's mum rang in hysterics about local racist thugs and asked him to come over because she still wasn't well and was frightened. He went, a little reluctantly, but knowing he hadn't visited her for days. Dixon sat in his counting house, counting out his eccies. He was too excited to wait for a safe amount of time to elapse before inspecting the bounty.

At ten-thirty Murray arrived home from the Prince of Wales where he'd had a few more drinks with Claude. He felt pretty good, what with being a fashion model and all. Seeing Dix's light on, he knocked on the door and poked his head around. 'What was in your parcel?'

'Three guesses?'

'Drugs, drugs and more drugs?' Butterflies beat their wings in the boozy cage of Murray's stomach.

'Yes, lots and lots of E's to cure my financial disease. And for good measure, some coke to use at my occasional leisure.'

'Wow!' Murray edged into the room and gazed at the pills and powder strewn over Dixon's desk. Alongside these treasures were the remains of an expensively bound financial year diary and a birthday card to one deceased Soren.

'It's all in the binding, you see.'

Murray regarded the two white lines that divided Dix's shaving mirror. Dixon followed his eyes.

'Seeing as you were good enough to ensure this reached me safely, perhaps I can tempt you with a line or two?'

Murray felt his bowels loosen with a shiver of excitement. 'I've never snorted anything before.'

'It's easy. Just don't breathe out through your nose or a million fragile dreams will scatter in a cloud of dust.'

Murray bravely irrigated his virgin nostrils with baby blasts of the bitter powder. Then he flopped onto Dixon's bed as excitement and blood roared through his brain. Dixon put a Stone Roses CD into the ghettoblaster; it began to play softly through the tinny speakers.

'Of course, I shouldn't be doing this, but it's important one knows the quality of one's investments, don't you agree?'

Murray exhaled ecstatically. 'Too right, old chap. How much do you have to pay to feel like this all the time?'

Dixon looked up from snorting his last line, his eyes wicked, his tongue poised at the corner of his mouth. 'That, Murray, is a question for the Devil himself. First you pay in money, then you pay by health and consequence, finally you pay by social exclusion. From there, who can say? It's a fine line between Heaven and Hell. Drugs are to be respected – good servants, bad masters.'

'I think they're cool.'

'Yes, well, just be careful.'

Dixon flopped onto the bed beside him, and Murray thought it would be great to massage his feet – not a notion that had ever occurred to him before.

'How'd the photo shoot go?' Dix raised himself up on one elbow.

'Okay. Claude's going to have me modelling in some catalogue, which is so ace.'

'I think you'll do very well. You're painfully handsome.'

Murray laughed and played absent-mindedly with a safe sex pack he'd found beside the bed. 'How can you be painfully handsome?'

'It's only ever painful to other people, you understand. They can't tell whether they are aching to have you or aching to look like you.'

'That's weird. Anyway, you're good looking. Like, you know, in that more mature way. Dudes go for that and, well, we all know what else they go for.' Murray's eyes travelled to Dixon's crotch.

'But you don't go for that so much?'

'I'm not saying I'm entirely uninterested, if you know what I mean. But I kind of like chicks too, and they seem to like me.'

'I'm not surprised. I don't think you're going to find too many people who don't like you at this point in time.'

'Just enjoy it, you reckon?'

'Well it doesn't last that long. I know when I was your age my looks didn't go unremarked upon either.' Dixon laughed, remembering Lady Asquith for a moment. 'I know it seems vain to think of one's self that way,' he parodied. 'The problem is people don't see anything else when you're young and gorgeous. They all want a taste of your beauty – they're not so interested in your mind.' Dixon realised he still wasn't sure whether Murray's mind was worth pursuing anyway.

'I'm not fucked-up about shit like that,' Murray shrugged. 'I don't mind showing people a good time. Hey, you're showing me a good time on this coke. You know, I thought you were pretty stuck-up at first, but I reckon you're actually alright.'

'Why, thank you.'

'I'm just spinning out a bit. Like Claude is so cool, and so is Bella, and Dũng, and Doc. I am fucking lucky, you know what I'm saying?'

Dixon ran his hand through Murray's hair. He sensed the boy was fit to burst from all the lust, adventure and fiasco that awaited him.

'And I don't know if I should tell you this, Dix, but I'm so horny I could explode.'

'Yes, I think I feel the same way. But what are we to do about it?'

'You're kidding me, right?'

'Well, we can either deal with it here, between ourselves, or venture out to where other people might see to our needs.'

'You know what I think we should do?'

'What?'

'Have a wank. Mainly because that humdinger of yours is something I could get into watching. And that way, it's not like we've had sex or anything complicated, is it?'

'No, it's more like what teenage boys do together over a porno mag.'

'What's wrong with that?'

'Nothing, it's refreshingly innocent and exquisitely nostalgic. Are you going first?'

'We have to do it together, ya daft Pom.'

'Ah, I see, together, is it?'

Murray heated the rock salt for a full half-hour in the oven before putting the Scotch fillet on it. He loved the sizzle it made. Eighteen minutes in a hot oven, the book had said.

'Dinner at eight on Saturday nights,' Doc had suggested as a good rule. Now he blew through the front door with just ten minutes to go, his nose red from having caught some sun at one of Brisbane's riverside cafés.

'You look sunburnt,' said Murray from amidst the steam rising off the cooker.

'I used the sunbed at the gym after work – stayed under a bit too long.'

'I should join a gym, I reckon, especially if I'm going to do this modelling stuff.'

'Come with me if you want. We could work-out together.'

'Cool.'

Dũng wandered in, spattered with paint.

'How's your mum?' asked Doc.

'Housebound. Some bastard at her shopping centre abused her about being Asian, and now she's too scared to go to the shops. Plus some Asian kid down the road got knocked off his bike by a bunch of hoods. He's in hospital and Mum's convinced they're after all the Vietnamese in the street.'

'Does she speak English?' asked Murray.

'When it suits her. Not at the moment.'

'Should I go and see her?' asked Doc.

'What, so you can fill her up with Xanax?'

'No, just to see if she'd see someone else, a counsellor or something.'

'I took her to her Vietnamese doctor this morning. He's promised to call in every couple of days. Trân and I are just going to have to visit on alternate days. She wouldn't see any Caucasian doctor right now.'

'At least you're there for her,' said Doc.

'Yeah, except I'm a greedy sell-out who's not only betrayed her, but my people as well. Even Trân got a serve today. She's going out with this quite nice, Anglo computer geek who, Mum thinks, will turn her against her own mother. History has swallowed my mother up and she has no emotional defences against all this new-right stuff.'

'She's clearly having some sort of breakdown – all that paranoia . . .' said Doc.

'Is she paranoid? Look at the constant, casual abuse we have to endure from the moment we arrive in Australia. Look at what happened to me. Not that I'd tell her about that. I said the bruises were from falling down stairs. It's awful.'

Murray cooked quietly. He thought migrants should at least be made to speak English before they came over and took jobs. But he didn't think it was a good time to express his views. He was beginning to realise that those sort of opinions might alienate him from the circles in which he now hoped to move.

Dixon arrived and the table was set. The mood became quietly celebratory. Dũng had finished his painting, *Murmurs of Genocide*, Doc had dislodged Angel – or so he hoped – and Dixon had completed his article on the Crest. Murray looked set to morph into a supermodel.

'We should all go to JC's tomorrow,' proposed Dix.

‘Why not?’ seconded Dũng. ‘Especially now that your eagle has landed, Dix.’

‘Indeed, and a fine bird she is too. We’ll ask Claude to come.’

‘And Bella?’ suggested Murray. ‘She’s just broken up with some married dude she’s been seeing. She caught him rooting some model at the studio.’

‘Sounds like one of Bella’s sordid tales,’ said Doc.

‘I reckon she’s pretty funny. She said to me if you’re going to power fuck – that’s what she calls it, power-fucking – always fuck upwards. She reckons it won’t get you anywhere, but you’ll know you’ve got your feet on the ladder.’

Doc looked up from his meal. ‘Or your legs wrapped around it. Ah, where would we be without the wisdom of sweet Bella? She’s a veritable post-modern Confucius.’

See All the Love

Claude was in the bathroom frocking-up for the afternoon's festivities. She'd just finished her eyes. 'Eyelashes are one part of a girl that can never be too fat,' she recited from a recent TV commercial. Mascara had returned with a vengeance she hadn't seen since the seventies – big, waxy clotted dolly-bird lashes. Part of her still wanted to be the perennial Saturday-night party girl, fixing herself up in front of the mirror while arrogant-looking boys waited in cars outside.

'Gettin' old,' she said to the mirror, which made no comment. She gave her lips a final layer of rich, glossy plum, pouted at her reflection and slipped into a dress she still wasn't quite sure about. It was clingy, minimal and she felt borderline-too-fat-to-wear-it. She put on knee-high boots which helped and which left a good measure of exposed, unstockinged thigh.

Finally, she donned her long black coat with the feather trim around the edges. She had to admit the whole lot looked pretty damn good. As she sauntered out the door, she could see Bella's car already parked in Juliette's drive.

Doc poured everyone a glass of Moët – undoubtedly, the most delicious thing to drink in a warm lounge on a cold winter's day.

'Cheers!' Bella lit a cigarette without asking if it was okay.

'Oh,' said Dixon instantly. 'If Bell's smoking it won't make any difference if I do.'

'Where's the ashtray, Doc?' asked Bella.

'Murray, get them an ashtray would you?' he snarled.

This was just the sort of thing that irritated Doc about Bella. She never seemed to think about other people's comfort. She also had a way of looking at Doc which made him feel she never took anything he said seriously. He sensed unfavourable judgements accruing just behind the mask of her Mona Lisa smile. Doc thought Bella homophobic, and she thought him a misogynist. They'd never really clicked.

Bella sprawled on the couch, billowing smoke and arguing happily with Dix about national identities.

'So what does being Australian mean to you, Doc?' she asked suddenly, fixing cool green eyes on him.

'Driving on the left-hand side, Medicare – however tenuously – Mardi Gras, Melbourne cafés and relative safety.'

'Too earnest,' Bella struck back without hesitation. 'Stick with the *Melbourne Star Observer*, it has all you'll need to know. Next! What does being Vietnamese mean to you, Dũng?'

'I'm not Vietnamese, I'm Australian, which opens up a whole new can of worms about what Anglos automatically assume about race and nationality. I didn't think you'd fall into that trap, Bella, especially having Italian parents. To me, being Australian means multiculturalism – however tenuously – football, a big sky, Housing Commission homes in Preston, and lots of trashy pub bands. Oh, and the National Gallery – next stop, the Metropolitan.'

'Hear, hear,' pronounced Dixon raising his flute.

'In other words you can read *Wallpaper* and get your hands on a few obscure cultural grants. And what does being English mean to you, Dixon?'

'Nostalgia, central heating, English voices raised in song and knowing all the words to "Tub Thumping" and "Jerusalem", and hearing six separate Ibiza remixes of "The Macarena" in four different languages. It means green grass and grey skies – except on washing powder commercials where they're always blue. And, of course, eccies that are vastly superior to anything you can get here.'

'Well, we all know who's the true patriot here!' proclaimed Bella, helping herself to a refill.

'Makes me wonder why you stay,' observed Doc, with irritation.

'One feels one must support Britain's ailing export industry, love, and I'm lucky enough to have the connections to do it. Don't think I'd be hanging around the bloody colonies a minute longer if I had to take those impotent fifty-dollar aspirins you so willingly call E's. God, even the Pommy ones don't do what they used to for me. Still, have to keep taking the wretched things. Empire, stiff upper lip and all that.'

'The only thing Britain ever exported was convicts and misery,' said Dũng.

'Ah, but what fine misery, and look at you all – I'm quite proud. You've done rather well for yourselves – doctors, photographers, artists and fashion models. A far cry from those rat-infested hulks near the Isle of Dogs you had to rot in a couple of hundred years ago. No, I think my report to the penal commissioners will be most favourable. Carry on! Jolly good show.'

'*Touché*,' cried Dũng and everyone laughed, even Murray, who found the pace of their conversation daunting. His pleasure, however, was unadulterated. He still possessed a childlike faith in adult cohesion, which didn't perceive the conflict around him – a blissfully naive belief that all grown-ups liked each other.

Just then Claudette arrived in her ankle-length feathers that begged to be touched. She added a tactile distraction, a sumptuous hint of glamour. Murray slipped off to lay the table with finger food he'd prepared to Delia, Stephanie and Jill's instructions.

Meanwhile Dixon offered their guests a powdery aperitif which added an extra dimension of enchantment to the champagne already in their systems. Murray watched in awe as the room exploded like a piñata full of booze, laughter and mischief. They trooped to the table and commenced their raucous luncheon.

Dix, still obsessed by Franz Zultman's tragedy, took a casual delight in holding the floor for longer than Doc, who saw hosting as his entitled role. 'It's all very intriguing, but I want to know how her father managed to take over all his building projects. It seems our dear Franz paid a hefty price for giving little Penny a social disease . . .'

Suddenly, there was a crash in the lounge room as a huge burning stump of wood fell from the fireplace. Doc leapt up to save the polished floor from its flames.

'Perhaps Franz is trying to tell us something?' murmured Claude. 'Murray, this chicken's yum.'

'Why, thank you,' said Murray in a fair approximation of his new mentor.

'Perhaps Dixon was Zultman in a former life?' continued Claude.

Doc jumped in, the log now safely back where it belonged. 'That'd explain why he's so tight with his money.'

Murray let the conversation flow around him, more interested in what there was to drink than eat. He felt better than Christmas.

The topic of Angel was mostly avoided. Doc simply said that she'd come to the surgery 'and had been no more pregnant than I am.'

'Which is saying something, given how frequently he mates,' quipped Dix, pointing an accusing chicken bone.

'Mating, mating, mating. Will everybody just shut up about mating,' shouted Claude. 'And are we to continue on with the champers or shall I open something else?'

The more cocaine Murray was given, the more he admired its source. People kept revisiting the little mirror for lines. He watched the girls clutch their straws with sharp painted nails and vacuum the stuff into their dainty noses. The illicit intimacy excited him. He looked at Dixon and couldn't help but conjure up visions of his impressive phallus at work on each and every member of the party. He started laughing at how gross his imagination was.

The living room had degenerated into a subdued mass of draped bodies. He peered at Claudette's pale thighs and the short dress that had ridden up even further.

Suddenly, Claude put her legs across his lap. 'You don't mind do you, hon?'

'Nah, make yourself at home.'

'We should think about making a move,' she suggested.

'Alright, I'm first in the bathroom.' Dũng made a dash that left no room for argument. Dixon handed Murray a pill.

'This is what you've been waiting for isn't it?'

'Excellent.'

'I'd only take half if I were you.'

'Fuck that.' And with a single gulp it was gone.

Murray got up to change into his new clubbing clothes. Claude began touching up her face in the lounge mirror while Dũng and Dixon sparred to have dominant reflections in the bathroom.

'Dixon, you're an octopus,' said Dũng, slapping his hands away as he tried to do his hair.

Bella wasn't going to JC's on the grounds that she got enough of fags, heroes and Barbie dolls in the studio. She decided she was going home to harass her ex-boyfriend's wife on the phone.

'You're all coked up, Bell, you shouldn't do that,' ventured Claude.

'I'll do what I bloody like – the bastard.'

'I thought you were only interested in him *because* he was married and played around. No danger of commitment and everything.'

'That doesn't mean I can't have my hysterics when he cheats on me.'

'But I thought you were going to come out and have girlie fun with me.'

'Claude, as you said yourself, it's been three years since you've had any real "girlie fun". I'm not giving up mine without a fight.'

'So you'd take him back?'

'Of course not, I've got my pride. But men can't be allowed to carry on with their rutting as if commitment doesn't count for anything.'

'You're such a hypocrite, Bella. You knew he was married!'

'Ah, but I didn't know there was no limit to his deceit. He's got to pay. You go out and do your fag-haggy thing, I've got grown-up women's business to attend to.' Bella poured them the remnants of the champagne.

'Where are those boys? Their faces take longer to put on than mine,' pouted Claude.

'Who needs them?' said Bella. Her voice dropped. 'Doc hasn't changed, has he? Still a bundle of nerves.'

'And steroids too, these days,' snickered Claude, her coke-induced confidence allowing her no guilt pangs at her betrayal.

All five piled into the Citroën which, of course, Doc shouldn't have been driving. Still, he hadn't drunk that much, and coke had made a God of him. Murray requested The Verve on the CD player, and as this was his official debut he was indulged. His vision kept blurring as the car moved along, and a wave of nausea made his skin prick with cold sweat. He was vaguely aware of the others having yet another bizarre conversation around him.

'A clitoris is not the same as a penis,' insisted Claudette.

'Whoever said it was? *Vive la différence*, I say,' enthused Dixon, all scrubbed up and glowing in his purple dealer shirt.

'But that's what you end up with, isn't it, Doc?' asked Claude.

'Something like that. The glans becomes the clitoral hood, the penile skin becomes the vaginal walls.'

'I couldn't imagine having it done. An opening made from my foreskin,' murmured Dix with a disturbed frown.

'Quite an opening in your case,' stated Doc as he swung onto Chapel Street.

'You boys are so off. I'd forgotten what going out with all of you was like.' Claude giggled.

Murray stirred and slurred, 'I don't want one of those fake cunts either.'

'There, there,' said Dix, patting him on the head. 'No one's going to make you have one, not today at least. Mind you, I can't see why anyone would do it. We boys already have a perfectly good hole, it just seems plain greedy to me.'

The rest of the carload popped their E's just before they pulled up outside the club. It throbbed and beckoned like a wicked beast spewing with exciting possibilities.

'God,' said Claude as she watched the procession of Sunday glamour-pusses making their entrances. 'They're all out today.'

Murray tried his damnedest to maintain some poise. His head cleared for a minute as they made their way to the door. A rush of pure love, peace and splendour went through him as he looked at the beautiful kingdom they were preparing to enter. He contemplated his companions: sweet, beautiful Claude, noble Dũng, mad Dixon, and the strange but irresistible Doc. Such friends he'd made! He grabbed Claude and Dũng's hands, as another glorious shard of Heaven pierced through his soul. Bravely, he kissed Claude on the cheek.

The bouncer nodded them through – so cool, thought Murray – and the solid thump of the music clarified into something more melodic. Scantily clad bodies of splendid proportions danced all around them.

'Dixon!' screamed Claude. 'It's our song, darling, from last week!'

'My God, you're right.'

As the song built to its peak the two danced at each other, mouthing the words with camp sarcasm. 'Open your eyes and see all the love – we've – got – enough – forever.' And, as Murray watched, an irrefutable truth flowed into him as clear as day. 'The song is so right – we *have* got enough love, forever.' With that revelation surging through him, he wondered how he could ever worry about anything ever again. He moved onto the floor with the other two, kissing them. He threw his hands heavenwards.

Dixon and Claude smiled at their charge. 'He probably wasn't even ten when we had our first,' Claude whispered.

'I know, breaks your heart, doesn't it? I could break his neck, I'm so jealous.'

Doc posed at the side of the floor while Dũng claimed a booth for them.

'Sweet Jesus, Dixon,' Claude exhaled heavily. 'This latest batch of imports have got a kick like a mule to them. I feel quite . . . the girl.'

'Yes, well, maybe you'll be hitching up your skirts tonight, my dear. Hitching and haunching – not that there's much to hitch.'

'Stop it, Dixon, you filthy hound.' She punched him in the shoulder. 'I can't even begin to imagine it, it's been so long.'

Claude looked at the dance floor, her hint of sardonic regret quickly overshadowed by something sanguine and alluring. A lynx she hadn't let off its leash for a long time had set itself free.

Murray was still dancing. Somewhere along the way he'd met some completely amazing people, like this chick, Vanessa, who worked in a Chapel Street homeware boutique called *In Casa*, but who was actually going to become a model. Murray was blown away by the coincidence. 'Far out, you know I'm just getting into modelling myself. I'm doing shoots for the Daimaru Christmas catalogue next week.'

'No way.'

'Absolute-fucking-way.'

'I don't believe it, this is *too* insane. My best friend, Jacinta, is a buyer for Daimaru – can you believe that?'

When he'd finished spinning out about the parallelism of it all, Murray could.

The synergy and perfect order of life had made itself abundantly clear to him. He wanted to keep dancing, but he also wanted to hang out with his friends whom he loved so much.

He slid into the booth beside Claude. She pushed a drink over to him.

'I just met these really great people.'

Claude pulled a cigarette from Dixon's pack and lit it. 'I think you'll find you meet a lot of great people tonight, hon. It kind of goes with the territory.'

'None as great as you, Claude.' He put his arm around her.

'Why thank you, honey.' She blew smoke as some frazzled black woman sang about lookin' for love in all the wrong places. For a moment, Claude thought her head was about to explode.

Then she felt the floor go from beneath her and her vision blurred into another dimension. 'Phoooo,' she sighed. She thought she'd already peaked some immeasurable time ago.

'They're like dogs,' she confided to Murray.

'Who?'

'The girls in this song – sniffing for a man.'

'You couldn't sing like that.'

'I've no intention of singing.'

'No, I mean if you were those black chicks sniffing for a root.'

'I'd never be that shameless. She's like a dog on heat that one – sexy though.'

They both started laughing, neither knew at what exactly. Claudette was surprised to be so Eccie-affected. She looked across at Dixon.

'Not a word, darling, we're bizz-bizz-bizzy over here,' he smiled.

'And I'm Miss-mess-messy over here.'

Dix was sitting next to Dũng and a girl who claimed she was psychic. She was telling them how she sensed something complex between the two, and how she 'had heaps of Asian friends'.

'Great. I've got heaps of Barbie-doll friends too,' murmured a totally whacked Dũng.

'What . . . like Ken and Skipper?'

'Oh, yes,' interrupted Dixon, 'and a camper van, pool and Barbie brothel.'

'She's got breasts,' offered the girl. 'She just hasn't got nipples.'

Dũng looked at her. 'Did you know there was a five-year-old girl in Charlotte, North Carolina, who cut off her nipples because she wanted to be like Barbie?'

'She'll never get into those kiddie beauty pageants now,' frowned the girl.

Doc was nowhere to be seen. He was, in fact, already on his way to the tubs where he hoped to release some of his pent-up stress. His E had worked, but these days he often felt outside of things on drugs. He knew Dixon was fucking Dũng – no one needed to tell him that – he'd seen them all over each other in that booth. Not that he'd say anything. The whole house'd fall apart.

Doc hung his clothes up and looked at himself in the full-length mirror. He mightn't have Dixon's cock, but his body was better. A young guy eyed him as he closed his locker and he felt the drug's energies focus in on his genitals. He shivered. Wrapping himself in a towel, he ventured into the corridors. On a TV screen above his head, Dannii dived into a pool, and he cursed the endless associations of everything.

Doc had reached a point where most of the passing trade looked exciting, so he ventured towards a group of men who'd gathered in the darkness. A hand whisked the towel from his waist, and darting fingers and hot mouths began to attend to him. It was rare to find himself the centre of so many attentions. He relinquished control and fell onto the vinyl bed. His body responded easily and mechanically, but as always his mind was filled with hellish visions. Doc smiled. At times like this, the conflicting visions created their own alchemy, an incendiary conjoining of Heaven and Hell.

The men's intrusions were getting bolder and more urgent. Doc offered no resistance, raising his legs and parting them on the sticky mattress edge. Amyl, eagerly dispensed by one suitor, arrived at his nostril and he took a greedy sniff. He felt the first prospective intruder to make sure he wore a condom, it was all the caution he could manage.

He rode with the rhythm, a pleasing, cooperative motion. Everything had always been a battle for Doc – ethical battles, financial battles, religious battles – but this was easy. This was his purpose. Come fire or brimstone, bacteria and pestilence, this was a moment of joy that nothing could hamper. And as the grunts and groans grew louder within his dark, unholy cloister, he thought, ah yes, this is definitely a snout in the trough scenario. He groaned a lusty giggle, almost daring himself to oink.

Abruptly, the guy pulled out. Doc felt for him blindly, eager for more. As the cock slid from him, he realised that it was unsheathed. A blind rage flooded through him. Doc sat bolt upright, and punched the guy. 'You cunt, you weren't wearing a condom. You took it off!'

His other attendants quickly fled on hearing this nasty turn of events.

'It was on when I started fucking you.'

'Well where the fuck is it now, hey?' Doc had the traitor by the neck. Then he remembered what happened last time he did this and let go. The guy bolted. 'You're fucked, man – seriously fucked,' snorted the wounded man as he disappeared.

Doc searched the dark mattress for a slippery jube that might have been the condom, but there wasn't one. Eventually, he wandered off, his heart racing at a sickening pace. His mind was filled with Gothic visions of weeping virgins and melancholy angels beating their broken wings and crying tears of blood.

Murray stood in the men's toilet, waiting for a cubicle. The throb of the music had dulled in here to a different percussion, a muted tangle of illicit suggestion. Other boys waited lethargically, their voices rising and falling in mysterious, delirious tones.

'I'm fucking over it,' said one to his mate. 'Let's go to Subway.' His gaze shifted blearily to Murray. 'You're hot!'

Murray tried to avert his eyes from the boy's intent stare.

'Wanna come and play with us?'

Murray felt butterflies in his stomach. He almost considered it, but realised he felt that way about most people tonight.

'I'm with friends,' he said.

'Oh well, your loss, gorgeous.'

Murray finally took his piss and worked his way back through the pump and grind. Dixon and Dũng had vanished into the crowd.

'I think I want to go now, hon,' said Claude. It was about eleven and they'd put in a good five hours.

'I'll come too, if that's cool with you.'

Outside, Claude waved down a cab while a car full of youths abused them for being poofs and dykes.

'I feel messy, Claude.' Murray snuggled against her on the back seat.

'Me too, hon.' She watched out the window as bright lights wove pretty patterns in her mind. Murray put his hand in hers and it brushed against her thigh, triggering a waterfall of electric charges. She tried not to think about it but the sensation wouldn't go away. Murray's hand touched her thigh more purposefully this time and Claude felt her neck redden. She hoped her three-year abstinence wouldn't send her into some dangerous erotic fit.

As if sensing her weakness, his thumb began stroking skin that was too far up her leg for the gesture to be interpreted as friendliness. She trembled at the thought that he might go higher and barely stopped herself from pushing forward to bring his finger in contact with her satin pants. She felt a rush of embarrassment. She knew she was monstrously wet.

'Wait,' she moaned softly.

They turned into their street and the taxi slowed. Murray looked at Juliette. Suddenly he stiffened, his eyes on the darkened turret. A grey figure seemed to move inside, a hand looked as if it was pressed to the glass. A chill dread went through him.

'Shit, Claude. Look!'

'What?' Claude raised her head.

'The turret. Look!'

But by the time she did, the figure seemed to have withdrawn, and Murray could no longer distinguish anything in the darkness.

‘Can I come into your place, Claude?’

‘Of course.’

Once inside, Murray flopped onto the couch and pulled out a joint he’d rolled earlier.

‘That’s just what we need now,’ she approved, hoping it would chill her out a little.

‘Do you mind me, you know, touching you, Claude?’

She shivered, lighting the gas log fire. ‘No, I’m quite glad you did.’ He passed the joint to her.

‘You want to do some more?’

His raw, uninhibited words started her engine again.

‘I’m not going to object to anything tonight, Murray. Those drugs are fierce – not that I don’t think you’re gorgeous, anyway. It’s just, I’m usually, well I haven’t done this for a while.’

‘Chill out, what’s the worse thing could happen? We fuck – people do it all the time, and love it!’

Claude grabbed a decanter of port and two glasses, and beckoned him into her bedroom. ‘Step this way. It’s cosier, hon.’

Murray sat down on a sea of white linen and gulped greedily at some sweet port. Claude arranged herself demurely against the pillows – a demureness which would be shockingly lost, very soon.

He kissed her clumsily while he tried to kick off his shoes. Then he kissed her more engagingly. Claude willed herself to calm down, though every touch seemed to increase the pressures and hungers resonating from within. Murray freed a breast from the bra that had struggled to contain it all day. His fingers busied themselves with a hard rose nipple, while his other hand secretly snuck back up to her thigh. She gasped with pleasure and surprise.

‘I wanna touch your cunt, Claude.’

‘I want you to, too, sweetie.’ She realised she’d done nothing herself so she pulled his shirt open and took his own dark meaty nipples between her purple nails. She felt a sudden desire to chew those chunks off him. What could a boy want with such chunky nipples? It seemed a waste. She twisted one and Murray groaned.

His hand fingered the delicate edge of her pants, the twisted hairs whispering crudely against the satin. She sensed his hesitation and pulled them down herself, leaving her dress hitched around her waist and her pie at Murray's disposal. He paused for a minute, his finger tracing the soft flesh of her outer lip. Her wetness spread quickly, his teasing finger smoothing the dampness along the entirety of her outlying curves.

'This is excellent,' said Murray. His fingers ventured further. Claude tensed as a long finger came to rest on her swollen clit, then let out an earnest cry.

She tore her dress over her head and laid herself out so Murray could really get to work. She unbuttoned his fly and from a nest of black hair his fleshy cock burst free. She sighed at its debut.

'Let me have a taste, honey.' Her sharp fingers guided him into her mouth. He shunted further in, almost gagging her. He closed his eyes – felt trains, trucks and packs of wild dogs thundering through his head. God help Claude when I come this time, he thought. He cried out as her mouth worked on his cock.

To Claude, it sounded like a sullen, schoolyard whimper. It excited her. He pulled from her mouth, and sprawled himself on top of her. Claude's legs splayed wide. He sought no consent, nor offered any protection. He just homed his shiny ingot of flesh in. Feeding time at the zoo.

3 a.m. is Eternal

Doc had no idea how he'd got to the turret nor where he'd found the rope. It was as if he'd been sleepwalking. He came to at the squeak of brakes from below, and watched as Claude and Murray got out of a taxi and went into her house. He was feeling very left out and down, but worse than that, scared. Mostly of himself. He stumbled back down to his bathroom, sat on the toilet and gave birth to the missing condom. Guilt overcame him at having punched the guy. He felt like crying. It dawned on him that he was losing control and he didn't know why. He showered and lay in bed, finally feeling clean but very, very alone.

Dixon and Dũng had been disgraceful. They'd snorted more coke in the toilets and had another E each. Dixon's trouser pockets bulged with cash as well as their usual wares and as they groped each other like alley-cats down the lane behind JC's, he nearly lost half his bounty when Dũng began to pull his trousers down.

Grabbing his hand, Dix dragged Dũng deeper into the laneway. It was littered with condoms from other such frantic encounters. Seconds later, he was on his knees, sucking as hard as he could on Dũng's cock.

It was quite unlike Dixon to go to so much trouble for someone else's pleasure, realised Dũng, touched. 'If you want me to come in your mouth, you're going about it the right way,' he groaned, spastic with excitement.

'Do it,' gasped Dix, taking a quick gulp of oxygen.

'You sure?'

'Mmnghh.'

'Don't ... speak ... with your mouth ... full ...' Dũng's genitals exploded with pleasure, brilliantly drug-enhanced.

Dix digested his order, then stood and brushed the dust from his knees.

Somewhat shakily, they began walking home. Dixon sang Soul II Soul along Punt Road; Dũng danced to it.

'Just do what I say,' said Dix.

'Why?'

'Because I understand Doc better than you ... you've just got to throw him a bone once in a while.'

'But you can't chew my bone ...' sang Dũng.

'No, seriously, we go in there – if he's home – and get into bed with him. I'll shag him senseless and he'll be happy as Larry.'

'I thought you said Doc was incapable of loving anyone. Now you want to go in and do that.'

'That, my dear, is love, I've decided. The family that lays together, stays together. Knowing when he needs us is as much love as I can muster. He doesn't repulse you, does he, Dũng?'

'Not particularly, I think it's more the other way around. I think he's got a yuk-factor about Asians.'

'I didn't notice it last time we threed.'

'Well, *you* wouldn't. We still haven't fucked, you know.'

'Of course I know, you pillock – I'm part of "we", remember?'

'And I need to take one, wait here.' Dũng disappeared down a lane.

They were whispering and giggling as they turned the key in Juliette's lock.

'Hello, is there a doctor in the house?' They stumbled through the hall to Doc's bedroom, but knocked first, in case he had trade in there.

'What are you two up to?' said Doc emerging from his Temazepam–Valium stupor.

'We wanted to curl up with you, darling.'

A grin of pleasure and relief spread across his face. 'Well, if you must.'

They plonked themselves on the bed, shedding sweaty garments as they went.

Dixon started kissing Doc while Dũng finished undressing him – fifty-dollar bills spilling all over the bed.

'I expect you'll be wanting a rogering tonight, Doc, though I dare say I won't be the first.'

'Oh, don't, Dix – I've had the freakiest night.'

'Where's baby?'

'Guess?'

'What's sauce for the gander is sauce for the goose?'

'Exactly,' Doc sighed.

Dũng went into the ensuite.

'What do you really want from me, Dix? Do you want love?'

Dixon groaned. 'Where love's concerned I'm something of a tourist, I think.' He flopped onto the bed. 'I loved Soren – I don't think I realised until he died, we were too competitive. I'm not a basket you should be carrying your eggs in, Doc. Still, I must love you a little, that's why we came in here. I'm human in my way.'

Dũng returned to the bed.

'What about you, Dũng?' Doc asked.

'What about me?'

'Are you a tourist too?'

'We all are, aren't we? On some insane package tour, the price not disclosed until we reach the end.'

'Where are the pills, Doctor? We need the peace, to say nothing of the torpor, they bring.'

Dixon kept Doc quiet by kissing him again and felt his cock hardening as he stroked it. Dũng's finger traced the seam of skin between Dixon's legs. Then it lighted on his sweaty arsehole and he grunted, increasingly lost in the gathering sexual tempo.

'The Doctor, the baker, the candlestick-maker,' he chanted as the trio gave themselves up to a queer and complex Tango.

Then their lips came together silently in a whirring synchronicity of lust. Shadows – the likes of which Franz Zultman never cast – danced on the walls. A nipple pinched painfully here, a deep burning penetration there, a groan, a whimper, a bark. Moonlight werewolves feeding on truffles and bones.

Cum Down

Murray woke to a face full of pussy. This time, of the feline variety. Missy twisted and padded her way over the two occupants in the bed. First, she offered Murray an uncensored view of her pink, puckered bum, then turned to give him a fishy-breathed miaow.

'Missy,' moaned Claude, whose head was all twisted-up in the dress she'd been wearing the previous night. Murray started laughing when he saw her.

'Oh my God, have we landed?' Claude opened eyes ringed with runaway mascara.

Murray bounced sickeningly on the bed. 'Yes, but remain seated until the craft has completely stopped moving.' He grabbed her tits. 'Emergency airbags, in case of sudden impact.'

'Careful, they're real – you don't find that too often these days.'

Murray leapt out of bed and waved his dick at her. 'Watch out – this is real too, and I've got a fire to put out.'

He went into the bathroom; Claude wondered whether he'd leave the seat up. From there he went to the kitchen and got them both some juice – a gesture that impressed her mightily. She dragged on her kimono, her inhibition resurfacing in the cold hard light of day.

'What a rad night,' said Murray, bouncing back on to the bed and making Claudette a little queasy. The phone rang.

'Oh go away,' she pouted in a little girl voice.

'Claude. Bell. Just ringing to show you that my demented–scorned woman routine also extends to phoning friends who are too hung-over to answer the phone. Call me when you are able.

By the way, Murray's prints are back, mmm mmm mmm. Just tell him they're okay, don't want him getting too big a head, do we?'

Murray laughed. 'When can I see 'em?'

'Oh, I'll pick them up later – don't pester me. It's bloody Monday, I'm a wreck and I've got a million things to do for this catalogue. I'll be lucky if I have time this week.'

'Hey, wasn't that weird what I saw in the turret?'

'It was probably just the drugs, hon, they do play havoc with the imagination. Are you hungry?'

'Now I think about it.'

'Let's have some brekkie. Are you going to tell the boys about last night?'

'Well, I'm not going to not tell them. They probably guessed anyway. They've got filthy minds.'

She nodded. 'Do you feel okay about it?'

'Yeah, 'course.'

'I hope we can still be friends, you know . . . I don't expect . . .'

'Yeah, yeah, yeah. Let's not talk about all that stuff. I came on to you, I reckon, and it was fun, wasn't it? Who can blame you if I'm *simply irresistible*!'

She clouted him over the head with a packet of bacon.

'Bell's right, we don't need to make your head any bigger.'

She grilled bacon and cooked toast as he flicked through a folder of her ads. Claude was thinking how outrageous it was that she'd had unsafe sex. What disturbed her even more was that according to the Man Ray calendar on the wall, it was exactly fourteen days until her period. What would coke and eccies do to a foetus, she wondered.

Three mouths yawned, groaned and reluctantly returned to consciousness and a cruel, mundane world. Each oral cavern tasted like the bottom of a bird cage.

'Boy-oh-boy,' said Doc. 'What a night and where's the water?'

'Oh God, is that the time?' cried Dixon. It was nearly ten. 'I'll have to phone in sick – and I am – splitting bloody headache.' He dragged himself from the bed and went into his own room to call work.

A key turned in the front door and in walked Murray. The first sight to meet his eyes was the open door to Doc's bedroom and both Dũng and Doc in the bed. Murray shook his head and hoped Claude was right – perhaps he was still seeing things. He changed into his tracksuit and set about cleaning up yesterday's lunch, as the others showered and returned to the grim prospect of a winter Monday. It seemed no one was going to work.

'So you enjoyed Claudette's hospitality last night?' asked Doc as he wandered into the kitchen. Murray was stacking the dishwasher.

'I got a bit freaked out. I thought I saw someone in the turret when we got home. Claude reckoned it was the drugs, but I know what I saw.'

Doc coughed. 'I was up there when you got home.'

'Why?'

'I don't know, I thought I heard something – music.' He *had* heard music but that wasn't what lured him up there. Nor could he remember how he'd gotten there. It concerned him. He didn't want to concern Murray, however.

'Not piano music, was it?'

Doc nodded. 'Usually is, I'm afraid.'

'I've heard it but when I have, I've been up there and it sounds like it comes from somewhere in the house.'

'Well my senses were way out of kilter last night.'

'I thought it was the ghost, that's why I went and stayed at Claude's.'

His eyebrow tilted slightly. 'That's why, is it?'

Murray went on with his work remembering what Bella had said about men and sex: 'It's always better they know too little than too much.'

Later Murray caught Dũng in the kitchen. 'Are you shagging Doc too now?'

'What's it to you? You're doing alright, aren't you?'

'What does Dixon think?'

'Who knows how his cesspool of a mind works. But it might be wise for you to keep out of everyone's way over the next couple of days and not be asking questions people don't have answers for. Tempers can get a bit short and egos ragged after a weekend like that.'

'What, like coming down?'

'Exactly.'

Murray took to his room. He thought about Claude and fucking her without a condom. He still felt pretty horny so he tried to pick up Nina's story but he was finding it a bit repetitive: all that plaiting her hair and pretending to be a Nazi Fräulein. He climbed up to the turret to see if there was any decent porn in the boxes there and noticed a coil of rope that he was sure hadn't been there before. He smoked a joint and spied on Claude. She was sitting at her table near the window but all she seemed to do was talk on the phone, wave a pen around and type on the computer – boring. Then the phone rang and he clattered down to answer it. It was his mum.

'So, whatcha been up to, Shane?'

'Mum, I told you – Murray.'

'Oh, that's right. Sorry.'

'It's okay. I've been out partying a bit. I've been going to these really ace clubs and I've got a job modelling in this department store catalogue. I've already done one shoot and Bella, the photographer, and Claudette – she's my agent – reckon they're hot photos.'

'Well, haven't I got the handsomest son? Perhaps you'll end up plastered on billboards all over the Hume Highway.'

'Who knows? But I've been meeting some really cool people. Is Tree behaving?'

'Oh, as much as you'd expect, I'll put her on later. Why I'm calling is that we're coming down Saturday week to see the *Rocky Horror Show* as a treat for her birthday. Do you want to come with us? It'd be great if you could.'

'Sure, like, if I don't have to be at the studio or anything that day.'

'Don't put yourself out for us or anything.'

'I didn't mean it like that, Mum. I'm sure it'll be fine.'

'Can we come and see your house?'

'Ah, maybe . . . I guess it should be okay.'

'What are you, a prisoner or something?'

'No, it's fine.'

'Well if you're going to be embarrassed by your own family, we'll just meet you in town.'

'I'm not embarrassed.'

'Sounds like it to me, Shane. Now have a word to your sister . . .'

three

'What's got over the Devil's back
must be spent under his belly.'

Thomas Middleton, 1607

Rocky Horror

An eerily mundane order had descended over Juliette in the fortnight that followed their wild bacchanalian weekend. Claude had been busy with work and the boys had retreated somewhat into their own little worlds.

Saturday morning dawned breezy and quiet. Dũng, feeling extra creative, locked himself away in his studio and feverishly added finishing touches to his latest painting. As he grandly applied the final stroke, the doorbell rang. Throwing down the brush, he went to answer it and was surprised to find a woman and a girl on the doorstep.

'Hello,' said the older one, smiling nervously. She looked around forty with blonde-tipped hair and freshly applied pink lipstick. She was wearing a parachute silk tracksuit in purple and aqua, and carried a blue shoulder-bag on a silver chain. As Dũng's eyes travelled to her feet, he realised she'd chosen the bag to match her shoes.

'I'm Phyllis, Shane – I mean Murray's – mum. This is his sister, Treecia. Is he about?'

'Oh, yeah. I'm Dũng. I'll get him. Have a seat.' He pointed to the lounge.

Phyllis and Treecia walked into the room.

'Oh, Mum, check it out!' Tree pointed to the painting above the fire.

Phyllis looked at it, perplexed by the violence of the images before her. 'It's quite something, isn't it?'

Tree was already going through the CDs.

'Oh yuck, I hate Green Day, bet that's Shane's. I haven't heard of most of this stuff. Oh, Mum, you'd like this – best of the seventies.'

'See, I'm more with it than you two think.' Phyllis pulled a pack of cigarettes from her bag and was about to light one when Murray came in.

'Hi Mum.' He kissed her. 'Ah, Doc's kind of funny about smoking in here.'

'Oh, sorry. I won't have one then.'

'I guess it's alright, Dixon does half the time.'

'No, it doesn't matter, love. You're looking well, maybe a bit skinnier.'

Murray shifted self-consciously in his jumper. 'I'm not skinnier.'

'Well it's nice to see you, love.' She put her arm around him and stared up at his face. 'Are you going to give your sister a birthday kiss?'

'Come here then – teenage trouble.' He kissed her.

'I'll be allowed to drive in four years.'

'I don't think so, Sis. Not with your mental disability.'

'Shut up!' Tree gave him a friendly shove. She was clearly pleased to see him.

'Aren't ya going to show us around?' asked Phyllis before the banter could degenerate any further.

'Yeah, let's see your room. I bet it's full of gay magazines now. Murray Fox, what a wank that sounds.' Tree giggled.

'Careful, Tree. I was gunna show you something cool for your birthday, but I don't think I will now,' sneered Murray, reviving his recently forgotten sibling rivalry. 'Mum, I think Tree is retarded. I recommend shock treatment – immediately.' He grabbed her head and she screamed.

'Don't you two start. I thought you'd be glad to see each other.'

'Whose room's that?' asked Tree as they passed Doc's door.

'That's Doc's, he owns the house – he's at the surgery. And

this one's Dixon's.' Murray pointed down the hall towards Dix's door. 'He's asleep. He went to Oxford or one of those posh Pommy joints. Dũng's studio is out through the kitchen. You've already met him. He's a painter. His work's pretty political, especially about Asians and stuff. The National Gallery in Canberra's got one of 'em. That's one of his in the lounge room.'

'It's very . . . interesting,' said Phyllis.

'They're post-structuralist or neo-something,' offered Murray with a nonchalant wave of his hand. 'They're all, like, really successful guys, but they still know how to have a good time . . . This is my room and because it's your birthday, Sis, I'll let you up into the turret.' Murray opened the door. 'Beware, there's a ghost in there.'

Tree clambered up the stairs. Murray and his mum followed more slowly behind.

'Mum, check this out, you can see the water,' she yelled.

'Well, Murray, it's quite a set-up you've got. Who'd have thought all this in a month.' Phyllis looked at her son.

'Oh ye of little faith,' he said, imitating Dixon. 'I can even cook a whole lot of new menus now, like Stephanie Alexander's stuff.'

'Who's she?'

'Earth to Mum – just the most famous cook in Australia.'

'Well, pardon me. You've been buying new clothes too, I see. You're looking quite the young man about town . . . I hope these blokes don't expect you to do more than, um, the housekeeping . . .'

'*M-u-m.*'

The three sat in a café overlooking the steel grey sea. Around them, Sunday crowds gathered in black coats to sip coffee and wine while plastic awnings protected them from the gusty southerlies coming in from the Tasman. Buskers and loonies wove around each other on the pavement. Phyllis watched the handsome waiters, pseudo-intellectuals, jugglers and colourful street-life in amazement while Murray ordered a macchiato.

'A mucky what?' said Tree.

'A long black with a dash of milk, Miss Border Bush Pig.'

'Well up yours, Mr Arty Farty Poofter Pants.'

'I still like my cappuccino. We've got a dispensing machine at work that does them now. Tea, chocolate, the lot. You just push a button,' Phyllis joined in.

'I bet they're not as good,' proclaimed Murray, sniffing the rich aroma of his first macchiato.

'Can we go to Luna Park?' Treecia pointed to the roller-coaster over the road.

'Not today, the show starts at five. Perhaps your brother'll take you tomorrow so I can go shopping?' She looked at Murray, daring him not to.

'Yeah, I'll take you. Where are you staying?'

'In the city. The Welcome Hotel it's called. A bit pokey but central. We got one of those deals.'

'It smells like old farts and Chinese food, and it's full of Asians,' said Tree as she slurped her iced chocolate.

'Don't be so racist, Treecia!' said Murray.

'Well you used to be.'

'Yeah, well I've learnt a thing or two, and Dũng's been a really good friend to me since I've been here.'

Phyllis just sipped her cappuccino, looking at him. She missed him, he could tell. Tree soon wandered off to watch a busker.

Phyllis pounced. 'So are you seeing anyone? Girl? Boy?'

'Not really, Mum, just want to play the field, you know.'

'Ah, the field. It doesn't throw much my way these days.'

'You should get out more – meet some blokes, become a lesbian.'

'A lesbian in Albury – can you imagine what Ron at the station would say? As for picking up blokes, I'm too old for the disco and I don't fancy spending my Saturday nights on the pokies at the RSL. Not when there's a new Harrison Ford or Mel Gibson movie at the video store.'

'God, Mum, they're even older than you.'

She threatened to whack him on the head with her bag. 'You should try and come up now and again, bring some friends if you want, we've got plenty of room.'

'Yeah, I will, Mum. I just got here.'

Murray thought about taking friends home to Albury. How boring it would be to all the people he wanted to hang out with. He felt sorry for his mum but at least he'd given her an excuse to get to the city more often. Her eyes were a little wet as she stubbed out her cigarette. They both knew something precious was finished. He'd grown up now and was being lured into all the perils that entailed. Phyllis realised sadly that she was somehow middle-aged. Her boy, half her pride and joy, was gone.

Desperate Measures

Selling drugs is all well and good if:

a) You don't have your nose in the trough all the time. (You may as well be stealing from the till of your own business.)
b) You don't spend all the proceeds on fifteen-dollar cocktails for a bunch of beautiful ne'er-do-wells who you'll never see again.
c) You don't lose bundles of cash while stumbling around darkened sex venues, drunk as a skunk and whacked to the eyeballs.

Finally, and most importantly, if you are aiming to pay off a British Barclaycard with Aussie dollars, it helps if the dollar is worth a little more than 35 pence.

Dixon sat on his bed with a bunch of bank statements and threatening letters, kindly forwarded by his mother. At first he couldn't remember spending $280 at Café Greco but then he had a memory flash of a messy, late-night excursion to the casino where he'd charged-up five people's dinners and they'd fixed him up with cash. Then there was $180 at Candy Bar. 'Surely not,' he moaned. After a time, however, it came to him that they'd been kind enough to accept his card during an embarrassing midweek scene in which he found himself penniless.

He had already paid £1000 off his card but he still had over £2000 to go. It was an outrage that $3000 should reduce to such a paltry sum in Sterling – still, what did he expect in some tin-pot country at the furthest reaches of civilisation and empire?

He'd also fallen well short of his projected profit – dismally short, in fact. If he was honest with himself – and it was almost more than he could bear to be – he had salvaged just over $4000, considerably less than his initial expectations of $10,000. He had $500 left in cash which, given the value of the dollar, seemed neither here nor there as far as his card was concerned.

How to stop Barclays bank speeding up the inevitable extradition process?

He looked at the two crushed ecstasies and the dusty white residues of cocaine that remained. There was nothing he could do with them except take them himself at some future time – after all, who was going to buy something so unattractively presented? Nor, with his credit limit now trampled in the dust, could he repeat the venture in the hope that more rigorous accounting might achieve better results.

He had to think of a way to make some money quickly and clear this maddening debt. He couldn't borrow from Doc. The price was just too high. But Dũng?

Dũng's paintings, even the small ones, fetched hundreds – even thousands – these days.

Dix wandered out of his room. The house was as silent as the grave. Doc had gone out for lunch with friends and Murray had said something about taking his sister to Luna Park. Dix pushed open the door to Dũng's studio, still debating whether he could bear to ask for a loan. The room was empty. Dũng must be at his mum's again, Dix thought, relieved.

He glanced around. There were at least thirty or forty canvases stacked against one wall. Perhaps he could just charm one of them out of Dũng? Dix flipped through the collection, lighting immediately on his own portrait. It shocked him momentarily; he looked older than when he'd last seen it mounted on the easel. Was it the light or had Dũng worked on it since – added weight to the jowls and darkness to the eyes? 'Enough with the Dorian Grey already,' he muttered, and continued to flick through them. Most had been there since the day Dũng moved in. 'A senseless bloody waste,' murmured Dix as two tiny inconsequential works presented themselves at the rear of the stack.

Would he miss a couple? He probably didn't even want them – probably thought they weren't good enough, or some precious, arty rot. These, thought Dixon, were desperate times. They called for desperate measures.

Dũng parked the car outside his mother's bank and checked he had her power of attorney with him. Getting her to sign that had been an ordeal in itself. He was going in to write a cheque for the balance of her mortgage. Then she could sell her house if she wanted and buy a flat somewhere else. It was the only solution he could think of to his mother's new agoraphobia. Perhaps in a new neighbourhood she'd be less fearful. Trân had agreed but as soon as they'd spoken to Mum about moving, she'd become attached to the house, the neighbourhood and her memories of Bà nọi.

'She makes it sound like gran would turn in her grave if she moved house.' Trân gave a grim laugh. 'What are we going to do, Dũng? She's going crazy.'

'It's probably just the menopause.'

'She had that nearly ten years ago. You can't blame everything on the mysteries of female reproduction, you know.'

'No, I'm serious, Trân. She probably needs to be on HRT or something. I can't talk to her about that, but you should.'

She looked up from her coffee. 'Thanks.'

'Well I'm paying off the mortgage so that no one can kick her out of the house when the White Australia Policy returns. I've convinced her she'll have "native title" then.'

They both cackled.

Dũng's thoughts turned to Dixon though he wished they wouldn't. They'd barely spoken recently, and Dũng wondered if perhaps their bubble of sexual tension had burst and vanished into thin air. Dũng wished he could have sensible relationships like his sister, then had to admit that would be a bit boring. It seemed quite clear to him that Dixon Brearly enjoyed toying with people to see what would happen. He just liked to see if he could hook people in. Dũng had thought himself a shrewder judge of character than Doc, but if he was honest, he'd been just as much a fool.

The pregnancy testing kit sat in Claude's bathroom cabinet. She was going to wait a few more days before she used it, after all it wasn't the first time she'd been late. But kit or no kit, she had an inkling.

Murray's behaviour towards her had been ambiguous since they'd fucked. He was more familiar with her but she had retreated somewhat. Even if he wanted more from her, Claude wasn't at all sure she could be bothered attempting a relationship with a bisexual boy fifteen years her junior.

'They're at their sexual peak then – and you're at yours now. It should be perfect,' said Bella, who'd become impatient with Claude's deliberations. 'Why don't you just enjoy it while it lasts? I bet those boys next door have been drooling to get into his pants, and you did it. One-nil for GIRL POWER!'

Claude hadn't said anything to Bell about not using protection. The truth was, she'd started hoping her fears were fulfilled. It shocked her to think that a negative test result would disappoint her. All at once, it seemed the perfect time for her to have a baby. She could just about cope financially, she couldn't imagine meeting Mr Right any more, and she suspected she'd become too set in her ways to negotiate the endless compromises marital relationships entailed. She never planned any of this, but now it seemed like providence.

They were midway through their week-long photo shoot and Murray had already done several sessions with Bella. Claude took another look at the transparencies on her light box. She decided he looked more comfortable in leisure wear rather than suits. He'd probably never worn one before.

He'd also just had his first salon haircut and had given Claude a detailed explanation of what products he needed to use if he wanted to keep it in the style: long at the front, short at the back and slicked to one side. Murray felt it was a bit poncy, but Claude's hairdresser had fairly gushed at the result.

Grinning, Claude picked up the phone to let him know she was leaving for the day's shoot.

'You ready, Murray?'

'Yep, I'll be there in a tick.'

There had been some friction between Claude and the modelling agency. She'd cancelled one of the male models and threatened to dump them all if they made her pay the $1500 booking fee. Murray had come in to take his place and was made to feel like a novice by the others.

'What have Imogen and Pierre got against me?' asked Murray in the car.

'Who knows, hon? They probably think you're too good-looking, or they're friends of Nathaniel, who we didn't use. Don't worry about it.'

'It just shits me, you know – I haven't done anything.'

'Ah, but you're doing something now. You're in the game, and it doesn't matter what business you're in – once you're in the game, you make enemies. The trick is, don't play it. Hey, isn't that the girl who was harassing you guys?'

'Shit, it is too.'

Angel was standing at the lights on Grey Street, waiting to cross. Claude stopped as they changed to red, and Murray wound the window down.

'Don't say anything to her,' urged Claude.

'Why not? Hey, haven't seen any Angels at my window lately!'

She came over to the car and peered in, then put her hand to her forehead. 'You.'

'Yeah, me. Ya boyfriend showed up yet?'

'Yeah, he has. Hey, maybe you can tell that doctor sorry from me – Mitch is back in Queensland, he wants me to go up, get back with him, but I'm not going up there. Not after he pissed off on me.'

Claude leaned over. 'You're probably better off getting yourself together here.'

'Yeah, right,' she said with a sarcastic snarl. Claude smiled sympathetically and shifted into gear. They took off.

'A weird chick that one – pregnant, ha! Why do all these chicks get pregnant anyway?'

'Murray, you know very well why chicks get pregnant.' They looked at each other shyly, new combatants in some gender game. 'You're old enough and wise enough to ensure it doesn't happen! How do you know I'm not pregnant?'

'Yeah, but you're older.'

'I haven't been through the menopause just yet, thanks.'

'Yeah, but you know what I mean.'

They drove on in silence, Claude wondering for all the world what Murray did mean.

Ricky sat in Doc's office, fidgeting nervously. Doc stared at him coldly from behind his newly acquired glasses which he was mostly wearing for show at the moment.

'See, thing is, I need a repeat on the Valium and those green things you gave me. They calm me down. The fuckers I live with are trying to nick stuff from me, including my pills. Cunts.' He looked over his shoulder as if they might be there.

'Let's see your arms.'

'No way, man. I haven't been whacking stuff up.'

'Well why won't you let me see then?'

'Yeah, after what you did to me.'

Doc thought about what he did. The idea of it repulsed him

now. 'You know very well I never did anything.'

'You really fucked me up.'

'That's why I've seen you peddling your arse in Shakespeare Grove, is it? Because I fucked you up? Now listen, if you'll give someone a blow-job in their car for fifty bucks, I can't imagine why you'd be scared to show me your arm.'

'I'm not fucking scared of anything. I don't like working down there but I'm not rich like you are. I could have been a doctor too, but people like me can't get jobs.'

'Ricky, two years ago you worked in a record store. You worked there for at least a year – I bought CDs from you. You can't get a job because you're speeding off your dial all the time, simple as that.'

'I'm not using at the moment, honest.'

'I only have to look at your eyes.'

'You're just like my family and everyone, fucking turn against me.'

'Well the next part is even worse, Ricky, and it's going to hurt you more than me. I'm not prescribing for you any more. It's going to be crazy town in your head from now on.'

'I'll fucking blow the whistle on you, Doc. I'll get you for what you did to me.'

'Good.'

'Wadda' ya mean – good?'

'Well, in order for anyone to believe your word over mine, you'll have to straighten out. I'm going to give you the names of several places you could check into, and the contact numbers for Narcotics Anonymous. No one, Ricky, will believe a junkie suffering from speed psychosis, much less a patient who has continued seeing me and who never reported the alleged incident at the time. You're not in a good position, old chum, and you're in even lousier shape. Your teeth are rotting, your skin is a disaster zone and your bones have already been irreparably damaged. I'd give you another two years max the way you're heading. So nothing would make me happier than to see you all fresh-faced in the courtroom, in, let's say six months.'

'You're an arsehole, Doc.'

Ricky stumbled out and slammed the door to begin the rounds of every twenty-four hour clinic in search of a sympathetic ear or a roving hand. Doc felt strangely elated despite the fact that his own grip on the world was faltering. Ricky was out of his hair and he'd even taken the Post-it note with the numbers on it. Why had he let it go so long?

Winter's Heart

The pictures had sat in Dixon's wardrobe for a week. He'd really just meant to borrow them but he couldn't see the harm in at least letting a gallery appraise them. Dixon vaguely knew Merrily Davis. Her gallery was downstairs in the same building as his office. While she possessed the accoutrements and manners of a charming Toorak matron, Dixon suspected butter wouldn't melt within a mile of her mouth.

This became apparent the minute he indicated he was there to sell something, not buy. The shift in demeanour almost frightened him.

'Merrily, I have been given two Dũng Ngo's, which I'm terribly fond of, but you see I'll be travelling again soon and fear I'll damage them.'

She raised her eyebrows. 'We're not living in the Dark Ages, you know. It is quite safe to send works abroad these days, galleries do it all the time. Send them in an Artpack, for God's sake.'

'I'm afraid it's also a question of money. I know how valuable his works have become, you see, and the path of the itinerant journalist is a costly one . . .'

'So you want to cash them in? Dixon, this is Toorak, people hock stuff all the time, but I have to say these paintings are not our usual style.' She put her glasses on and looked more closely. 'Not our style at all. My clients go strictly for still lifes, pastoral scenes, landscapes and portraits. My lot haven't come to terms with modern yet, much less post-modern and beyond.'

'The National Gallery paid twenty-seven thousand for one of his paintings, you know.'

'Yes, and they paid over a million for *Blue Poles* twenty-odd years ago. But I don't think you'll find one of my customers, even now, who approves of that decision. Still, he is going places. Tell you what, I'll give you two-fifty a piece.'

'Two-fifty,' he said incredulously. 'These are selling for two-and-a-half grand a piece.'

'Not here, they're not. And I'm sure you've got your reasons for bringing them to such an inappropriate gallery. This is Toorak, Dixon, we're nothing if not discreet.'

Dixon was in the bidding now, he'd already forgotten he was only having them valued. He felt incensed. He couldn't let this woman undervalue Dũng's worth to this extent.

'I couldn't take less than twelve hundred for the pair.'

'You don't know much about gallery margins, do you?'

Dixon said nothing. Merrily sighed. 'Nine hundred?'

'One thousand, no less.'

She looked at him and shrugged. 'Alright, I should get you working for me.'

'Can I?'

'Only joking, barely enough to sustain me, I'm afraid.' She tore a ragged cheque from the book on her desk. 'A pleasure doing business with you, Dixon dear.'

Dixon arrived at his desk to a most unexpected surprise. A cheque for two thousand dollars.

'You little beauty, Brearly,' shouted Brian. 'They've just sold the hotel, three million plus.'

Dix looked at the cheque and felt a hideous pang of panic and guilt. He grabbed Merrily's cheque and legged it back down to the gallery.

'I'm sorry, Dixon, you're too late.'

'What do you mean – too late? I was just here.'

'So was Gabriela Rossini, we keep an eye out for each other, you see.'

Dixon felt like begging her, but he didn't know how to begin. He felt sick. Now Dũng's paintings would be on display in Fitzhi Rossini Gallery, right on Fitzroy Street. Dũng was sure to see them. Worse, Gabriela would be on the fucking phone!

'I can't believe it.'

'Sorry, darling. We've all got to make a living.'

'How much did she pay?' He couldn't stop himself from asking.

'You don't want to know the answer to that question, dear. You just don't want to know.'

Dixon had to remain composed. He couldn't look like a thief. What had he been thinking? It was as if he'd gone into an evil trance and now the damage was done. He briefly considered using the two thousand dollars to try and get them back, but it would be too humiliating. Besides, he now had three grand. Not much in the larger scheme of things but better than a poke in the eye with a sharp stick. Still, what about Dũng? How could he ever look him in the eye again?

Lady Asquith had thought the soft music a dream. She lay still, and listened again. Age seemed to dull everything except the pain of her angina and memories. Her heartbeat was sluggish, each throb dislodging some particle of her life and bringing it to her attention as if for consideration. Conversations, conflicts, childbirth and acquisitions. She could barely find the energy to move from her day-bed now. But a Chopin piece she remembered all too well seemed to be playing in the next room. With effort, she lifted herself from the nest of blankets to see if anyone was there.

'Caroline? Caroline darling, is that you?' There was no answer.

She struggled with her stick, resting on it at two-step intervals, breathless. The light was playing strange tricks on her, it had been doing so for days.

'All of them coming at me,' she muttered with precious breath. She heard her father's laughter, cruel and terrible, smelt the cigar smoke that used to waft from his den. The smell of men and their precious, bumbling power.

She remembered her maid, Enid, rushing into her room with notes and secret flowers – the hushed whispers of their conspiracy. 'Miss Penny, Mr Zultman's car is down at the back gate. He said he'd wait there for you.'

They'd titter about her secret loves, her wicked rendezvous. Then she'd disappear into the lush, green summer garden, her pale, beaded crêpe dress a vibrant coruscation darting through the rustling trees. She'd hitch it high, giggling as she scaled splintery palings to reach Franz or one of the others who waited for her in their shiny cars. In her memory it was always summer, and Franz had been special: romantic and exotic. Now she could barely recall the trembling delights he'd brought her. How eager men had been to bring pleasure to a pretty young heiress. And how quick to scorn her behind her back. Not Franz though, he'd been discreet.

And such a fuss about an infection. They may as well have been living in Victorian England. She never went near that doctor again, not after he'd gone to her father with news of her predicament. She could still feel the flush of shame.

She thought again of Franz. Her own voice echoing back from the past:

'Daddy, it was Franz. I wasn't to know. I'm so ashamed.'

'Get out of here, Penelope. You have fossicked in the gutter and you've seen exactly where it gets you. I learnt what your mother was like, I should have known her sins would blot through the page to stain her daughter. Be thankful I'm still mindful enough of you to see this put right.'

'Daddy, you musn't hurt him!'

'It's out of your foolish hands. You have a lot to learn, my girl. Now get yourself upstairs and finish your packing, or God help you.'

Lady Asquith reached the conservatory door, trembling as the music faltered. She stood gasping in the heavy dusk that had taken hold of the room. Her eyes strained through the murky soup of evening. 'Franz, is that you? Have you forgiven me, sweet . . .'

She let out a frail cry as her cane fell from her grasp. A strange and ugly chord reverberated as she slipped to the floor.

'Caroline, my pills. Darling, my pills . . .' Her voice trailed off as she sat against the cold tiles of the hall. The ceiling arched high above her. So high. 'Oh dear, it was a terrible thing, a terrible thing.'

Flight of Fancy

The following morning Dixon loitered outside a travel agency, like the criminal he was, for a full fifteen minutes. He lit another cigarette, reeling at how disgusting it tasted so soon after the last.

He was tortured by guilt and racked by the tension of not knowing when he would be found out. Undone. He couldn't bring himself to go in, but knew he couldn't stay to face the music. He could never bear anger. He'd spent hours as a child behind the gardening shed, fearfully dodging his father's wrath over some measly broken window or a few paltry stolen pounds. The thought of the righteous anger of his peers, and his resulting humiliation – well, it was insupportable.

Dixon read down the tired old chalk menu of world destinations: Bangkok, Cape Town, Dublin, Frankfurt, Rome, New York, Tokyo, London. Why had he done it when he'd been so good, so far?

'Because, *leibling*, it's in your nature,' came Soren's reply from deep in his head.

'Who asked you, you're dead,' he snapped back, then realised he'd spoken out loud. A passing woman was giving him the strangest look. He blushed.

Each destination conjured up postcard snapshots of possibility as he read through them. New York – no, too big and greedy, and he hadn't made the grade yet. Tokyo – nah, far too governed by the work ethic and prone to earthquakes for Dix's liking. The eyes had already been picked out of all the former Eastern Bloc countries, and Moscow was too desperate and savage. He'd heard the stories about people having their throats cut for a pair of Levis and a Sony PlayStation. He thought about Cape Town, well and truly liberated from the tedium of apartheid but still a bit messy politically. Dublin, romantic for a writer, but expensive, and a little too Catholic and underpopulated for one such as himself.

Dixon focussed resolutely on what lay ahead. What was done, was done. He knew that there would be anger, disappointment, perhaps even broken hearts in the wake of his decision, but at the end of the day he was just an old broom sweeping dirt. It was grossly indulgent of him to think people would not get over his betrayal. And forgiveness is the perennial lesson of existence – it would be nothing without its subjects.

He booked a flight to somewhere hot and cheap for the Friday after next – the day after pay day. He hoped Dũng's paintings would not surface before that time. He needed one more injection of income before he left.

Dũng had agreed to show fifteen new works at Fitzhi Rossini Gallery in September. Gabriela had wanted more but Dũng felt he'd be struggling to have even fifteen. *Murmurs of Genocide* was so large it had taken nearly three months to complete. He looked at Gabriela, seated across from him, her piled-up hair speared by three chopsticks, her lipstick vibrant red against her livid complexion. She was a half-Dutch and half-Russian Jew, the widow of an Italian painter whose work she alone had brought to prominence during the eighties. She held her glass of coffee in gloved hands.

They were at her favourite café in Fitzroy Street, surrounded by similar arty-types. The sun was vanishing and trams filled with workers eager to begin their weekend were trundling past.

'Don't you like *Lẫm bẫm diệt-chửng*?'

'I like, darling, but you have done better paintings.'

'You said you wanted a big one, a political one – something Gothic.'

'I still want to show it, someone will buy it, but I don't want to put more than fifteen thou' on it.'

'Fantastic, I'll make about eight grand for three months' work. I'd rather do small paintings if that's the case.'

'Sorry Dũng, it's the best I can do on it – maybe next time you do a big one, we'll get fifty thou'.'

Dũng pouted. 'Maybe I'll just destroy the bloody thing. No one likes it.'

'Don't do that, darling, it's good, I do like it, but you can't expect everything to be a masterpiece. You know, I just bought two Dũng Ngo's the other day. Someone is selling your works already – you see how much your value goes up in the last two years? A good sign when works circulate.'

'What paintings are they?'

'I don't know, I haven't seen them yet. I buy on name purely. They're small and beautiful says Merrily when she rang. I'll pick them up next week.

Dũng's eyes were on the passers-by; his mind was far away, thinking about his mum, about Dixon and their first kiss by the grave of a dead basher.

'One she said is a little girl, the other, a little boy. A pair, I think. They must be old because I don't remember them. No one will buy them from her gallery, it's too conservative.'

'What?' Dũng looked back to her; he hadn't been listening at all.

'I'm talking about the paintings.'

'Oh yeah, let me know when you get them – I like to know which of my buyers are art lovers and which are investors.'

'And which ones are short of cash, darling, yes?'

'Hmm, yes, that too.'

Claudette was a week late. The pregnancy test had shown positive when she'd used it. She swore Bella to secrecy and let her hopes bubble over.

'You are joking?' For the first time in their long friendship Bella sounded stunned. 'Claude, you're mad.'

'You're jealous.'

Bella sighed on the other end of the phone and lit a cigarette. 'How are you going to cope with a baby on your own?'

'The same way I've coped with everything else on-my-bloody-own.'

'Have you been to the doctor yet.'

'No.'

'It might be a good idea before you start broadcasting the news all over town.'

'Bell, I'm not broadcasting anything all over anywhere. I'm just telling you. Hoping you'd get all conspiratorial with me. What would you do?'

'I don't know,' she sighed again. 'Probably the same as you. We're pushing thirty-five. Alright, I'm jealous and in shock. It's the last thing I expected to be hearing from you.'

'Well it wasn't planned at my end either. I'm still in shock from the sex to say anything of its consequences.'

'You'll have to stop drinking.'

'Everything has its price.'

'Murray'll freak out.'

'Maybe, but I hope not. It's not like I'm planning to put any demands on him. Once he knows that, he'll probably think it's "cool". Who knows, he might even be of some help – at least in the garden.'

Bella was laughing. 'Weren't you the one who always said that women turn into cows when they have babies.'

'Moooo.'

'Well, darling, congratulations. I suppose we should celebrate but you can't indulge.'

'I've never heard it said that a couple of glasses of champagne can cause foetal alcohol syndrome. For God's sake, the thing was conceived on an eccie, it'll probably be a slow learner.'

'Dumb and happy, which is fine if it's a boy. It'll need to be dumb, happy and pretty if it's a girl.'

'Let me get through the birth, please, before I have to face the prospects of adolescence and beyond.'

Murray sat in Doc's waiting room – waiting. He and Doc were going to the gym together after surgery closed. Doc was still with his last patient in the consulting room, although everyone else had left for the day. Brochures littered the table – information about combination therapies, HIV and living for the future. He looked through the different pamphlets: 'Safe sex is hot sex – if it's not on, it's not on'. He grabbed a magazine and flicked through the glossy pages, 'Breast Implants: Like 'em or Lump 'em'. He looked at pictures of breast supplementations that had gone hideously wrong. He wanted to think about something else. Anything rather than HIV and how he'd been raped and then fucked Claude – raw. What if . . . he thought, as the last patient departed.

Doc wandered out and Murray broached the subject. 'Doc, do you reckon I could get one of those blood tests for HIV?'

'Are you concerned?'

'Not that concerned. It's just something happened to me once and, you know, I'd like to take it – just to make sure.'

'Well, come in. We can do it now. In fact, I'm overdue for one myself so we'll send them off together, hey?'

'It'll be just like junkies shooting up together, except the opposite – unshooting up!'

Doc handed Murray a tourniquet. 'Can you hold this for me?'

'I don't know how you can do it to yourself – I'd freak out if I had to draw out my own blood. Have you seen those breast implants in the magazine out there – talk about gross.'

'I know, I left them there as a deterrent. Not that I get many women coming for plastic surgery referrals, just trannies mostly, and their eyes seem to glaze over when you start talking about the risks involved.'

He turned to Murray. 'Your turn.'

'I don't like to watch.' He held his arm out as Doc swabbed it and tightened the tourniquet. He looked towards the window and felt the pin prick.

Doc sat the two vials of blood on his desk and went into the office to get some labels. Murray held them up to the light to look at the blood. Was one darker than the other?

'Blood. How the fuck does it know so much?' he muttered.

He put the vials down and went to the window. The sun had disappeared. It was *Shebat* and people were making their way to the nearby synagogue. Doc returned.

'Those Jewish dudes have the weirdest haircuts and the women all look like they've got wigs on.'

'They have got wigs on.'

'Why?'

'Oh, it's something to do with vanity and keeping your head covered in the presence of God, a show of respect. The really strict ones shave their heads.'

'I reckon all that religion stuff's a bunch of crap.'

'It's easy to say when you weren't brought up eating the body of Christ and drinking his blood at communion.' *Sin is in your blood, brother.* The placard's message flashed before him as he sealed the Pathology courier bag.

'When do these results come back?'

'Oh, about a week. I'll let you know.'

'Are you worried, Doc?'

'I always used to worry. But the whole situation has changed in the last couple of years. There's all these combination therapies now which can save people from getting sick for who knows how long.' He was turning off the lights and switching on the answering machine. 'Still, no one wants to be taking bucket-loads of pills every day for the rest of their life.'

'On the radio they reckoned if your ancestors died from the Black Plague, you had a natural immunity to it.'

'Well that's all well and good if it's true, but how are you going to find out if they did?'

Murray shrugged. 'It'd be great if that vaccine came out, people would be rooting like rabbits.'

'AIDS never stopped that happening for long.'

'I'd freak if I got it. The only modelling I could do then would be for Benetton.' He laughed again.

'Well, come on, let's get out of here and focus on the living for a while, hey?'

Dixon didn't plan to give any notice when he left work, nor did he plan to advise members of the household. He decided it was better for everyone that way. He wasn't one for emotional (or acrimonious) goodbyes. His flight left at four in the afternoon so he'd just sneak out of the house with his laptop and a few other valued possessions. He believed in travelling light.

Bev stopped by his desk on her way out.

'I suppose you've heard.'

'Heard what?'

'About Lady Asquith.'

'What about her?'

'Oh, she's at death's door again, only this time it's for real. She was rushed into Saint Vincent's yesterday, and they're all saying she won't come out. Heart attack or something. *Women's Weekly* and *The Melburnian* are hotting up the presses for when she goes. You might even get some more mileage out of your lovely visit and chat. No doubt the family have already called in the developers and subdividers. Can you imagine the money when they start selling river-front apartments off the plan?'

Dixon rolled his eyes. He was thinking about subdividers and developers fishing about in the well. It looked as if he'd timed his departure perfectly, he thought.

'The house and surrounding buildings are heritage listed, of course,' continued Bev, 'and there's a well dug by convicts too, which is protected.'

'Yes, I've seen that, it's quite a distance from the house. It'll get in the way of any development I'd expect.'

'Oh, you know what developers are like. They'll just fill it in, keep the façade and then build some vaguely heritage-influenced condos.'

Dixon grunted and thought about the Zultman files he'd amassed. He'd discovered that Franz had a younger sister, now also deceased, and that she had inherited everything that didn't go to paying her brother's debts. It seemed it had been a matter of egotistical obsession that Penny's father take over each failing enterprise in the lost Zultman empire. But the piano remained a mystery. Perhaps Franz had left it to Penny as his apology for sullying her expensive reputation?

Bath Time

It was early Saturday afternoon, Dixon's last weekend in the house. Bored and restless, he remembered his few remaining narcotics. Might as well make the most of them, he thought. One final hurrah. Dũng was out and Murray was off with Claudette, but Doc was home and he had all the right equipment to send the gear straight to one's vital neural cortex. Dix strolled into Doc's room, waving the tiny plastic bag like a semaphore flag.

'Doc, how about you and I whack up these remaining Es and coke?'

Doc looked up from his computer. He'd been planning to visit the gym in an hour or so. Now Dixon was compromising him. A shiver of delight passed through him as he rapidly unmade his plans for the rest of the day.

They sat in Doc's bathroom, Dix perched on the toilet seat. Doc leant over the vanity, as he syphoned up the solution into the syringes through cotton wool balls. 'How much is there in this mixture of dregs?'

'Not really sure. I'd say one to two Es – possibly a little more if we're lucky – and a wee dusting of coke. Just enough to jazz things up a bit.'

Doc sniggered evilly. 'As if they need jazzing up!'

'Well, it is the last shout, I'm afraid, I'm not importing any more. Despite all my calculations, forecasts and feasibility studies, I'm not making any money as a dealer.'

'I only hope I don't lose time like I did the other week. We're not as *Dũng* as we used to be.' Doc had been quietly relieved to see whatever it was subside between those two.

'He's not that *Dũng* either. He's just got some sense that's all. Not a state of clarity I've ever aspired to and clearly something I'll never attain.' Dixon felt a pang at the mention of Dũng's name. It hadn't been enough to win him over as he had. No, he'd had to go and do one of the worst things he'd ever done. He thought back on his growing catalogue of other 'worst things'. The Visa card he'd 'borrowed' from a German boy in Mykonos, the dance party ticket scam he got himself involved in at Gay Pride, and the sixteenth-century manuscript he'd liberated from the Cambridge archives. He realised he'd done worse in the past – and lived to tell.

With the truth serum about to run in his veins, Dixon reminded himself that men governed nothing with more difficulty than their own tongues. He knew it would be all too easy to say too much.

Dix turned away as Doc perused the crook of his arm for the choicest vein.

'Are you ready?' Their eyes met for a minute: Doc's searching and wet, Dixon's glazed from the gauzy layers of deceit that were amassing over them.

'Consent granted. Fly me to the fucking moon.'

He looked away from the needle and felt it prick. Doc released the tourniquet and the hammer fell. Champagne rushed down his spinal cord and he felt the sweet intrusion of an angel's tongue searching the nerve ends of his arsehole.

'Oooooh,' he sighed as the toilet tried to suck him down into some wild, wet and awesome nether place.

Doc released his own tourniquet with the sexy, illicit know-how of an expert and bowed his head in front of the vanity mirror. His secret HIV fears flew off on the heavy wings of black crows.

Doc's feral eyes made the slow journey round to Dix, who sat like the proverbial 'Thinker' on the toilet. He and Dix were alone now, an intimacy that had been getting more and more infrequent. Dix was so utterly drug-fucked that for a moment he thought he was Franz Zultman. He lifted his head, wondering if he hadn't just lived an entire lifetime in this shiny, tiled place.

'God, Doc, are you okay?'

'I think so.' No sooner had he said it, than it came true. He was better than okay – he was flying. 'I love this bathroom, Dix, I can really chill out in here. Let's have a bath, a sacred ritual of sorts.'

Dix thought briefly of sacredness and found a yawning cavern in his psyche. He knew that Doc looked, however misguidedly, for the goodness in others. There was some kernel, some glittering nugget of love missing in Dixon's make-up – a nugget he suddenly pined to possess.

'Do you think we're remembered for the good we do, or the bad?' asked Doc, as if he'd somehow tuned into Dixon's furtive cerebral meanderings.

'Both,' Dix replied. 'I think those we remember the most are people whom we are ultimately unable to attribute to either. People who are irredeemably good *and* bad. Take Schindler, Garland, JFK, Brett Whitely and Maria Calais, for example. We love paradox and I have every intention of being one myself.'

'I just feel too much guilt.'

'What about? Not our murder most foul, surely?'

'Not about that. Even in the context of traditional Catholicism, I have no doubt I can be forgiven for that.'

'Well, if Dũng's right and we get to play every different role throughout our historical progression of lives, we shouldn't fret about anything, just coast along.'

'Like now.'

'Yeah.'

'Dix, you sounded like Murray then. Let's have a bath.'

'Okay.'

Dixon brushed Doc's fragile face with his hand. Poor Doc, he thought. He hugged him and felt within him that tremor of frailty. He wondered if he might not stay, perhaps they could all love and shelter each other somehow. But Dixon knew he would only do further damage once his stay-by-date elapsed.

Dũng had pretty much finished getting the exhibition paintings together. They were all stacked in his room, awaiting delivery to the framers. Gabriela had wanted him to mount them in frames of perspex and chrome. Dũng had thought them hideous and said so. They looked more like 1970s nightclub fixtures than capsules for his genius. He was sticking with his lavish gold frames which were actually cheaper, more expensive looking and far more enduring.

Returning home from a final meeting with Gabriela, Dũng was greeted by the sounds of splashing and cavorting coming from Doc's ensuite bathroom. His heart sank as he recognised Dix's voice intermingled with Doc's. Murray was home too, sitting in the kitchen, nursing a cup of tea.

'What are they doing in there?' Dũng braced himself for further testimonial to Dixon's roving mercurial passions.

'Fucked if I know, I think they've gone crazy.'

Murray seemed decidedly ill at ease with the situation.

'Why? You're not scared are you?'

Murray shrugged. 'They're in the bath, splashing around – they've been in there for hours. They just keep filling it with more hot water – that's how I know they aren't dead. And when I went in and yelled through the door if they wanted dinner, Doc spent half an hour howling "Murray-urray-urray" like a poisoned dog, while Dix just went "yadda, yadda, yadda". No joke, half an hour. I started flipping out a bit, you know. It's like they're possessed by the devil or something.'

'Well, you're probably half right. They've been possessed by demon drugs is my guess. You will see this sort of thing from time to time in our sweet abode. At least they're safely in their zoo. They'll come out when they're hungry. We can go out if you like. They're both giving me the shits a bit at the moment, anyway.

Let's walk down to Acland Street and along the pier. It's quite windy today, they always say it excites the more aberrant brain cells in mad people.'

'They were singing too.'

'What song?'

'I don't know. "The Look of Love" or something.'

'ABC. They're reliving their youth – bit before our time, Murray.'

Only the really brave were out on the pier. Murray and Dũng leant their weight against the wind. It was bloody cold. The Squall Café glowed like a beacon at the end and, when they reached it, they ordered coffee just to feel the heat from the cups.

'Do people actually live out here, upstairs from this café?' asked Murray, recalling the Edwardian balcony above them with washing flapping frantically on it.

'I think so. It'd be weird, wouldn't it?'

'Even more spooky than our house, I reckon. Claudette and I saw Angel the other day, you know. She said she'd caught up with her boyfriend in Queensland or something.'

'Short of Siberia, that's probably the best place for him.'

'I've never been there. The weather'd be unreal, I reckon.'

'Yeah, but there's something about the tropics which makes agendas more conservative and behaviour more corrupt.'

They stared idly at other fearless walkers battling the wind on the pier: a little girl being dragged along by a huge dog, a couple kissing while a scarf snaked free and skipped along the wooden planks, boat owners in the marina trying to moor their crafts in impossible conditions.

'So, is it like a threesome with you guys?'

Dũng looked up, frowning. 'What?'

'Well, how you all bonk each other. I don't get it.'

'There's nothing to get, it's just, well . . . People get older, they get jaded and they like to experiment. And when everyone's taking drugs and partying, things get harder to explain.'

'Are you in love with Dixon?'

Dũng cackled bitterly. 'Love and Dixon, surely I wouldn't be so stupid? Maybe I would. I've loved worse people than him before. Dixon's clever and funny, but he's an imperialist in the deepest sense, a man for all seasons. He takes from the weak and sides with the strong.'

Murray understood the last part and nodded thoughtfully. 'There's this model, Imogen, who's like that at the studio. Like she really hated me when I started modelling, but once she realised I was in with Claude and Bella she's like, "Oh, you should come out clubbing with us some time." She reckons they get VIP booths at Mink and know all the door bitches and shit, but I can see straight through her.'

Dũng was watching Murray, aware of how intense his desire for knowledge was. He smiled, remembering the bitchy dramas of being a nineteen-year-old. 'I've had one of the booths at Mink, it's no big deal.'

The deep green of Claudette's back lawn drained to black as Saturday night descended. Claude stirred a bolognaise sauce with a wooden spoon. She was deep in thought, her gaze out the window unseeing. It had just dawned on her how huge a responsibility the baby would be, and how lonely a journey it could become. For the first time, she felt fear and dread in the pit of her stomach.

She blinked back tears that had started with onions but were now backed by real emotion. She suddenly felt she'd been short-changed in missing out on all the dreamy hetero-romance and companionship enjoyed by the lucky ones. While she'd always kept a sturdy cynicism in place, a different truth had broken abruptly and painfully through her protective shell. Now she wondered if, by having a child, she'd be complicating her situation even further, denying herself all hope of finding anyone ever again.

Claude thought of the two books she'd bought on pregnancy and birth. She'd hidden them away in the same manner that teenage boys hid pornography. Having a baby suddenly seemed an incredibly radical and subversive thing to do. Up to now she'd always thought it hideously banal and conformist.

She felt a pain in her hand. Looking down, she saw it was covered in blood. She'd been so engrossed in thought that her fingernails had cut into her palm where she'd clutched the spoon. She gasped and put her hand under the cold tap. She wondered whether she might not be the sort of mother who drowned her baby in the bath because she was too busy thinking about which designer to use for the next winter catalogue.

Steam clouded the bathroom. Doc and Dixon played like toddlers on the fresh towels that littered the floor. They had already fucked each other several times and Dixon was playing with the Doc's arse. His fingers and rings glistened with lubricants, poking and twisting like tendrils. Even his own arse had the loose, wet feeling that comes from extensive penetration.

Doc had finally made them get out of the bath, fearing they'd have heart attacks from spending so long in hot water when they were so drugged. They'd looked like prunes for the next half an hour. Now they were like newborn babies, raw and juicy, each using the other's cock as a dummy, their cum bitter, tainted by toxins keen to escape their systems. They'd kept the shower running because they needed the steam, although they couldn't remember why. If a stranger had entered their kingdom it would have smelt like the douche room on a porn set.

But no one had intruded and so it remained sacred. At least to Doc who, in allowing Dix's huge appendage to plunder his viscera, felt sure that Our Father would be impressed by the toil of his loins and his Saint Augustine style of martyrdom.

Dixon saw it differently. Certainly the sense of plunder was indeed a thrill, as was the kneeling worship of this sweet mortal physician. He wondered why he felt such power and potency on drugs but never questioned it. Why would he? Why would anyone? Drugs reveal our archetypes, no more, no less. Would Doc ever find the match for his desire? Would Dixon ever find the ultimate challenge to his arrogance?

Where does something like this go? thought Doc. Surely this was something that couldn't be replicated too easily, with too many others?

He'll remember this, thought Dixon. He may never again know this amount of pleasure in his life. That hungry orifice will close and pucker once more, feigning modesty for future prospectors. I can only hope that they will forever be substitutes for what I have left behind.

He lowered himself to lick the wound he'd opened, flickering his tongue like a snake. Doc trembled with pleasure and fell forward. Dixon knew Doc was sentimental about these things, and would probably take it the wrong way. But even animals licked each other's wounds, even they sniffed their mates to make sure it was their own scent and not another's that had left its mark.

Requiem

'Murray, Murray,' she called, running down Juliette's hallway towards his bedroom. She held her belly which had bloated obscenely with pregnancy. Her own weight was making her lose balance in a sickening, drunken way. Someone was after her with a knife. She was terrified and Murray was nowhere to be seen. She was in his room and the stairs to the tower were her only escape. She knew they were a hopeless dead-end, but her pursuer was too close behind to think of another plan. It was the rapist, she sensed suddenly, and he had come for the child. He'd cut it from her if she couldn't foil him.

She looked down and saw she was wearing a one-piece swimsuit; it seemed the only thing holding the baby in. She pushed herself into the stairwell and began to climb, only to discover she wore high heels. They caught on the tiny stairs, which had become more like vines or tree roots, hopelessly twisted. 'Not my baby, not my baby,' she cried as she lost her footing and began to fall . . .

Claude woke, trembling and tearful. The street-light outside her window cast a knife-like shard of illumination through the grey winter dawn. Jesus Christ, she thought, what was that about? She got up to take a sleeping pill, but then remembered she was pregnant. Like most useful, helpful and pleasurable opiates, they too were probably no-go.

Grumbling, she went in search of the herbal tablets in her kitchen cupboard. Filling a glass of water at the sink, she looked out the back window. A flicker of light shone from the turret. It looked as if there was someone up there, lighting a cigarette. She peered through the gloom and was sure it was Dixon's silhouette.

He took a drag and for a second his face was illuminated. The shadows gave him a moustache, the dawn light made his pallor blue, and it seemed as if he was far away and almost not Dixon at all. He looked down and must have seen her in the kitchen, for he winked at her. But there was something weird about it, evil almost. Claude shuddered. What did he want up there, especially after she'd had that dream? She shuddered again, from the cold as well as her thoughts and felt her stomach. 'No big old nasty's going to hurt you, my love,' she vowed.

The last thing Dixon expected first thing on his final morning at work was a phone call from Caroline Asquith, heiress-in-waiting.

'It's about my mother, Mr Brearly. She keeps saying she wants to see you.'

'Why on earth does she want to see me?'

'I really don't know, but she's single-minded about it. She hasn't let up for two days and she's really in a bad way I'm afraid. Could you possibly come? It would mean so much to her. I'll send a car, of course.'

'Is she in the hospital?'

'No, we're at home. It's what she wanted.'

This was not Dixon's usual sort of gig. He'd done the deathbed thing with Soren, though he hadn't been there at the very end. His death had reminded Dix of how Soren would pick up trade at clubs while they were out together and vanish without a word, leaving Dixon on his own. Soren's mum had phoned him with the news. He'd expected at least a few more visits, but then Dixon always hoped for a bit more of everything. With Penny Asquith, it seemed absurd – embarrassing – that she should call upon him at such a personal, private time in her life.

'Lady Asquith's car has arrived for Dixon Brearly Esquire,' said Bev in her plummiest voice. 'What have you done to warrant this private audience?'

'Never you mind, dear. Aristocracy, like misery, loves company.'

'Huh,' she uttered as Dixon's coat-tails flapped past her.

Lady Asquith was rigged up to a drip in her usual day-room, two nurses in attendance.

Caroline clutched his arm. She seemed less self-assured than on his previous visit. 'She's rambling quite a bit, Mr Brearly. She seems to be caught up in the past. She's convinced someone's been playing the piano. I haven't heard a thing, of course, she's imagining it. I hope you can help her make sense of things.'

'Lady Penny, it's Dixon Brearly. You wanted to talk to me?'

'Dixon, they found you, did they?'

Her eyes, the sole remaining evidence of her continued presence in the world, were tiny, sunken, watery pools. 'Caroline thinks I'm hallucinating, but he's been here, you know.'

'Who?'

'Franz, of course, playing the piano. Chopin was his favourite, you see, that's how I know it's him.'

'Did he leave you the piano, Penny?'

'Yes. I didn't want it in the house, but Father knew how much it was worth. He liked to keep trophies of his conquests. When Daddy died, I meant to get rid of it, but then Caroline learnt to play and . . .'

'Did he leave it to you as some sort of apology? An apology for his impropriety, for the . . . social disease . . .'

She seemed to choke for a moment, then let out a sob. A solitary tear leaked from the corner of her eye. 'Him? Apologise to me? I don't think so. He killed himself because of me, because of Father – because of all of us.'

'Why? Because of the guilt for what he'd done? Was the remorse too much for . . .'

'Me,' she growled desperately. 'It was me.'

'But I don't understand. If he disgraced you with a social . . .'

'He didn't give it to me,' she rasped impatiently. 'I gave it to him. Don't you see?'

He was beginning to. 'So your father, how did he know?'

'The doctor, of course. I was stupid to go to him, he belonged to Daddy's club – they were all very ho-ho with each other. Men! But I didn't know what was wrong with me, you see, until it was too late.'

'And your father, he blamed Franz?'

'Well of course he did. I told him it was Franz. There were others, you see. I never told Father that, never told him the half of it. Had to protect the family, the name.'

'Your name?'

'My cousin. He was responsible, you see. But I could never have told Father about that . . .' Her head rocked slowly, another tear sneaking down the ravines of her face. 'Father was horrid, put all sorts of stories about. Made them up before the gossips could. I told you nothing could ever have come of Franz and me. I don't know what Father would have done if he'd known I'd been with my cousin, Archie. He was in Daddy's employ, you see. And married. I had responsibilities.'

'But not to Franz?'

Her head roved ever so slowly around the room. 'I was too young, women didn't have the power then and no one wanted the Jews taking over everything. Now it's the Asians, of course, you wait and see. There was just too much at stake. You understand that, don't you, Dixon?'

Dixon was about to ask what exactly had been at stake but realised the answer was in her wandering gaze. The Louis XVI chairs, the Chesterfield lounges, the Royal Doulton porcelain, a profusion of artworks. All this. Cluttered pricey chattels that would soon be vibrating to the thunder of Sotheby's gavel. Everything looked dusty and lacklustre in the room, blocked from light by the huge tree she had planted herself. Dixon knew that lives were often expended for but a fraction of what Miss Penny had stood to lose had her father struck her from his will.

'Dixon, there's something I want you to have. A gift for Juliette. I've explained to Caroline that when I'm gone you're to have the piano.' She handed Dixon a letter of bequest and the photograph of herself and Franz. She'd been clutching it like a rosary and it was even more creased and crumpled now.

'The piano should be back there. Perhaps it can play sweeter music for you than it ever has for me. Thank you for coming, Dixon. I feel better, lighter of heart now.'

Dixon wandered out to the hall where Caroline stood, her arms folded. He was, he thought, a most unlikely choice for priest and confessor. Still, he had a photo and a story now. Alas, there was nothing he could do about the piano. He'd have to leave it for Dũng – payment for the stolen works. He cringed to think of its value. It was probably worth over $30,000. But even Dixon wasn't blind to the morality of the tale he'd been charged with.

'Caroline, your mother's explained to me about the piano and while it seems awful to broach the subject at a time like this, I must let you know I'm going abroad on business for a few months. I'll give you Juliette's address so if it becomes necessary you could send it there to my housemate, Dũng Ngo, in my absence.'

Caroline nodded as he wrote out a card for her. He wondered for a moment at the extent of the family greed and whether the piano would ever leave the Asquith fold.

'I'll be in contact with Dũng over the next few months,' he said, labouring the bequest.

'Of course, Dixon. I would not betray mother's wishes, though someone will be expected to pay for the delivery.' Her eyes were cold as she saw him to the door. 'All the very best on your travels. Goodbye, Dixon Brearly.'

As he travelled back to work he pondered Lady Asquith's sin. Did it have the makings of a book? he mused.

Doc had been far more nervous about his blood test than he'd let on to Murray. He'd been in no hurry to get the tests back. His heavy heart lost about fifty kilos when he saw his own negative result tabled under the alias of Simon White. (He had no intention of his staff finding out his status if it had been positive.) Murray, alas, was not so lucky.

What could Murray have got up to, Doc wondered painfully, then realised that beat sex in rural areas was probably not well-resourced enough to get the safe sex message across. There were probably hundreds of married men who fucked boys like Murray without condoms, convinced by wedlock that they were somehow not in the HIV demographic.

Still, even without talking to Murray about his sexual exploits, Doc felt that he himself was more deserving of this diagnosis. He'd have to get Murray in for another test. He felt a pang of regret – he had a deep fondness for Murray. It hadn't even been two months, but he'd brightened everyone's life, as if opening a window in a stuffy, old room.

He picked up the phone and pressed the 'home' pad.

'Murray? It's Doc. Can you pop into the surgery?'

'Why? Is the blood test back?'

'Yeah, but I need you to get another one.'

'Why?'

'Just come down could you?'

'Was it positive?' Murray felt his skin go cold.

'We've got to check, so just relax. It'll be alright. Just come here.'

Murray remembered his father saying, 'Just come here, swim out.' A bleakness began to descend. Not that, he thought, please not that now – so soon – just at the fucking beginning.

'Are you coming or do you want me to come and get you?'

'I'm coming,' he murmured.

He walked through the park, past the gossiping clusters of women who fed the ducks while their wheezy husbands played chess. In his panic, he'd forgotten his coat, so he stretched the sleeves of his jumper to keep his hands covered. His arms wrapped around himself just as they had that day in the weir. He was, once again, on the verge of totally freaking out.

'Murray, how do you think you might have got infected?'

'Fucking one time – one time. This guy raped me. It was my own stupid, fuckin', dickhead fault. I shouldn't have gone with him. "You love all that cock up your arse," he told me. I didn't fucking love it. I told him not to.'

Murray clenched his eyes shut as the tears gathered. He didn't say anything about Claudette, he couldn't even face thinking about that. 'It wasn't my fault, Doc.'

'Of course it wasn't. Listen, come here.' Doc put his arm around him. 'Do you know where the guy is?'

'Oh, Perth or something. He's fucking married, or so he reckoned. I don't even know his second name. I got away from him as quick as I could.'

'Alright, alright. But first, we're doing another blood test. There could be a mistake.'

'Sure, like how often does that happen?'

'It's been known to happen, believe me.'

'Here?'

'Yes, here, but that's not all. Whatever the outcome, you're not going to die, you know. We don't get off that easily any more. I'm afraid it's probably decades of life for you unless you walk in front of a bus. I'll give you some stuff to read and you'll need to see a counsellor – unless you'd rather wait till after we get this test back. Alright?'

Murray nodded. 'Please don't tell the others, *please*. I mean if any of those models knew, if anyone . . .'

'Of course not, this is absolutely confidential.'

Doc almost mentioned Claude, but he felt confident that she of all people would have kept her head together when her legs were apart.

Murray wasn't having any of Doc's positive outlook shit. He was heading for the nearest blood house to do the most grown-up thing he knew. Get hammered. He sat in a truly appalling pub in Brighton Road. The bar was lined with alcoholics, their eyes fixed on the satellite sports channel that flickered annoyingly in the corner. A couple of old women pumped coins into the pokies. One coughed phlegm onto the gaming machines, a cigarette still burning between her knuckles.

This wasn't what he'd hoped for, this was no *Boulevard of Broken Dreams*.

'Whatcha want, young fella? Does ya mum know you're out?' asked a crimson-faced barman of sixty-plus.

Murray wasn't in the mood. 'Just two double vodkas and tonic,' he said.

'Young lady joining ya then?'

'No. They're for me, alright?'

He took his drinks and slunk into a dark corner. He lit a cigarette from the pack he'd just bought. May as well start smoking now, he thought, and immersed himself in misery. He wasn't cooking anyone's dinner tonight. They could all go without.

Adieu

Dear Dũng, Doc, Murray,

Trashy, I know, to do a runner on you all like this, dears. I can only apologise and hope that Franz Zultman's piano, which will be with you very soon, will go some way to making amends, Dũng, for the paintings. Yes, I'm an art thief as well as a wretched cad.

Can you believe Lady Asquith has bequeathed Franz's piano to me? It's worth a great deal of money so if you wanted to split the proceeds you could all cheerfully travel the world, find me and exact your terrible revenge.

I'll miss you all.

Dix stamped the card and put it in the post box as he fled from his office into a waiting cab.

An hour later, Dixon sat in a mock-Italian restaurant at Melbourne's Tullamarine airport watching aircraft move in and out of their boarding gates. He just hoped he wouldn't be stuck next to anyone too repulsive – though, in any case, he had his tranquillisers. Thankfully, he was only looking down the barrel of an eight-hour flight this time.

Two bags and an open laptop lay beside him. One bag, a stapled, plastic duty-free number, held his allowance of booze and fags – never enough. The other contained his hand-luggage. His small suitcase was already in transit.

He stared at the old sepia photo Lady Asquith had given him, and began to type.

The Avon River has long channelled the melted frosts of the English countryside to the sea. The water is dirtier now, but its swirling currents remain as fatal as they ever were. Lady Caroline Foxbridge had withered, lost the necessary strength to stroll along its banks . . .

'Do you mind if I sit here, fella?'

Dixon looked up. It was an American. There really were no other empty tables so hopefully the man wasn't one of those tedious international travellers with a penchant for globetrotting chatter.

'No, of course not.'

'Nice notebook, I've got one just like it. Where you headed?'

'Jakarta.'

'No way! Me too, I'm living there right now.'

Dixon looked at his clothes, hair, shoes. Definitely professional. 'Oh, do you work there?'

'For the time being. I'm with the UN. Things have been a little shaky there, as I'm sure you're aware. I get shipped off to these countries for my sins.'

Dixon looked at him more intently, wondering if he might speak a more international and wordless language. The big American's smile – pearly toothed and milk-fed – indicated that he might. 'I imagine that must get quite stressful?'

'It has its moments. Hey, what say I buy you a beer?'

'That's very kind of you . . .?'

'Seymour, Seymour Albright.'

'Any relative?' asked Dixon hopefully.

'No, alas. She's a fine woman for sure.'

'I'm Dixon Brearly. I'm a journalist.'

'So you're covering events?'

'Not at all, I'm covering myself with tanning lotion and writing a novel.' Dixon smirked inscrutably. Seymour laughed and swung towards the bar. Dix noted his trim, not entirely objectionable figure, and judged him to be in his late thirties. He felt a sudden appetite for Yankee Doodle. Despite what Bella said, Dixon knew there were times one had to get connected to get well connected.

A flutter of possibility activated his nerves and senses. How could some incumbent de facto ever compete with the thrill and the mystery of an exciting new possibility? And how could any red-blooded boy ever settle down when every bar, departure lounge and café yielded yet another stranger with a glint in his eye?

Bella was probably right about one thing, Claude reminded herself. She should at least tell Murray about the baby. She'd made her decision and Murray, whatever his reaction, was hardly going to influence the course she'd embarked on. These thoughts crowded her mind as the front doorbell rang.

Murray had downed three double vodkas in that awful pub and, as he walked down the street, it occurred to him that he might just have the courage to tell Claude what he'd found out. Every nerve in his body jangled with anxiety when he thought about it. If she was just some stray shag it wouldn't have bothered him so much, but Claude was family.

Claude opened the door with a pen in her mouth, clutching a handful of mock catalogue lay-outs. 'Hello, Fox, *entré*. Which do you think is classier, this or that?'

Murray stared dumbly at the two pages she held, and shrugged. 'They're both great, Claude, I don't know much about design and stuff.'

'Have you been drinking?'

'Oh, I just had a couple with this friend at the pub.'

'Well if you're liquored up, it's probably a good time to talk to you about something – sit down.'

Murray did as he was told. Already Claude was taking over the situation and his resolution to inform her was ebbing away.

'Murray, I want to tell you something because I think you've got a right to know. Now I don't want you to panic or anything – I'm not asking anything of you – but I'm pregnant as a result of our wild and lovely little night together.'

Murray looked up at the picture of Claude in her bondage suit. His mouth opened but no words issued from it. He felt as though someone had knocked him over the head with a brick.

'I'm going to have the baby, hon. I've decided it's the right thing for me to do at this stage of my life. I'd like to be a mum and, well, if you want to be involved at all, you're quite welcome. I think it's important for a child to know who their dad is.'

Murray nodded mechanically while nausea overtook his stomach.

'Are you okay, hon?'

'Yeah.'

'A bit of a shock, eh?'

'Yeah.'

'Do you want a drink or something?'

'Nah, I've had enough. Gotta go. Cook dinner.'

A look of distress descended over Claude's face as Murray took his hasty leave. She sunk into the sofa. She felt fragile and wounded. Slowly the feeling blossomed into anger. 'Who do these men think they are? Not an ounce of control when it comes to their desires and not a skerrick of empathy when it comes to the consequences!' she shouted at Missy. The cat threw her a disdainful look and stalked out. Claude shook her head. What had she expected from a nineteen-year-old? She began to get teary again. It would always be just her on her own, at the end of the day. Stupid, romantic Claude biting off more than she could chew. Good-old-always-there, please-everybody Claude. Idiot Claude, who was foolish and naive enough to think Murray would give a damn.

'I don't believe it! Where did you get these?' Dũng stared at the paintings of a little boy and little girl.

'I told you, darling, I bought them from Merrily Davis,' Gabriela pouted.

'Who the fuck is Merrily Davis?'

'She has a gallery in Toorak.'

'But I never sold these paintings! To my knowledge, they're still stacked with the rest of this exhibition in a corner of my room. You can't sell them, they're stolen.'

'Merrily is very respectable. I told you she's in Toorak.'

Dũng laughed sarcastically, and felt his stomach turn to lead. He tried to push the thought away but he already suspected someone else in Toorak who wasn't quite so respectable. 'Did she say where they came from?'

'I don't give respectable galleries the third degree. I trust her. We often buy or swap.'

Dũng drove to Toorak and found the gallery. He waited impatiently while Merrily laboured the virtues of some dime-a-dozen landscape to an expensively dressed patron. Finally, the customer left.

'Hi, are you Merrily Davis?'

'Yes.' She looked quizzically at the sloppily dressed Asian man.

'You bought two of my paintings.'

She shrugged. 'I did?'

'Yes, and sold them to Fitzhi Rossini.'

'Oh, you're Dũng Ngo. I'm afraid they weren't our sort of thing, Mr Dũng. I thought Gab would be more interested.'

'Where did you get them from?'

'I, er, well they were from a chap whom you'd given them to.

I think he was a little embarrassed to have to sell them . . .'

'Not an English *chap* by any chance?'

'Why, yes, he just works upstairs if you want to speak to him . . . The *Courier* . . .'

Dũng left her talking and jumped in the elevator. He approached the *Courier*'s California-blonde receptionist whose bust strained for release against her tight, pink leather dress. 'Is Dixon Brearly here?'

'No, he left early. Going away for the weekend, I think.'

Dũng's bullshit antennae went up. Dixon never went away for the weekend: he was broke for one thing. Dũng knew for a fact the only trips Dix had taken this year came from drug dealers. His stomach started to eat itself while his mind exploded with rage.

'Where's he gone?' asked Dũng, his expression unable to disguise the emotions he felt.

'Sydney, he said.'

'But he's back on Monday?'

'As far as I know.'

Dũng's rage was fairly bubbling as he escaped from Melbourne's stuffiest suburb in his modest little car.

An endless refrain of disaster and alarm rang through Murray's head. A cacophony of internalised recrimination. He lay on his bed sweating from the horror of what he'd done – the lives he'd ruined. He smoked a joint but that only made things worse so he took a stolen Rohypnol – just one so he could sleep. What would he do? What could he ever do about this? He rocked on his back moaning softly. There was no one he could talk to. Perhaps he should run away to Queensland or Perth. If only he could leave his head behind. Sleep came heavily like a baby grand dropped from a great height.

'What's wrong with him?' asked Dũng, eager to discuss a more pressing matter. He'd come running in the door, straight into Doc who'd advised him that Murray was ill and dinner would not be forthcoming. Dũng was still shaking from the shock of Dixon's betrayal.

'Flu, he came to see me today. He just needs some rest,' said Doc. 'Fancy a pizza?'

'I'm not hungry. Did Dixon say anything to you about going to Sydney for the weekend?'

'He was talking about it, he didn't say when.'

'I reckon he's done a runner. He's just stolen two paintings of mine and sold them to a gallery in Toorak.'

'No, he wouldn't.'

'He fucking would, and he did – for much less than they're worth. I could kill the bastard.'

'You really think he's gone?'

'Yep.'

'He owes two weeks' rent too, the cunt.'

Together, they headed down the hall. En route, Doc paused to look in on Murray. He was fast asleep, sweating a little. Doc sat on the bed and tried to wake him gently.

'You alright?'

Murray frowned, annoyed at the disturbance. 'Sleeping, leave me.'

Dũng swung open the door to Dixon's room. His PC was gone and all his shoes.

Doc joined Dũng in Dixon's room and poked around. The CDs and his Christopher Chronis suit were also missing. That did it for Doc. A mixture of emotions went through him: betrayal, loss, but perhaps also relief. Dix had always said he would vanish one day. Doc had just never imagined he'd go without the proper civilised procedures of saying *adieu*. A lump formed in his throat. Dũng came and sat by him on the bed.

'He's shafted both of us, love.'

'Despicable really, wasn't he?'

Dũng nodded as Doc's eyes misted with tears. He put his arm around Doc's shoulder.

'I'm a fucking idiot, Dũng. What's wrong with me?'

'With us, *em yêu ơi*. Perhaps we'll see things a little more clearly now.'

'It's just so fucking rude and disrespectful. What's so maddening is that he told us in advance he was like that. I always thought he was talking theoretically, when in actual fact he was warning us the whole time.' Doc sighed. 'Are you going to report those pictures to the cops?'

'I feel like it, but no. I'll go after him one of these days and extract my own sort of justice. People like him can always be traced. They leave a trail of vain fools who spend hours, years pontificating about him rather than recognise the grim, ugly fact that they were willingly duped.'

Moon or music woke Murray. His mind was still murky from drugs but no less haunted by his thoughts. His limbs felt like lead. There were no murmurs or movements in the house, but a blue and white haze thickened the darkness of his room like cornflour in gravy. He had woken into a midnight precinct of ethereal gloom. His heart grew as heavy as his limbs when the knowledge of his present predicament weighed down on him again. He almost smiled to think how he would be happy now to be just HIV positive, to not have Claude . . . He couldn't even venture there in his mind.

He rose from the bed wearing nothing but his boxers. His skin turned to gooseflesh, his nipples to pellets with the crude shock of the cold. In the mirror, he looked pale and emaciated. 'The moon paints a different picture of us, she knows our frailties and makes us confront the darkness in our hearts.' Had Dixon said that, or Nina in her book? Or was there another voice somewhere, feeding him cimmerian thoughts? Murray shivered and took another pill.

He'd keep taking them, keep sleeping, as long as they worked. He whimpered as he realised how short that time would be.

Almost absent-mindedly he went through the door to the turret. The stairs were steep and his legs like treacle. How could legs weigh so much and steps stretch so far? As he reached the summit he was struck by the moon's forceful light. It was as if he had stumbled on the gleaming, eternal light people claimed to have witnessed on life-after-death documentaries. He slumped onto the window seat, shuddering like a kitten in the snow.

The moon's slender, silver fingernails picked out the details of the room, drawing his gaze inextricably to the rope. 'No,' he cried out, with a sputter of tears and bubble of snot. But the rope had been chosen for him. He negotiated for a minute, tried to make deals with destiny, but he knew there was no use. The matter was out of his hands. He knew no one would ever like him again, he could never be loved or respected. As soon as the situation with Claude came out he'd be sent from the house. He'd be no better than Angel or any of the other desperate trash roaming the pavements. He'd had his chance and blown it big-time.

A piano played sweetly and ever so softly in the distance. A voice somewhere coaxed him to pick up the rope. A sudden yank, a second's burning and his spinal cord would pull away in a fibrous, sinewy clump from the brain. It would be as quick and effective as pulling a plug from a power point. He cried, stifling his sobs, thinking of his mum. He'd never been so scared, but so many had gone before him this noble, gruesome way.

He opened the window and proceeded to tie the rope to the window frame, fastening a strong reef knot. A good knot's important – how did he know that? He brushed away the tears and mucous with the back of his hand. Still grizzling, he strengthened his resolve. He tightened the cord around his neck and sat for a moment in the cold, open window while frosty splinters scratched his legs. 'Up and over,' a voice murmured. Bravely, he heeded the command and sent himself plummeting into the night.

Rope

Claude came shuddering out of a disturbed slumber to the sound of shattering glass. She pulled on her kimono and ran to the kitchen. The turret was yawning, two whole windows missing – glass, wood frames and all – as if a meteorite had struck it. She blinked in disbelief. 'Oh my God.'

She ran out. At the side of the house she could make out a clump of something and, as she moved closer, she became aware it was a clump of someone. 'Oh Jesus. Doc, Doc . . . Quick! For Christ's sake.' She realised she was screaming, and lights were going on up and down the street.

Dũng woke from some infernal dream. The scream had seemed so real. It sounded like Claude. He staggered out, Doc close behind in his tracksuit.

'Oh God.' Doc moved Claudette away and knelt beside the prone figure, his fingers searching the twisted throat for a pulse.

Dũng dashed inside, grabbed the cordless phone and rang for an ambulance.

'Don't move him – anyone,' commanded Doc in official tones.

'Is he alive?' asked Claude.

'Yes, but Christ knows what he's done to his spine.' He took the phone from Dũng. 'We have a post-hanging victim. Male. He's suffered a five-metre fall. He's unconscious; breathing – just; haemorrhaging from the nose; compound fractures of the left arm and left leg. He hasn't been moved. Suspected damage to the spinal cord.'

Murray lay surrounded by glass fragments and splintered,

friable wood from the turret. The glass had missed him somehow but his weight had easily taken out those ancient rotted windows.

Claude stood with her hand over her mouth as the medics braced and moved Murray onto a backboard. A few die-hard sticky-beaks, undeterred by the cold, stood around in their dressing gowns.

'I'm going in the ambulance. Are you two going to come? It's the Alfred hospital.' Doc was still in professional mode.

'Yeah, we'll dress and go in my car,' said Claude, sniffling tearfully into a tissue she'd pulled from her pocket. She shook her head, dazed. 'I can't believe it had this big an effect on him.'

Doc looked at Claude as he climbed into the ambulance. 'So he told you about testing positive?'

'What . . .? HIV?'

Doc nodded from the back of the vehicle as the doors closed. The shrill siren began to reverberate through the night. Claude took hold of Dũng's arm, her face disintegrating in the flashing lights.

As Claude accelerated recklessly down St Kilda Road, Dũng rang Phyllis on the mobile.

'Hello,' she said, her voice thick with sleep. It was 3 a.m.

'Phyllis, it's Dũng, Murray's housemate from Melbourne.'

'What's wrong?'

'He's been in an . . . accident.'

'Is he . . .'

'We're just going to the hospital now.'

'What hospital? I want to drive down.'

'Why don't you wait until we're there?'

'How bad is it?'

'I don't know. He's broken his arm and a leg.' Dũng said nothing of the neck.

'Oh God,' Phyllis moaned. 'Who was driving?'

'It was a fall.'

'A fall?'

'I'll explain as soon as we get to the hospital. We're going into a tunnel so you're going to drop out.' It was a lie, but it worked. Claude was still sniffling and wiping tears from her eyes with her coat sleeve. 'Oh Dũng, what am I going to do?'

'What are *you* going to do? What about him?'

'I'm pregnant, Dũng.'

'Oh shit.'

'That's why he did it. I told him and he couldn't face me with the news.'

Dũng was silent for a while, digesting the enormity of the drama that had suddenly unfolded before him. He shook his head. 'Claude, I'm sorry, but let's get through his crisis before we deal with yours, okay?'

She nodded obediently. 'What if he's paralysed, Dũng?'

'I don't know. Let's just see what's happened.'

They pulled up in front of casualty and parked illegally.

Whether holding public or private health cover, all patients must first visit the emergency ward. Dũng and Claude found themselves surrounded by people quivering on the brink of this world and the next: broken limbs, heroin overdoses, road trauma, burns. They went in search of Doc and found him at the coffee-vending machine.

'So?' they chorused.

'A bit early to tell.'

'What can they tell?' asked Dũng with an impatient edge.

'Well, he's critical – he's suffered an anterior displacement of the C2 – the second vertebra on his spine. Technically, he's broken his neck, but they won't know more until they run an MRI scan. They're still stabilising him, so that will have to wait. He's unconscious. They haven't ascertained yet if he's got any movement, and we don't know if he's bleeding internally. His arm and leg are broken, as are two ribs, maybe three, and he's probably got a fractured skull. It ain't good.'

'Do you think he'll die?' asked Claude, softly.

'How would I know? We can only hope and pray his spinal cord holds. If that goes, well . . .'

'Let's hope, then.' Claude's voice quavered, then strengthened. 'We've rung Phyllis. You want to give her the spiel, hon?' She handed Doc the mobile phone.

'Like a hole in the head – I'll take it outside. I don't want them taking me to task for using it in here.'

Claude and Dũng sat down on the plastic chairs. 'Where's Dixon anyway, did he sleep through it all?' Claude enquired.

Dũng shrugged. 'He's pissed off, we don't know where.'

'A shame. I could use one of his cigarettes tonight.'

'What about the baby?'

'Well, the way things are going, there may not be any baby. Oh God. What a fucking mess.'

River Deep

Murray picked his way along the river, lush and green like in September. Mossy scents permeated the air. He could see the rope he used to bomb his sister from; he looked for her but she wasn't there. Just then he noticed some guy in a flannel shirt, kind of swarthy and handsome. Suddenly he knew he was in a different place.

'Are you God?'

'Hardly.'

'Jesus?'

'Not quite.'

'Why are you here then?'

'Let's just say I'm here to introduce you to someone.'

Another man came out of nowhere. A dapper, handsome fellow like those dudes in old black and white movies. 'Franz Zultman, at your service.' He bowed stiffly from the waist.

'No way! That Jewish guy?'

'The very same,' said Franz with a puff from an obscenely phallic cigar. 'That'll be all, Judas.' He dismissed the swarthy chap. 'So they tell me you're at the proverbial turning point?'

Murray looked ashamed, his eyes downcast as he poked the earth with a long stick he'd been wielding. He felt miserable. 'I fucked it, didn't I? I put my hand in the noose while I was falling.'

'Well, it saved you – potentially.'

'So I do get a choice?'

'Looks that way.' Franz tossed his cigar into the river. It fizzled and disappeared with a pop.

'But I don't want to be paralysed.'

'Look Shane ... Murray ... whatever, you're in a bad way. I won't lie to you. You've broken quite a few bones – you've even succeeded in breaking your neck – however, you still might make it through. You're not the only one who ever had it up to pussy's bow, you know.' Franz looked over his shoulder, lowering his voice to a whisper. 'They make you watch all the things that would have happened if you'd not topped yourself and believe me, you can do without that. If I'd known then ...'

'Well, even if I get better I've still got AIDS, Claude's still pregnant. All that shit, man – I dunno.' Murray felt himself waver. 'I couldn't stand for her to hate me ...'

Franz looked at Murray with paternal hope and concern, his own agendas undisclosed. 'Look.'

Suddenly Murray could see his body all braced up in a cot. His mum sat beside him. Claude and Dũng were pacing the corridor. Tree was telling him about the latest Smashing Pumpkins CD and how much he'd love it.

'You see, your mum's not had an easy time, Murray, bringing you up on her own. You'd break her heart.'

Murray began to get teary.

'Now, now, none of that.'

Murray felt a change. He looked towards Franz. 'Will I remember any of this?'

'Oh yes, the essence, the realisation – an enlightenment, if you will.'

All at once the peaceful river setting was gone. Murray had apparently made his choice, and before he knew what had happened, he was in darkness once again.

There were footsteps, trolleys, a confusion of whispered voices. He felt his body pulling at strange angles. He had no underpants on, just a light smock. His left leg was pulled up, hanging. He couldn't move.

'I don't know, Tree, go and ask one of the nurses, love. I'm staying here . . .' Tree's footsteps echoed down the corridor. 'I'm waiting for as long as it takes to get my boy back.' He felt a feather touch on his forehead, a finger flicking his hair and tracing his brow. 'Because I don't know what I'll do if my Shane doesn't get better.' He realised he couldn't move his neck, it was in some sort of brace.

Phyllis dropped her head into her hands as if she was praying. Then she looked up and screamed.

His eyes were open, grey as the Melbourne sky.

'Mum,' he croaked.

'Oh, Shane, my darling, you've come back to us, thank God.'

She was kissing him in a frenzy, wherever she could find a patch of skin. Her tears sprinkled his face and he could smell cigarettes. He was home.

'Easy, Mum. I'll have a shower when I'm good and ready.'

'I thought we'd lost you. The doctors reckoned you'd come around, but this last day or so were touch and go . . . I've prayed, I've done the works. But you're here. Sister, come quick, he's awake. Tree, your brother's awake. Shane, I mean Murray. He's all right.'

By seven that evening Murray was surrounded by a sea of silver helium balloons, expensive flowers and a Daimaru hamper from Claude. All these things were cheerful but it was only the morphine pump that gave him any relief from the pain that threatened to engulf him. The matron was concerned there was too much going on for someone who'd been out cold for three days and clinically dead for thirty seconds. Tree sat by the bed, eating a Mars bar.

'You should've seen Mum when you died – she went spastic. I hoped they'd zap you with those things like on *ER* but they gave you a needle instead. When you started breathing again she went even more mental. "I can't stand it," she shouted and went running up and down the corridor like a headless chook. Doc gave her a pill which turned her into a space-cake for six hours. Best six hours we've had since we got here, thanks to you.'

'I could've died if I'd wanted to. This dude asked me if I wanted to stay or go.'

Tree started humming the X-Files theme. 'Don't bullshit me. What's it like having a broken neck? You look like Frankenstein with those steel bolts.'

'Better than having no brain.' Murray grinned at the ceiling.

'Bastard, I can't even hit you in case you bloody die again. Everyone could see your dick when you were first in here. It was gross.'

'That's a matter of opinion.' Doc walked in and kissed Murray.

'Gross, boys kissing,' whined Tree.

Doc looked at her. 'You'll see worse.'

'If she lives long enough. Piss off, Tree, go and pig out on more chocolate.'

'So how are you, Mr Franz Zultman, almost the second?'

'Okay. I'm sorry, Doc. I just . . .'

'Well, before you go any further, let me tell you a few things. The HIV test was wrong.'

'You're joking?'

'Far from it. Somehow those blood samples had the wrong labels on them. I don't know how I could have done it.'

Murray remembered picking up the samples when Doc had left the room. He must have put them back wrong. No point in saying anything now.

'I've been losing the plot a bit lately, so perhaps that explains it.'

'Does that mean you are . . .' Anxiety overlayed the relief in his voice.

'Positive.'

'Oh, Doc.' Murray felt a sadness well up in him. 'Are you freaked?'

'Well clearly not as much as you were – not that there are any windows left to tie a noose from, even if I wanted to.'

'Did I wreck the turret?'

'Completely, but it needed to be fixed, so you owe me.'

'Get Mum to draw some money out of my account.'

'I'm not concerned about the money. You can work it off like a dog in a few months when you get better.'

'Where's Dix?'

'Flown the coop, overseas. God knows where. Still, it's just as well because we've needed the two rooms for Phyllis and Tree.'

'They probably think they're in Buckingham Palace.'

'I'm sure they would have preferred to stay home in Albury, all things considered.'

Murray's face took on a hang-dog expression. 'It was because of Claude and the baby and giving them AIDS. I thought it was all over, Doc, that no one would ever forgive me.' He sniffled, then brightened. 'Hey, do you know who told me to come back?'

'Who?'

'Franz Fucking Zultman the first.'

'Sure.'

'No, he did. He really did.'

Dũng and Claudette strolled in. Claude wore her boots and a grey dress. She was carrying Nina's biography and a photographic proof sheet.

'Thought you might be interested in these, hon.' She kissed him. He blushed and closed his eyes. He'd been awful to Claude. His head was in a fixed position so he couldn't even look away. 'I've been a bit of a fuckwit – a total dickhead, I reckon.'

'Hear, hear,' sang Dũng. 'As punishment I've made a drawing of your dick which was exposed for all to see for hours. God knows I had nothing better to do than sit here looking at it. I'm going to turn it into a plaster sculpture and when your neck's strong enough, you can wear it on your head, *em yêu ơi*.'

Epilogue

There's a picture in Claude's kitchen of a beautiful young man lying across pearly Swiss Balls which, blurred by the camera, look like huge, real pearls. He's wearing a bright green shirt and the background is a vibrant sky blue. The photo looks like a David La Chapelle shot. It's not. It's one of Bella's, and the model is Murray.

Outside, it's one of those beautiful May, autumn days, which offer a brief reprieve from winter's onset. The sun is shining and Cora, Claude and Bella lie on a blanket amidst her thriving back garden. Cora is nearly a month old, still uttering puzzled murmurs at her recent rude awakening to the world. Murray is planting bulbs, his stiff movements those of a much older man. He's been very sweet since the baby was born, running around for Claude, doing the shopping, even learning how to change a nappy. Dũng's next door, trying to learn piano. If they've heard 'Greensleeves' once, they've heard it a thousand times.

'Have you heard from Dixon?' asks Bell, her voice as vague as smoke in the languid sunshine.

'I got one letter, just after Cora was born. I'm still reeling in shock that he's written at all. He's been back in England since January – must have run out of money seriously this time because he's at his parents' home in Bath. Living with Mum and Dad must be quite a compromise for one of Dixon's age, penchants and appetites. He's written a book, a mystery based on all that Lady Asquith, Franz Zultman stuff – there's even a murder in it. Apparently some publisher in London's interested. Needless to say it's all set in England, about some old Duchess. As much as he loves

Australia, blah, blah, blah, it lacks the ambience and marketing potential he perceives in the UK, or some such shit.'

'Bloody typical, isn't it?' says Bell, as she toys with Cora's single crest of downy brown hair.

'Still, despite all he got up to, I liked him.'

'He was more fun than Doc.'

'Poor Doc, you've always been so mean to him. He's a changed man these days. Does meditation, Reiki – hardly touches drugs. He's more together than he's ever been. He's been great with Cora too, hasn't he, darling?'

'Is Murray interested in more than just co-parenting?'

'I don't know. Don't know if I am, either.'

'You're a scaredy-cat.'

'He's too young, the writing would be on the wall from the start. It's better like this.'

'What are you two bitching about?' Murray looks towards them, squinting and grinning.

'Nothing, hon. You want a drink or something?'

'Yeah, and a joint when I finish.' He is still intent on the soil before him. 'That was the worst thing in hospital. The only joints I ever got were the ones you and Dũng brought in. Then I had to go down three floors to the garden to smoke them, and all those nurses went tut-tut when they got a whiff. Should've given them a puff – blown 'em away.' He tosses a spade full of soil in the air. 'Kapow.' He lies twitching on the ground, moaning.

Bella and Claude giggle and resume their gossip.

'I don't know how you resist. I think we should get him working again,' Bella muses. 'He looks kind of different since the accident – more serene or something.' She grins. 'Maybe Cora would like a brother or sister.'

'One's quite enough for me, thanks.'

'I'm not talking about you.'

Bella looks towards Murray.

'You wouldn't?'

'Worth a try. I could wear that bright red nighty-dress-thingy while I'm photographing him, it rides up something shocking when I squat.'

'Stop it, you evil bitch. Just let him alone for a while – he's not a sperm bank.'

Murray came over and picked up his daughter. 'Your grandma wants to see you – yes she does!'

Cora gurgled.

'When's Phyllis down?' Claude asked.

'Next weekend. She'll stay in Dixon's room.'

'Hmm,' says Claude. 'Nearly a year and we still call it Dixon's room. We should name it the Empire Suite, reserved for visiting dignitaries only.'

The sun is sinking. They move into the kitchen as an evening chill descends. Through open French doors they view the sturdy new window frames that have been installed in the turret. Then Claude puts the kettle on and Bella reads Dixon's letter.

Missy curls by the fridge, purring. She keeps her distance from the squirming new resident. She'd have Cora's eyes out if Claude ever turned her back.

The kettle whistles, the baby cries, the phone rings. On the radio a woman reading the news says, 'The badly decomposed body of an unidentified man was found this morning by excavation workers in Toorak. The site, formerly owned by Melbourne's prominent Asquith family, has recently undergone subdivision. Police, as yet, have no leads on the case . . . '

'Well that'll teach Dixon. Now there really is a mystery and he's not even here to follow it.'

Murray pipes up with a mouthful of cake, 'Dũng reckons Dix was a trouble-maker – less drama now he's gone.'

'Maybe,' says Claude. 'But I bet any money, both those boys would be only too pleased to see him back.'

'You mean *you'd* be only too pleased.' Murray shrugs. 'They won't find who did that murder, those rich dudes never get caught.'

'What would you know and who said it was murder? Perhaps Dixon knew something about it, maybe that's why he fled,' suggests Claude in a dramatic stage whisper as Cora sucks sloppily on her nipple. 'After all, he must have done something to score that piano. I wonder what it was. He's a dark horse, Dixon.'

Murray sniggers. 'Yeah, and doesn't mind who's in the saddle.'

Claude laughs hard, her breast coming loose and spilling milk all down her front. 'Look what you've made me do, you filthy sod.'

Missy licks her milk from the floor, Murray wants Claude to put some in his tea and Cora still wants more in her mouth.

'God, I'm bounteous Mother Earth and all cups overfloweth. Where are the saucers for all the spilt milk?'

Glove Puppet Neal Drinnan

Little Johnny's earliest memories are of cheap, paid sex – grim, hasty couplings glimpsed through the bedroom door of a squalid English council flat. His mother's death and a chance meeting with a brilliant, handsome stranger put Johnny on the cusp of a new life in affluent Sydney, where he becomes as popular with the boys as his mother was.

Youth and sex are forbidden currencies that Johnny loves to spend. With the seeds of ruin planted deep in the pockets of his genes, he'd sell his soul. If only someone would buy it . . .